THE FORTUNATE FALL

BY

OLIVIA ALMAGRO

ISBN: 978-1-7373337-5-3

Dedication

I dedicate this book to my brother,

the late Charles Michael Almagro.

I hope I am making you proud.

Table of Contents

Acknowledgements: i

CHAPTER ONE ----- GENESIS----- 5

CHAPTER TWO -----PATHETIC MEDIOCRITY----- 14

CHAPTER THREE -----I'M NOT ALONE----- 25

CHAPTER FOUR -----VENGEFUL----- 31

CHAPTER FIVE -----WAITING IN VAIN----- 39

CHAPTER SIX -----CRIMINAL MINDED----- 48

CHAPTER SEVEN ----- AMBIGUITY----- 56

CHAPTER EIGHT ----- ESCAPE FROM REALITY----- 64

CHAPTER NINE -----TRUST NO ONE----- 72

CHAPTER TEN -----THE NAKED TRUTH----- 81

CHAPTER ELEVEN -----KING'S GAMBIT----- 91

CHAPTER TWELVE ----- FALLACY----- 99

CHAPTER THIRTEEN ----- SINS OF HIS PAST----- 108

CHAPTER FOURTEEN ----- GHOSTLY----- 118

CHAPTER FIFTEEN -----REVELATION----- 126

CHAPTER SIXTEEN -----INDICTMENT----- 133

CHAPTER SEVENTEEN -----THE SMOKING GUN----- 141

CHAPTER EIGHTEEN ----- MALFEASANCE ----- 149

CHAPTER NINETEEN ----- CONSEQUENCES ----- 157

CHAPTER TWENTY ----- A DOUBLE LIFE ----- 165

CHAPTER TWENTY-ONE ----- DELIBERATIONS----- 172

CHAPTER TWENTY-TWO ----- CHICKENS COME HOME TO ROOST ----- 180

CHAPTER TWENTY-THREE ----- LOYALTY PAYS-------...188

CHAPTER TWENTY-FOUR ----- WHO'S IN CHARGE-------196

CHAPTER TWENTY-FIVE --------FACING HIS WRONGS------
.... 204

CHAPTER TWENTY-SIX --------BURDEN OF PROOF------ .212

CHAPTER TWENTY-SEVEN --------DEATH KNOCKING AT THE DOOR------ 220

CHAPTER TWENTY-EIGHT --------PROVOCATION------ ...229

CHAPTER TWENTY-NINE - WHO YOU ARE AND WHO YOU WANT TO BE-.. 241

Epilogue.. 245

Alternate Ending: Unfinished Business.................................. 253

Acknowledgements:

I would like to thank my Heavenly Father for giving me strength and guidance and for never leaving my side.

My parents Charles A. Brown and Alicia Almagro - Thank you for giving me life and for being the best parents a girl could ask for. I love you both. Until we meet again.

My oldest sister Alicia Zayas - Words cannot express how much I love you. Thank you for always reminding me who I am as a woman and that Mommy's strength lies within me.

John Almagro- Thank you, my older brother, for always being there for me and believing in me. I don't know what I would've done without you. Love you forever.

To my brother Robert Almagro Sr. and my daddy's twin - I love you dearly!

Atiya Almagro - To my niece, you are truly a rock star. Thank you for your valuable support.

To my best friends Kimberly A. Morrow and Dr. Stacie A. Morris - Thank you for thirty years of friendship. Your friendship means the world to me. I am so blessed to be on this journey called life with you both.

Ms. Tinker – Thank you for being our extension to Erica. You mean the world to me!

Chanel Taylor - You're my sister and friend. Thank you for always being by my side and telling me when I am wrong.

Eva Jane Bunkley – I appreciate your friendship and sisterhood. Thank you for cheering me on all these years. I love you!

Anna Mariotti - We go back since Hartford City Council. I look forward to many more years of friendship.

My cousin Caroline Brown from the UK – I am just loving our budding friendship and cousinship as grown women. Love you!

Karen – Thank you for always encouraging me, especially those days when I am feeling doubtful.

My childhood friend Tiffany. What would I do without you? Love you!

To my childhood friend and sister Verlecuia "Lisa" Mitchell - Thank you for your support. Love you.

My editor Gina Salamon - Thank you so much for supporting me and my business. I appreciate our working relationship.

Rebecca Amodeo – Thank you for being my accountability partner. I appreciate your support.

Morshe - Thank you for all that you do. I'll never forget your words of encouragement. I appreciate you.

My favorite professor in the whole wide world Frederick Taylor. Thank you for taking my calls and listening to my crazy ideas.

Upper Albany Neighborhood Collaborative Family - Thank you for your support!

My Morris Brown College Family – I am indebted to you all.

"Show me a hero, and I'll write you a tragedy."

F. Scott Fitzgerald

CHAPTER ONE

----- GENESIS-----

The morning sun forced its way into the hotel room as Rachel explored Bernard's bare body stretched out across the bed. The only evidence he was alive was the crescendo of loud snores and heavy breathing followed by a brief silence. On a small table across the room, two empty bottles of champagne and a half-eaten pizza sat as remnants of the night before. Bernard's custom-made suit jacket, shirt, and tie lay bundled in a ball on the floor, and the bedsheets were wrapped around his waist, exposing the shape of a diamond seared onto the left side of his chest and a tattoo of his daughter emblazoned on his forearm.

Rachel leaned over, gently kissed him on the cheek and whispered, "Goodbye."

"Come back to bed, Rachel."

"No, I have to go. Text me later," she whispered.

She gathered her purse and keys from the nightstand and scanned the room for the last time, finally locating her red lace thong under the bed. As she walked toward the door, Bernard quickly rose and hurried toward her. He caught Rachel at the door, his hard penis pressed against her butt, the heat of his body searing Rachel through her dress.

"I want another round."

"I can't, baby," she whispered, and in response, he kissed her passionately.

"Okay, promise me, we'll see each other soon."

"Yes," she replied and stared longingly into his eyes.

"I'll call you before I get on my flight," he said, and when she looked back, she saw he still watched her as she hurried to the elevators.

Rachel's relationship with Bernard Davidson was complicated, and if you asked her friends, they would say it was more like a nightmare. The kind where you could predict a not-so-good ending. They were two hopeless romantics constantly forced to find a way to meet up. Different cities and different hotels, always where the creaking of a mattress, heavy breathing, ass slapping, loud moaning, and headboard banging against the wall, told a story more compelling than a Prince album.

Ten years and counting, six hundred and seven miles apart, and a wife and a kid couldn't keep Bernard away. While Rachel loved every ounce of him, she had always known their affair wasn't good for either of them. Despite his promise to be with her, it was evident Bernard has no intention of leaving his life with his wife and child. So Rachel was left to either accept their arrangement or move on, and still, she couldn't find it in herself to end it. Instead, she had spent all these years settling for the occasional no-shows and disappointments, the lies, and missed opportunities of meeting great men who genuinely had an interest in her.

She just didn't know what life would be like without him. She'd become accustomed to his inability to love her unconditionally and couldn't free herself from the situation. She loved the way he made her feel when they were together. It was like them against the world. So she lived with it and accepted their choices.

Rachel stepped outside to a beautiful Monday morning. The wind danced its way into her car as she headed toward the freeway, her natural coils blowing endlessly from the sunroof. The sultry sounds of Anita Baker singing "You're my Everything" crooned across the airwaves. While Rachel made every attempt to sing along, her tone-deaf voice was unmatched to Anita. So instead, she hummed to the music.

This was going to be a great day, she told herself, or so she thought as those feelings would suddenly change. When she drove into the office park, a line of cars stood piled up waiting to enter the garage. Each new passerby slowed down to witness the commotion while a police officer motioned everyone away. "Keep moving," the officer yelled.

The noise from a helicopter hovering above was deafening. As Rachel got closer to the building, she saw that a sea of blue and red lights encased the area. A forensic crime unit van and paramedics were stationed along the median of the property. Yellow tape cordoned off most of the building, and going by the looks on their faces, the news reporters with satellite vans were awaiting a briefing about something big.

Rachel found her co-workers inconsolable. They had been ordered by the police to exit the building slowly, one by one, with their hands on top of their heads. Their clothes were disheveled and torn with blood smeared everywhere, showing evidence of a struggle.

She quickly snatched up her cellphone and began calling everyone she knew.

FIVE YEARS EARLIER

Rachel couldn't believe she had an interview. She had not been in front of anyone vying for a new position for four long years. But this time was different. This time, she already had a job, and while she made decent money, Rachel felt it was time for a change. She was ready to embark on a new opportunity and confident that she could excel in this new position as spokesperson and media liaison for the Empowerment Agency. Rachel was up for the challenge. The interview was scheduled for 6:00 pm with the executive director and the human resource manager, but they were running behind, so here she was, patiently waiting in an enclosed glass area lobby.

Rachel was greeted by the receptionist, a chubby Nuyorican, named Elizabeth Reyes, with long black hair and blonde highlights. Her pink and sparkling silver nail color matched her outfit. When she walked into the room, her opaque pantyhose rubbed against her thighs and made a swishing noise. Elizabeth handed Rachel a packet of information to read, and she could see tears perched from Elizabeth's eyelids. She told Rachel that she had just received a call about her dad being rushed to the hospital.

"Are you okay?"

Elizabeth quickly wiped away her tears with a nod and smeared what was left of her mascara across her face. Hoping to break the awkward silence that followed, Rachel struck up a conversation and began asking her questions about the job.

With a heavy accent, Elizabeth replied in a robotic manner, "Everyone is friendly, and Mr. Williams is really nice." But something didn't seem right to Rachel about her response. It sounded rehearsed. She wasn't sure if it was the news about Elizabeth's dad causing her to speak this way or if she was simply embellishing the truth.

While Rachel waited to be interviewed, Elizabeth opened up about her life, and Rachel listened intently. Elizabeth explained she was a single mom of three and had moved from Spanish Harlem to Miami to be closer to her ailing uncle, who was like a father to her. But then she abruptly stopped in the middle of our conversation with a terrified look on her face.

"Oh, h–hi, Kimberly," Elizabeth stuttered . Rachel, this is Kimberly Goodwin, our human resource manager."

Kimberly smiled and offered to escort Rachel to the conference room, where the interview was to be held. She seemed startled to find Elizabeth and Rachel talking. Rachel said goodbye to the receptionist and wished her father well, then was quickly whisked away.

Kimberly was an attractive woman of Scandinavian descent in her thirties with short blonde hair. She struck Rachel as a carbon copy of the news anchor Meghan Kelly. Kimberly wore a navy pencil skirt with a pearl necklace draped around her neck and kitten pumps.

When Rachel entered the conference room, Roger Williams, the executive director, stood, smiled, and shook her hand. "Roger Williams."

"Rachel Gibbs. Nice to meet you."

"It's a pleasure meeting you."

Mr. Williams stood six feet, two inches tall, and had a rotund belly. His skin was the color of a charred raisin. His hairline was noticeably receding, with flecks of gray saturating his temples. His symmetrically round pouty lips and broad nose were prominent features on his face, and his posture and build gave her an immediate impression of someone who once played sports. Behind his sleepy eyes, Rachel saw something mysterious and dark.

He wore a well-tailored smoky gray suit and brown leather Florsheim shoes that complemented his entire outfit. Rachel saw instantly that this was a man who occupied a room the moment he entered it. His presence alone demanded authority, and at times he came off as aloof.

Throughout the interview, Kimberly seemed to choose her words carefully, speaking much like a child fearful of saying too much in front of her parent while Mr. Williams listened intently and jotted down a few notes. He asked several questions but allowed Rachel to do most of the talking. While chatting about more personal things, he stated that he was born and raised in Baton Rouge, Louisiana, and attended the University of Florida for undergrad and graduate school. He explained that in his role as director of the agency, he was responsible for implementing social services programs for residents. Those services were provided in Empowerment agencies. While some people admired him for his work, others disdained him.

Rachel was pleased with the interview and went home feeling confident that she had the job. A week later, she was offered a position and happily accepted.

Rachel handed in her resignation with her current employer the next morning, and on her last day, her co-workers hosted a farewell luncheon at a local Mexican eatery. They laughed and drank Margaritas for hours, talking about the good ole times. As they said their goodbyes, she felt excited and scared at the same time. Deep down inside, she wasn't entirely sure she had made the right decision.

"Good luck, Rachel," my former supervisor said as he walked toward his car.

On her first day with the new agency, she reported to the office at 9:00 am and was greeted in the lobby by Kimberly, who smiled and welcomed Rachel with a warm embrace. Kimberly showed her around the office and introduced her to new colleagues. Everyone helped her feel at home.

Her office was small and cozy. After a few hours, Rachel became thirsty and decided to take a break. She noticed the four water fountains along the corridor were broken, and she found no water coolers anywhere. During her search, she came across Elizabeth, who was once again acting strange. She seemed agitated. Rachel didn't know if she should keep walking or stop and ask a question.

"Do you need help with anything?" Elizabeth asked.

"Yes, where are the water coolers?

"You can purchase water in the break room," she said and stormed off. With that, Rachel decided to skip the water and head back to her office. She would discover later that this was just one more clue that everything wasn't as it seemed here.

Rachel loved most things about her new job, and the fast pace was exactly what she desired. But after several months, things began to change. The morale was low. Resumes were constantly left behind at the printer. The working relationship between Roger Williams and Rachel became difficult to comprehend.

Most days, he was angry at the world. No one wanted to cross his path during those dark moments. When staff was called to his office, they were cursed out or told their job was on the line. Rachel quickly discovered that it was better to avoid him at all cost, so she stayed mainly in her office. When he caught up with her, he would chastise Rachel about things that were out of her control. As time went along, she somehow turned into one of his targets, and it became increasingly difficult to garner the energy to go to work.

Bernard assured Rachel that things would get better between Williams and her. "Baby, he's just under a lot of pressure. You know how they do us black men."

"Here we go again," she mumbled to herself. She wasn't in the mood. *Save that shit for your wife.* Rachel complaining to Bernard about Williams always came with resistance even though Bernard had never met the man.

In Bernard's mind, black men could do no wrong. Rachel's boyfriend was part of what she called a "silent fraternity" of successful black men who felt disenfranchised by the white establishment. While they'd done well for themselves, they believed they were often not given the same opportunities at work as their white counterparts. In fact, most black men in her life believed this to be true. But this wasn't the case, not in this situation, at least, and she wanted Bernard to have her back.

Deep down, she believed this was Bernard's way of avoiding having to deal with anything of significance to her. It was obvious he just wasn't that emotionally invested in her. Besides, he had a wife and child to deal with at home, and their time together was supposed to be about having fun.

But she wanted more from him than he could offer her, so one night over dinner, Rachel finally got up the courage to end their ten-year affair. She'd had enough of his bullshit.

"What's wrong? You haven't said a word to me all evening? And why aren't you eating?"

"I don't have much of an appetite," she replied.

"Are you not feeling well? Wait, are you—"

"No, I'm not pregnant," she replied before he could finish his thought. *Don't you dare ask me to stop at a Walgreens either.*

"Let's take our food back to the hotel and chill," Bernard suggested.

"No. I want to go home. I can't do this anymore."

"Can't do what anymore?" he asked in a raised voice. His entire demeanor changed.

"Us. You and me. This monthly fling. I want more of you," she demanded.

He reached over and gently caressed her hands. "Come on, Rach. Look, things haven't been going well at home. Max and I have talked about possibly separating for good this time. I've been looking at some lakefront condos. I just need some more time, baby, to explain it to my daughter. You know she's my world."

"I've been down this road with you before. You'll find another excuse to stay." As she rose to leave, he grabbed hold of her arm, lowered his voice and said, "Let's go back to the hotel room and talk about this some more."

Last thing she needed was to go back to his hotel room and be drawn back into his web of lies. "No, you don't have a right to hold my love hostage anymore." Even though she wanted to make love to him one more time, Rachel had to hold on to her emotional dignity. She stormed out of the restaurant.

Bernard was pissed and texted her throughout the night. He even sent a picture of him holding his large erect penis. "You'll miss this," he wrote.

She replied, "No, I won't."

Over the next several months, Rachel heard nothing from Bernard. He changed his cell number, and their mutual friends claimed to know nothing about his whereabouts. It was like he'd fallen off the face of the earth, or at least, he wanted her to believe he did.

At first, Rachel trolled his wife's IG page, hoping to learn something new. But it was too much to bear seeing him in photos with his wife, seemingly happy and in love. So while social media gave a false illusion of his amazing life, Rachel wasn't about to stick around to find out if anything had changed. She became determined to move on for good this time and focus on work.

CHAPTER TWO

-----PATHETIC MEDIOCRITY-----

He pulled off her blouse, what was left of her clothing, and exposed Rachel's ample breasts as she straddled him on the chair. She instinctively moved her body up and down as he moaned and whispered he loved her. He held her waist tightly, and his round lips sealed firmly to hers. His angular face and the intensity in his almond-shaped eyes slowly began to fade away.

Moments later, Rachel was brought sharply into focus by the sound of a rambunctious alarm. She pressed snooze and realized she was home in her bed—alone. She peered through the window and saw the morning sun piercing through the rain clouds. Clutching her pillow, she began to sob uncontrollably. This was not the first time she had dreamed about Bernard, even though it had been nearly a year since she last heard from him.

Since their big blowup, it was painfully clear they would never lay eyes on each other again. She learned from a mutual friend that his company's business dealings had gone terribly wrong, which led to him downsizing and filing bankruptcy. Unfortunately, this didn't stop his wife's excessive spending habits. The last time

Rachel checked, he was still on IG, pretending he was the black Bill Gates, and his wife was Beyoncé with a bad weave.

Rachel wasn't quite the dating optimist, so instead, she replaced Bernard with carbs and gained an extra ten pounds on top of the weight she had gained the year before.

Rachel slept in on weekends, ate strawberry gelato by the pint, and binged-watched reruns of *Good Times*. She had no interest in doing anything else. As the months went by, joining a gym seemed inevitable, and although it was near the top of her list for the new year, it was a promise she knew she would break because even higher on her list to remedy was her situation at work, which had gone from bad to worse.

She barely made it into the office on time that morning. Congested traffic and droves of angry protestors were partly to blame. Men and women of all ages marched defiantly, flooding the streets and blocking the entrance into the building. The security officer she came to know saw her struggling to fight through the crowd as the chatter of Haitian Creole and English grew intense and louder. He reached out and took hold of Rachel's hand to pull her inside the building.

She spent her first work anniversary sitting at her desk, chowing down on her lunch and fielding calls from anxious reporters wanting to know the future of the Empowerment Agency office in Little Haiti.

"I'm ending the contract with the operator of the Little Haiti office," Williams said to his secretary Claire as he stood by and watched the angry crowd grow in size. "The agency will close indefinitely."

Roger Williams knew the closest alternative for the Little Haiti community was on the other side of the city, which meant a heavier caseload for that agency, and they were already overworked and underpaid. On top of it, his timing couldn't be any worse; the holidays were quickly approaching.

To make matters worse, he refused to address the protestors and even threatened to call the police if they came inside the building. He also refused to issue a statement to the press choosing instead to let the situation fester into a major problem. He, at least, owed an explanation to staff, who didn't know when they were going to receive their next paycheck, but that didn't seem to bother him.

Little Haiti was a community made up of hardworking Haitian immigrants who worked low-wage-paying jobs and didn't have access to many employment and political opportunities, as did the neighboring Cuban communities. Its close proximity to downtown made it desirable to wealthy white investors wanting to cash in on its potential. Williams was simply making way for gentrification to invade this thriving community built on the backs of immigrants responsible for its culture and million-dollar charm.

There were rumors that Roger Williams had personal issues with the administrator of the organization, and hearing this rumor didn't surprise her. After a year at Empowerment Agency, Rachel learned that Williams was not your average boss. He was a thug, dangerous, and a master manipulator who was great at using his charm to position himself to get what he wanted at anyone's expense.

If Williams felt threatened by someone, he would do anything in his power to malign their character. He charmed everyone in town, including the movers and the shakers, and in their eyes, Roger Williams could do no wrong.

He had a political machine backing him, too, fueled by his contributions to multiple political campaigns, churches, and community-based organizations. He wasn't doing it for the goodness of his heart, but merely as a way to garner support whenever he found himself in hot water. He sat on practically every influential board in Miami, and his wife was a socialite.

Williams was convinced that no one could bring him down. He had a dark soul.

Rachel overheard him say to the VP, "I'm prepared to go to war at any cost until he's out of my sight." It didn't matter how many lives Williams destroyed. He showed no remorse even though he knew this organization was the pulse of the community. He demanded that the director of the Little Haiti office vacate the premises within twenty-four hours, which gave those employees under him no time to look for another job.

Mr. Williams issued a request that Rachel stop by his office one afternoon. What is it now? she wondered. Rachel's hands trembled, and she felt like she had a huge cotton ball rolling erratically inside the cavity of her mouth. She gathered her notepad and pen and hurried to his office. Rachel's heart pounded rapidly in her chest, while the sensation of meeting her fate and hell was her final destination rolled through her.

The comptroller rushed by Rachel with her head down as she entered. Inside Williams' office was Claire O'Brian, his secretary. "He just hopped on a call," she whispered. "You can have a seat, or you can wait in your office. He shouldn't be on that long."

Rachel decided to wait in the sitting area just outside of his office. She was afraid that if she walked past the elevator, she would muster up the courage to leave and never come back.

While Rachel waited, she sat and observed Claire working. She was amazed by how much courage Claire had to work so closely with Williams. Rachel believed she would literally die from anxiety being that close to him every day. The thought made her nauseous.

Claire was a transplant from Columbus, Ohio. She had worked for the agency for seven years and spent five of those years as Mr. Williams' personal secretary. She was insanely organized and kept him afloat. Neatly adorned on her desk were shamrocks of all sizes, celebrating her Irish heritage, sharpened pencils, a variety of pens, and green sticky notes with affirmations spread all around. Rachel thought back to every time she walked by since she started working here and how Claire was always tidying her desk or sanitizing her hands. Frankly, she thought it was her nerves—why else would the woman clean her desk every two seconds. Roger Williams' office space, on the other hand, was a pigsty. From documents to candy wrappers were strewn everywhere from his desk to the floor.

"He's ready for you," Claire announced, interrupting her thoughts. Rachel jumped up and almost lost her balance, then proceeded into his office with trepidation.

"Hello, Mr. Williams."

"Rachel, please come in and close the door."

Sweat poured down her temples, and circles of perspiration formed under her armpits. Closing his door usually meant she had done something wrong.

For the next three hours, she sat staring at her blank notepad while Williams typed on his computer and made repeated calls to different people. Around 6:00 pm, Claire peeped in to say goodnight, and a few other staff members came in and out, handing him documents. The hours continued to drag on. A while later, Rachel looked over at the clock, and it was now close to 9:00 pm. She had been in his office since about 3:00 pm. She was hungry and had to use the bathroom so badly, but she didn't dare complain.

Finally, he looked up and said, "Rachel, I am not happy with your report. You'll need to add more information."

Her hands shook. Rachel had already made several revisions to the report, and each time he said the same thing.

"Sir, exactly what information would you like for me to include in the report."

He pulled a report from five years ago from beneath a stack of crumpled paper and passed it to her. She continued to ask more questions but received no direction.

Instead, all he said was, "I would like to send the report off first thing tomorrow morning. I'll need it done tonight."

She nodded and returned to her office, then spent the next few hours mulling over the five-year-old report to see what else she could add to her report. By this time, she was suffering from mental fatigue and simply didn't know what he was looking for. Finally, an influx of energy came over her, and she finished the report as best she knew how then texted Williams as he instructed to get his approval.

"Don't leave until you've heard from me," he replied.

The building became so quiet that she could hear the elevators traveling from one floor to another. Rachel paced, pouted, and even dozed as she waited some more. Eventually, the clock showed close to 1:00 am and still no word from Williams. She decided to pack her things and leave. She'd had enough.

When she stepped off the elevator and reached the lobby, she found the security officer, Cliff, asleep at the front desk with his head leaning back and his mouth wide open. Rachel debated if she should wake him to ask if he could escort her to her car, then decided against it.

Rachel bravely walked alone to her vehicle. The temperature had dropped, so Rachel draped her shawl around her shoulders and made her way quickly toward the parking garage. As she reached it, she saw Mr. Williams driving away and heading toward the main road.

She wondered how long he had been outside and why. Was he planning to come back to the office? He was known for showing up during odd hours of the night, but it was 1:00 am, after all.

But as sleep deprivation and hunger pangs were getting the best of her by this time, she tossed those questions aside and drove home. The next morning, she saw Mr. Williams in the hallway and stopped to inquire about the report. He never asked why she had left without his permission or even acknowledged that he received her report at all. He acted as though he didn't know what she was talking about, so she just went along with it.

Rachel was so ready for this day to end, and it still had a long way to go. The protesting outside added to the already tense mood in the office, and Roger Williams was like the walking dead. She truly believed it was his mission to shatter the dreams of others.

The day of their annual holiday luncheon soon arrived. The smell of cooked holiday food traveled throughout the corridors. Festive decorations and a beautifully adorned Christmas tree added to the holiday ambiance. Staff waited forty-five minutes for Williams to arrive to bless the food. When he finally did, he gave his infamous prayer that had a sort of overly hyped-up emotional vocal inflection eerily similar to a preacher. For a moment there, Rachel thought she was in church and hoped someone would snatch the microphone from the drunk deacon.

"We are thankful, dear God, for allowing us to see another day. Pray for those without, dear God," he shouted. Sitting next to Rachel, her co-worker's stomach growled as Williams rambled on for thirty minutes. She opened her eyes about ten minutes in to see their executive director shrugging his shoulders and shaking his head as if he'd caught the spirit of foolery. The hypocrisy in Williams' prayer was enough to anger anyone. Roger Williams was indeed a character, and it didn't take Rachel long to see that everything he did was a performance.

About the time the new year began, the stress at work and Rachel's recurring dreams about Bernard were taking a toll on her. So, she decided to see a therapist at the suggestion of a friend.

While she waited in the therapist's reception area, Rachel noticed a disheveled man who looked to be in his mid to late forties and appeared extremely depressed. She wondered what was happening with him. Had life thrown him a major curveball as it did with her?

Rachel was so exhausted having to put on this armor of strength all the time. Williams was clearly trying to break her. Just days before, things got so bad at work that she just wanted to quit.

While in deep thought, a woman with a New York accent called her name. Rachel stood and followed behind her as the woman led her into the doctor's office.

The therapist, Dr. Rosenblatt, was a petite woman with short grayish-black hair. She had a tough stance about her that Rachel admired immediately. She had authored several books on workplace bullying, as well as psychopathic and narcissistic disorders.

Rachel told her about her working relationship with Roger Williams and how she had ended her longtime affair with Bernard. It was hard to share her inner feelings with a stranger. *How could she possibly relate to me?* Dr. Rosenblatt was old enough to be her grandmother.

Rachel stumbled on her words, and at one point, Dr. Rosenblatt stopped her mid-sentence. She assured Rachel that everything would be okay. Over the next hour, Rachel began to open up to her. Dr. Rosenblatt had a way of helping her to feel at ease, and eventually, Rachel let her guard down.

"Take your time, Rachel," she said.

Rachel's eyes welled up with tears until the diplomas and family photos encased in black frames on her wall became distant. Dr. Rosenblatt stopped writing on her notepad, leaned forward, and handed her a tissue.

"No, it's not uncommon to have dreams about an old lover. Sex was the only way you could express your love to him. This is why you're having those dreams."

They went on to talk about work and how Rachel felt it was affecting her emotionally. She explained to her that Roger Williams was fiercely competitive, and if something went well, he made a point of taking the credit. If it didn't go so well, he would blame others. He seemed to get off on pitting workers against each other to create an atmosphere of distrust.

"If I report him to HR, things will only get worse for me," Rachel said. "Mr. Williams is a bully, and bullies tend to target people who pose a threat. But I'm not a threat to him. I don't want his job, nor could I do his job."

"Dear, your personality exudes strength," Dr. Rosenblatt explained.

Desperate for some shred of hope to continue in that work environment, Rachel asked for advice.

"Unfortunately, Mr. Williams will not change his behavior, and he'll continue to intimidate you. Bullies are uncannily similar to spouses who are physically and emotionally abusive to their wives or husbands. He wants to control his target at all costs. Bullies tend to perfect their craft over time. It's likely he's done this before."

Rachel nodded. "He does have a certain way of using his charm to deceive people."

"It sounds like he knows how to gain people's trust, and those he keeps around him never suspect his true nature."

Rachel was surprised to learn how her affair with Bernard and her working relationship with Mr. Williams were intertwined. "Your feelings of unworthiness are the root of your problems," Dr. Rosenblatt explained. Before Rachel could gather her thoughts and respond to her statement, Dr. Rosenblatt looked at her watch and said, "The session is over."

Rachel was actually relieved and couldn't wait to leave her office. "See you in two weeks," Dr. Rosenblatt said as Rachel walked out the door.

The hour session with Dr. Rosenblatt was just what Rachel needed. For the first time in a long time, a sense of hope filled her that she could rise above the drama in her life.

It was so refreshing to finally have the afternoon off from work as Rachel had no plans to return that day. Besides, there was no way she could go back to the office after her session with Dr. Rosenblatt. She needed time to emotionally process everything they had discussed.

Rachel decided to meet up with a friend to have an early dinner at a new swanky pub in Wynwood. When she walked into the restaurant, the temperature difference immediately struck her. The air conditioning in the restaurant was up so high, she began to rub her hands as though she was standing outside on a snowy day. But after two glasses of Chardonnay, she warmed up. Her friend Courtney Hansen called and said she was stuck in rush hour traffic, so she ordered another glass of wine and watched a couple who sat a few tables away.

They seemed so much in love. The man caressed his date's face. She had his full attention, and it was obvious they were into each other. Rachel wondered how long they had been dating and did they have any plans on marrying. She couldn't tell if either of them had on rings. Rachel tried not to stare, but they were so cute together.

Finally, Courtney walked in wearing fitted blue jeans and a white t-shirt that read *This Is What Democracy Looks Like*, with a cat wearing a pink hat. Rachel choked back the tears that threatened to fall and waved to Courtney as she saw her scan the room until she found Rachel sitting at a corner table.

As she always did, Courtney came in practically bouncing with happiness and good cheer. She was an interesting white woman who had grown up in New Mexico. Although she had a law degree and was licensed in Florida, she taught art classes by day, ran an illegal weed grow house, and on the weekends, she read tarot cards to tourists. Courtney lived out of her studio on South Beach with her boyfriend of seven years. Bob was a struggling writer, and they both lived on the bare minimum. Courtney lived by her own rules and standards, which Rachel admired about her.

They were so different in many ways, but Rachel could always depend on Courtney when she needed someone to talk to. Friendships are not always based on how much you have in common but on how willing you are to come together in times of adversity.

After their food came out, Rachel began to share with Courtney her session with Dr. Rosenblatt.

How was it?" Courtney asked.

"I told her about everything."

"And what did she say?"

"She said that Mr. Williams' personality traits are consistent with a person who suffers from a psychopathic personality disorder."

"Are you fucking kidding me?"

Rachel ignored Courtney's brief outburst and continued. "She suggested that I look for another job. She's worried about my well-being."

"Well, kiddo, you should start looking for another job right away."

"The job market here sucks, and more than likely, I'll be looking at a huge pay cut."

"Well, you can always stay with Brian and me."

"No, I'll be fine. Thanks."

"Well, our home is always open to you."

After dinner, Courtney and Rachel walked around Wynwood. Around 11:00 pm, they called it a night, and she drove Courtney to her car. They exchanged goodbyes, and Rachel headed toward the city streets to avoid the highway. On her way home, Rachel began to think about work and how much she wanted out of there.

CHAPTER THREE

-----I'M NOT ALONE-----

While signing for a package at the front desk at work, Rachel saw her colleague Jennifer Levy abruptly leave Mr. Williams' office, visibly upset. She was so distraught that when the receptionist asked if she was okay, Jennifer mumbled her reply. Rachel could barely make out what she said. Jennifer quickly gathered her belongings and stormed out of the building.

After graduating from the top of her class with an MBA from Wharton School of Business, Jennifer was hired as Development Officer at Empowerment Agency. She was responsible for managing and coordinating fundraising. She worked closely with the executive director and other management in establishing private funding priorities and providing guidance on a wide range of policies and procedures for individual donors, contributing members, corporations, and foundations. She had raised millions of dollars, and most of those funds went toward programming. Jennifer was a badass. She was instrumental in raising money for the new Parent Student Adult Education Empowerment Center, located in the heart of Liberty City in Miami. It was said that

Roger Williams had no qualms in letting everyone know that she was an asset to the agency.

But about a year into the job, Mr. Williams began to berate Jennifer in management meetings. He stripped away some of her core responsibilities, including communicating with donors without his permission. This often hindered her ability to adequately raise money because most of the funding grants were time-sensitive. When she identified opportunities, her request would sit on his desk for weeks.

One thing about Williams, he did not like anyone to pester him, as he would say, "about anything," even matters that were important.

He also took away Jennifer's mobile issued by the agency, her parking permit, and her laptop. Rachel learned all this from overheard conversations.

Jennifer was a tall, beautiful woman with glistening cocoa brown skin and coils that cascaded down her back. She could have easily been a runway model. Her confidence alone could light up a room. At work, she wore tailored suits and designer shoes to match her purse. Jennifer was the youngest of three siblings who migrated from Haiti. She spoke three languages. While in undergrad, she spent a semester at the Université Paris-Sorbonne studying French Literature. Upon graduation, Jennifer received numerous job offers to work on Wall Street. Instead of settling into a cushy corporate gig, she chose to work in social services. She was extremely ambitious, and her work meant a lot to her.

Jennifer not only exuded confidence but had a zest for life. She often treated her staff to refreshments and made a point of celebrating their birthdays by bringing in a cake for everyone to enjoy.

But Roger Williams slowly chipped away at her confidence and began to question everything she did. After a while, Jennifer became a recluse in the office and would only communicate with her staff through emails. The CEO had turned everyone against her, and she had to watch her back. Donors often complained that she wasn't returning their calls on time. During lunch, she would sleep in her car and often seemed out of it, as if she was on some form of medication. When Rachel first started working for the agency, she made a few attempts to speak to Jennifer, but each time, the woman quickly walked away.

Eventually, Rachel asked around to find out what the deal was with her. A few people told Rachel that she'd had an affair with Williams and had suffered a nervous breakdown. None of those rumors made any sense to Rachel. It became clear that Jennifer had been branded the enemy of the agency, and no one was allowed to talk to her.

One day as Rachel entered the building, she saw Jennifer leaving for lunch. When Rachel spoke to her, Jennifer looked around to see if anyone was watching. Jennifer warned Rachel that she didn't want to get her in trouble, so they walked to a closed-off area where no one could see them.

Jennifer began to ask her questions. Rachel told her what she'd heard about her, and Jennifer told her that none of it was true.

Jennifer had an enviable life outside of work. She was happily married with two children, Yael and Mathew. Her husband, Seth, parlayed his time in Washington, D.C. as the curator for the National Jewish Museum.

Williams had issues with Jennifer for some reason, and from what she learned from Jennifer, he'd made her believe that she was incompetent and not qualified to do the work, despite her many accolades before and during her tenure at the agency.

Jennifer was no longer invited to management meetings. Instead, Michelle, her assistant, attended the meetings on her behalf and provided an update to everyone. Michelle, who was less qualified, was now the lead on Jennifer's projects. And yet, when things went wrong, Jennifer was blamed for it.

Rachel could relate to Jennifer's work issues. She and Jennifer grew close as friends. They made it a point not to socialize at work because they were wary of their colleagues informing Williams of their budding friendship. Jennifer believed he was trying to destroy her career and that anyone he felt threatened by, he went in hard on.

Her predecessor met with Jennifer at a coffeehouse and told her to be careful of Roger Williams; he was manipulative and conniving, she'd said. The predecessor had been blackballed around town.

Rachel asked Jennifer how the relationship had devolved into him despising her. She told Rachel that there were a few times when Williams demanded that she falsify information on federal documents. To do so could have landed her in prison, so she refused. Williams warned her that by not signing those documents, she showed that she was against him and would pay greatly.

One afternoon, Jennifer stopped by Rachel's office to say hello, and Williams caught her. He ordered that Rachel meet him in his office immediately. Once there, he demanded to know what Jennifer and Rachel were talking about.

Rachel told him that Jennifer had a headache and had come by her office for Tylenol. He refused to believe Rachel and said he was sure they were plotting against him. He became irate and told Rachel that Jennifer was stupid and didn't know what she was doing. That Rachel needed to stay away from her. In his cynical and jaded voice, he reminded Rachel that her fate was in his hands.

By this time, Jennifer was contemplating resigning. Her husband no longer wanted her to be associated with the agency. People began talking in her husband's Washington circle, saying that Roger Williams was dangerous, and they recommended that his wife resign immediately.

Jennifer certainly didn't need the money; her husband did extremely well financially. Aside from being a curator, he was also a founding member of a successful tech company that a couple of his former classmates had launched while in grad school. Jennifer was independent, though. For the first few years after her children were born, she was a stay-at-home mom. While it was one of her most important endeavors to date, Jennifer said she felt a sense of obligation to have a career outside the home as well. Still, she was considering her options and discussed perhaps consulting, establishing a foundation, or working for another agency.

The next time Jennifer and Rachel met up, Jennifer told her that a secretary from one of the donors' offices told her in confidence that Roger Williams had met with her boss and told him that he was planning to fire Jennifer because there were some questionable things that she had done at the agency. She later found out that Williams had spoken with several others too. Many of the donors were no longer returning her calls, and when they did respond, they appeared elusive and reluctant to provide her with any pertinent information. If she sent an email, the donors would reply and copy Mr. Williams and Michelle on the email. Jennifer told Rachel that she had never experienced anything like this before. She believed Williams was trying to destroy her credibility and the relationships she had built with donors, even those she had worked with prior to her coming to Empowerment Agency.

It became clear to Rachel that this was Roger Williams' modus operandi. Destroying livelihoods.

Soon after, Rachel was also banned from communicating with certain offices. Williams had reached out to a well-known anchor turned public relations professional. He wanted her to train Rachel on improving the newsletters and other communiqués.

He called Rachel into his office, and with her sitting right there, he got the woman on a conference call. "Miss Gibbs is having difficulty communicating my messages," he told her, "and I believe your assistance would be a great help to me."

While he spoke, he looked directly at Rachel and kept a smirk on his face. Clearly, this was his way of painting her as inept. She was so upset and humiliated in the meeting that she began to cry.

Later, despite several calls and emails made to the businesswoman, she never returned his or the assistant director's calls.

The more Rachel learned about Roger Williams and his manipulative ways, the more she grew not to trust him.

CHAPTER FOUR

-----VENGEFUL-----

It had been two months since Jennifer resigned from the agency, a day that did not go as planned. And as luck would have it, Rachel was out of the office that entire day in business meetings.

Jennifer had left her several messages wanting to meet up for lunch, and Rachel was anxious to see her, only partly because she had some questions about what really took place that day. Rachel heard rumors, but she wanted the whole picture, and for that, she needed to hear it from Jennifer directly. When they finally met up, the truth was even worse than she imagined.

Jennifer told Rachel that on her last day, she confronted Williams about federal documents that not only showed inflated costs and other expenses not associated with a certain grant but that her signature had been forged. She also accused him of mischaracterizing the grant and not using the money for its real purpose. Jennifer threatened to expose the fraud, and to put it mildly, their conversation went awry. And he did not take her threats lightly.

Her former assistant, Michelle Porter, was a petite, and racially ambiguous female often mistaken as a Latina. Her pixie haircut and slender body made her appear a lot younger than her actual age and certainly not a mother of four. Michelle's oldest child was born when she was a freshman at Florida A&M University, where she studied architecture. Michelle had been a track star on a full academic scholarship when she found out she was pregnant. She left school and began working odd jobs to make ends meet.

She was the daughter of a renowned pastor in Miami, and Williams had handpicked her for the position she held at Empowerment, even though Jennifer had interviewed five people for the position and had chosen a young man named Greg, a recent graduate with a business degree from Nova University. Jennifer believed he was perfect for the position and offered him the job. But Williams had other plans and demanded Jennifer hire Michelle instead.

Jennifer told Rachel that things had moved along great with Michelle in the beginning and that she was a fast learner. Michelle and Jennifer had even formed a solid working relationship that extended outside of work. They had a lot in common. They were both married with children and often hosted playdates on the weekends. Jennifer believed that Mr. Williams's sole purpose of having Michelle on board was to spy on Jennifer, although Michelle had told her that he was simply returning a favor he owed to Michelle's father, Pastor Covington.

Pastor Covington had a tall, burly frame. He spoke like and resembled the Hollywood actor, James Earl Jones. He was a powerful figure in Miami politics and served as the mayor's confidant. During the presidential elections, all of the candidates, including Hillary Clinton, visited his five-thousand-member church to seek out the black vote. When the city was ravished with gun violence in the 90s, and five-year-old Tawana Smith was killed from stray bullets that ricocheted from a shoot-out at Liberty Square between rival gangs, Pastor Covington was able to assist police in talking to residents, which led to an arrest. As a way to help revive Liberty City, he formed a solar energy company and built a six thousand square foot hydroponic vegetable farm. Residents were not only trained and offered jobs but were able to buy shares at a nominal fee from their salaries into the company.

Jennifer shared with Rachel how she found out about the connection between Williams and Michelle during a visit to her family's church.

"Daddy, this is Jennifer from work."

"It's a pleasure meeting you, Pastor," Jennifer replied.

"You are as pretty as Michelle said you were."

"Thank you, how kind of you." Jennifer said a few parishioners were waiting to speak to the pastor when they were introduced, and he hurriedly stated, "Please be sure to tell Roger I said hello, and I will be in contact with him very soon."

Jennifer explained that as the pastor walked away, she was confused. Although she didn't think it was a big deal about Williams knowing Michelle outside of work, she couldn't understand why Michelle had never told her. Adding to Jennifer's suspicion that there was more to Michelle's installment as her assistant, after discovering the connection between Michelle's father and Roger Williams, Michelle began to act as though she was uncomfortable about withholding information.

***

They met at the Oak Tavern in the Miami Design District. Jennifer was running a few minutes late because she had to run some last-minute errands, so Rachel was already seated. Jennifer arrived at the restaurant donning a beautiful royal yellow sleeveless floor-length maxi sundress that complemented her beautiful brown skin, tortoiseshell Manolo Blahnik sandals, and a black Givenchy

Antigona bag. As the hostess escorted Jennifer to the table, Rachel could see that she'd lost a few pounds.

Once their drink orders were placed, Rachel leaned forward and spoke in a hushed voice. "So tell me what really happened that day you left."

"I confronted Williams about having my name forged on those documents. Instead of denying it like I expected, he called Michelle into the office. When she came in a minute later, she didn't even acknowledge my presence. She just looked directly at Williams. He handed her the documents and asked, 'Did you see Jennifer sign these?' Michelle looked at them and nodded."

Jennifer huffed out a breath and went on. "Williams then asked her, 'When did Jennifer sign the papers?' and Michelle told him, 'I believe it was a few months ago.' Until then, I'd truly thought Michelle was my friend. I was fuming mad, and as I stormed out of his office, I told him, 'You'll be hearing from my attorney soon.'"

"Unbelievable."

Jennifer nodded. "Tell me about it. And by the time I made it back to my office, the IT manager was already there, barring me from even touching my computer."

Good thing you had been planning to leave for months anyway and made copies of everything."

"Damn right. I've got all of my work files backed up in emails and in a file at home. So I gathered my family photos and other personal items, stuffed them in a box I had under my desk and left the building."

Rachel sighed and sat back. "And by the time Michelle got back to her office, everyone was already talking about it. Williams had everyone believing that you really did falsify information on grants and forged his name."

Jennifer shared with me that her family had just returned from a weeklong trip to the Bahamas. While they were away, someone had broken into their home and vandalized their property. This had never happened in the eight years they had been living in their home on Hibiscus Island, an exclusive community located near Miami Beach. Their five thousand square foot home overlooked Biscayne Bay. While a few things were missing, the police believed someone targeted their home to vandalize. Jennifer was pretty shaken up by the whole ordeal.

The server interrupted their conversation by placing their lunch on the table.

"I'm afraid for my life," Jennifer said. "I really think someone is trying to kill me."

"What makes you say that?"

"I've been receiving threatening calls almost around the clock on both my house phone and cell. I didn't tell my husband right away because I didn't want him to worry about me and the kids. But then someone hacked into my computer at home and sent threatening emails with nude photos of me to Seth. Whoever it was said we're having an affair. Seth confronted me, and I told him everything, including how the brakes went out on my car one morning after dropping the kids off at school."

"Oh, Jennifer. That's incredible."

"I had just dropped Yael and Matt off," she continued. "I was heading toward the highway when my brakes gave out. I thought I was going to die. I couldn't believe what was happening. I tried not to panic, and I slowly downshifted to a lower gear, and my car slowed down. Thankfully, I was able to pull over to the side of the road and turn the ignition off. I prayed and thanked God that I didn't get hurt, and my children weren't in the car with me at the time."

Rachel couldn't believe all that Jennifer had been through. She handed her a napkin to wipe her tears away. Jennifer told Rachel how Seth was convinced that Roger Williams was behind all of this madness, including when the school couldn't find her son Matt, who was autistic. One day when picking her children up from school, the administrator mentioned that they received a call from Seth wanting Matt to come home on the school bus. But Seth was in D.C. and had been in meetings all day. Besides, there was no way Seth would make arrangements for their children without informing her. She grabbed Yael's hand and ran out of the school's office, and drove straight home to meet the bus. Minutes before she arrived home, the bus pulled up with Matt. Jennifer grabbed Matt and sobbed; Seth was fuming mad.

Jennifer and Seth met with an attorney and also sought advice from the police. The attorney reviewed the documents and had notified the Ethics Commission about the forgery. The police informed Jennifer and Seth that no arrest could be made because there was no evidence linking Mr. Williams to the incidents. The phone calls were made from Google assigned numbers and were untraceable. Without Jennifer knowing, Seth went by the agency one evening to see Mr. Williams. He stormed past Claire and went straight into Mr. William's office.

Claire came running behind Seth, yelling for Mr. Williams when he refused to stop. When Mr. Williams saw Seth, he jumped out of his seat and said, "Oh, shit."

Seth forcefully grabbed Mr. Williams by his shirt collar and said, "If you come anywhere near my wife and kids, I'm going to fucking kill you. Do you hear me?" yelled Seth. He knocked the papers on Mr. Williams's desk to the floor. As Seth walked away, Mr. Williams said, "Call security right away."

Since the break-in, Seth had been working remotely from home. When he had to fly out to meetings in Washington, her brother-in-law, Jeff, would sleep at the house with Jennifer and the kids. A police officer at night would stand post in front of the house. Jennifer shared with me how Seth wanted to place their home on the market in Miami and make D.C. their permanent home. However, Jennifer didn't want to uproot her family in the middle of the school year. Besides, Miami was home and where she was raised. The kids loved their school, especially Matt. The school had an excellent program that integrated academics with hands-on life activities for students with mild cognitive delays, exactly what Matt needed. Since attending the school, Matt showed great improvement.

It was getting late, and Jennifer had to get back home to pick up her kids from school. "Thanks so much for meeting me. I appreciate our talk," Jennifer said.

"If you need anything, I'm here for you," Rachel said. As they were leaving, Jennifer gave her a huge embrace.

Things were rather quiet around the office. Roger Williams had been spending most days in and out of meetings downtown. Some of Rachel's colleagues were acting strange and not really saying much to her, while Williams ignored her in management meetings.

Then late one afternoon, Williams called Rachel into his office to discuss the status of the newsletters. Rachel told him that she sent him a draft last week by email. He denied receiving it. She went back to her office and forwarded him the email she sent to him. When she returned to his office, he opened the document and began to read the newsletter.

He asked, "You've been married, right?"

"No, I've never been married."

"When you're married, if you cook the same meal every day, your husband will become bored. You need to switch it up sometimes."

As he spoke, Rachel drifted in thought. She couldn't help but think about what Jennifer had shared with her. She felt so uncomfortable being in the same room with Williams.

Michelle suddenly appeared at his door, and he welcomed her into his office.

"You wanted to speak with me?"

"Yes," he began. "I want you to help Rachel with drafting the newsletter. You've worked on newsletters before?"

"Yes, in my senior year. I was the editor-in-chief for my high school's newspaper."

"Okay, great. Ladies, I would like to have a draft by this evening. Thanks, Rachel, you can leave now."

Rachel was angry, and she stood stoically, wishing she had the courage to tell Williams that she didn't need anyone's help to do her job. But she knew it would only make matters worse, so she collected her stuff and left. As Rachel closed his office door, she couldn't help wondering if they were plotting against her.

CHAPTER FIVE

-----WAITING IN VAIN-----

It had been two years since Rachel last saw her friends Alice Williams and Anita Jones in Little Rock, Arkansas. As she arrived, the echoing sounds of Alice and Anita screaming, "Diva!" greeted her. She looked up, and her friends smiled from ear to ear. They hugged as other passengers entered and exited the baggage claim area.

Her friends looked amazing. Alice's hair was swooped in a ponytail. She wore a tight-hugging tangerine-colored sundress that accented her cinnamon complexion and flesh-colored sandals. She looked as if she was Lane Bryant herself and fell off pages of a plus-size women's fashion spread. Anita, the oldest of the friends who looked the youngest, wore a loose-fitting cream blouse that fell slightly off her shoulders, with denim Capri pants and black ankle-strapped sandals with heels. She looked gorgeous, and her russet skin and loose curls that fell past her shoulders enhanced her medium build and height all the more.

Alice said, "You look marvelous, darling," in her pseudo-Eartha Kitt voice. They left the airport in laughter.

As they exited the airport, she gazed out the window and saw the beautiful oak and pine trees lining the interstate. The atmosphere was calming, like a beautiful painting with a sea of oranges, greens, and browns plastered all over. Rachel was happy to be with her friends and away from the madness she left behind in Miami.

Alice announced that they were invited to a barbecue that her boyfriend's fraternity was hosting at a lounge. Alice was dating the son of a prominent African-American Methodist Episcopal preacher. "I can't wait for you guys to meet my sweetie," she said.

After a quick bite to eat, the three of them went back to Alice's apartment to shower and rest up for the party, but not before they made themselves some sangrias and reminisced about the good ole times. Alice lived in a three thousand square-foot former industrial building that had been converted into residential lofts. It had high ceilings and an amazing skyline view of downtown Little Rock. The décor in the loft depicted Alice's personality so well. It was a perfect blend of southern charm meets urban contemporary.

A framed picture of the three of them at homecoming in 1999 sat on her bookshelf that extended the entire wall. Since earning her doctorate degree, Alice published several textbooks and authored several scholarly journals that were highly received by academicians around the world.

"When are you and Clarke planning to tie the knot?" Rachel asked.

"We're working on it." Alice smiled.

"Well, I need at least a year to shed these unwanted pounds, so be sure to give me ample warning."

"Trust me, you guys will be the first to know."

After a few wardrobe changes for the evening's event, Rachel decided to wear a pair of form-fitting black jeans, an emerald green blouse that fell slightly off her shoulders, and a pair of Nine West black heels. All of her friends said green complemented her honey-brown complexion. Rachel put on some sienna lip gloss from MAC, outlined with their chestnut-brown liner, and with her shoulder-length bob hair cut, she was relaxed, feeling good, and ready to enjoy some great music. She couldn't remember the last time she'd felt so confident.

Clarke met them at the door, and he was everything Alice had said, a nice-looking southern gent who had a professorial look to him. He was bald, with a salt and pepper goatee and black-rimmed glasses. He stood about five-ten, had broad shoulders, chestnut-brown skin, dimples, and a pearly-white smile. He sported bowties on the weekends and spoke with a very deep southern drawl. He was a student in the Integrated Computing Doctoral Program at the University of Arkansas. Clarke taught African-American studies at Philander College and served as the youth pastor for his dad's church. He was an active member of Alpha Phi Alpha, the second oldest intercollegiate Greek-letter fraternity founded by African-Americans. Alice and Clarke were making future plans together.

The lounge had a nice vibe to it. Most of the guests were in their forties and older. As they made their way around, Clarke introduced them to his fraternity brothers and colleagues. He was certainly the man around town. He was the president of the Phi Lambda Chapter of Alpha Phi Alpha. Alice boasted how Clarke was one of the chosen few appointed by the national committee of the fraternity to be part of the historic campaign drive that built the memorial honoring the legacy of Dr. Martin Luther King at the National Mall in Washington, D.C.

The party was a fundraising event to benefit the Boys and Girls Club of Little Rock. There was a mid-sized dance area with a DJ booth adjacent to it. Above the bar area were large flat-screen televisions. It was a beautiful night. Some of the guests relaxed outside along the River Walk area near the loading docks. A group of them engaged in a conversation about the federal government shutdown and its impact on impoverished communities.

Rachel stepped away and slipped into the bathroom. As she was leaving the restroom, she accidentally bumped into a guy and almost spilled her drink on him.

"I'm so sorry," she said, awkwardly reaching out to wipe his shirt. "Did I spill the drink on you?"

"No," he said in a deep baritone tinged with humor. "Close enough, but no." He had such a beautiful smile, a football player's physique and a caramel-golden complexion. He was tall, with a low fade haircut and wore black denim with a gray shirt.

"I'm Richard Douglass. And you are?" he asked, offering his hand.

"Rachel Gibbs. Nice to meet you."

"My pleasure. Okay, let me guess, you're from…?"

"Miami." Rachel quickly glanced over to the area where she had been sitting and noticed her group had disbanded. *Good.* She wanted to know more about Richard.

"Was someone waiting for you?" he asked.

"No, not really. Rachel had been talking to a group of people, but she could see they were no longer where she saw them last."

"Do you mind if I buy you a drink?"

"No, not at all."

As he led her to the bar area, she spotted Anita and Alice on the dance floor coupled up with Clarke and another guy. It reminded her of their days in college. They were never the type of women to stay huddled in a corner together. At some point, they would typically go their separate ways and meet up again at the end of the night.

"What will you have?" Richard asked.

"An apple martini." They took their drinks and worked their way outside to a quiet area.

"So, you're from Miami."

"Where are you from?"

"Galveston, Texas. I played football at the University of Houston and later played in the NFL until I retired in 2000."

"Let me guess. You were a linebacker?"

His expression said her assumption was accurate. "How'd you know?"

"I dated a linebacker in college, and you guys have a similar physique."

"Well, I was a lot bigger back then. I don't play much since I retired. These days I run a foundation. What do you do for a living?"

"I work for a government agency as a media liaison and spokesperson."

"Do you have any children?"

"No, I don't. How about you?"

"Yes. I have a twenty-one-year-old son. He's entering his senior year at University of Virginia." Richard retrieved his iPhone and showed her a few pictures of them together. His son was the spitting image of him.

They laughed and talked the entire evening. Rachel felt so good to engage in a healthy conversation with a man and a good-looking one at that. She introduced him to Alice and Anita when they came by to let her know they were planning to leave.

"Take your time," Alice insisted. "We'll be out front waiting for you."

Richard and Rachel exchanged cell numbers. "It was nice meeting you, Rachel."

"It was my pleasure."

"How long are you in town?"

"My flight leaves Sunday morning."

"Maybe, we can go out to dinner before you leave."

"Sure, I would love to." He walked Rachel to the car and gave her a warm embrace. He smelled so good that she thought she was going to pass out.

On the ride home, Alice and Anita teased Rachel the entire way about him. "Girl, he is so fine," Anita purred.

"He's okay looking." Rachel laughed.

"You should invite him to the barbecue tomorrow," Alice suggested.

"I'll text him now. Wait, I should text him in the morning. I don't want to appear desperate."

Anita said, "Well, I think you should text him tonight so that he doesn't make other plans."

"You're right." She sent Richard a text inviting him to the barbecue, and he immediately replied with a yes. Of course, she was then too excited to sleep.

Rachel woke up to the smell of breakfast and the pale morning light bursting through the windows. As she lay in bed, she thought about how much of a good time she'd had the night before. It had been a long time since she had so much fun.

"Breakfast is ready!" Anita and Rachel were stunned by the bounty of food Alice had prepared for them. She was very domestic and enjoyed entertaining people at her home. They nicknamed her the black Martha Stewart in college. Alice prepared eggs Benedict with black truffle hollandaise, Belgian waffles with strawberry compote accompanied with warm Vermont maple syrup, toasted pecans with vanilla whipped cream, Apple Wood Smoked bacon, and country sausage links, home fried breakfast potatoes, and an assortment of fruit. Before they began eating, they said grace, raised their glasses of mimosa and toasted to twenty-five years of friendship.

After shopping for some last-minute items with the girls, Rachel spent what time she had left figuring out what to wear the next time she would see Richard. While in the checkout line, Richard texted her, asking for directions. Flutters of anxiety and excitement rushed through her. It was really happening. She was going to see him again.

They arrived at Clarke's parents' palatial home in Pulaski Heights, an affluent neighborhood filled with white-collar black professionals located in the northern section of Little Rock for the barbecue. A line of cars was already parked along the circular driveway.

Clarke met them at the door, and the aroma from the grill led them to the backyard, where the barbecue was being held. The wall décor in the living room held family photos, including several of Clarke with an afro as a child, along with graduation photos of him in high school and college. The décor of the sprawling dining room and living room was soft pastel colors and plastic-wrapped furniture.

Clarke introduced them to a few family friends and his mom, who were in the kitchen preparing food. From there, they stepped through the sliding French doors leading outside.

Quite a few people had already arrived, including Richard. When she found him, they hugged each other like old friends who had not seen each other in years. The two of them filled a plate of food and made their way to Clarke and the others, who were engaged in a heated discussion. Clarke mentioned that he was not supporting any woman running for president because it wasn't a woman's place to be Commander-in-Chief. He believed a woman's place was to care for her children and the home.

Richard looked over at Rachel to gauge her reaction.

"I have to disagree with you, Clarke," Anita said. "This country needs a woman to run its affairs. The same way we can run boardrooms, classrooms, and our homes, we can run the White House."

Most of the women at the barbecue agreed with her. Alice seemed a bit taken aback and embarrassed by Clarke's comments. Clarke was barking up the wrong tree when he chose to debate with Anita. Debating with Anita was like being in a boxing ring with Mike Tyson. She taught U.S. History for ten years, and when it came to history, Anita was as good as Google.

As the discussion continued, Richard leaned close and whispered, "Do you want to go for a ride?"

"Sure, why not," Rachel said. She wasn't particularly interested in witnessing Anita's verbal slaughter of Clarke, so she mouthed to Alice that they would be back shortly.

Richard held Rachel's hand as they left the barbecue.

"Are you okay?" he asked.

"Yes, I'm fine."

"Clarke seems like a nice fellow. But he has conservative views."

"No, he's ultra-conservative," she corrected, and they both laughed.

Richard drove to a nearby park, where they walked around until they found a nice shaded area. For a short time, they played around and snapped a few selfies, then settled in and talked about their past relationships.

"I'm not ready for a committed relationship," Rachel told him. "I have a lot of issues going on at work, which take up a lot of my time." She paused and, with a smile on her face, continued. "However, I am inclined to meeting a new friend."

"Can I be your friend?"

"Sure, you can."

Richard told Rachel about Aim High, the foundation he created while playing for the NFL. The organization raised several thousand dollars in scholarships for underprivileged kids. Alice sent her a text to tell her that the barbecue was wrapping up, and she could head over to her place anytime. Richard drove her around town and gave her a tour of the city.

"Why did you move here to Little Rock?" Rachel asked.

"To be closer to my son. My ex-wife is from Little Rock." Richard went on to explain that he met her in college. It was getting late, and Rachel had a flight to catch in the morning. Richard drove her to Alice's apartment and walked Rachel to her door.

"I had so much fun hanging out with you," Rachel said.

"It was a lot of fun. Let's keep in touch."

Rachel felt like a school-aged girl with a crush. She wanted him to reach over and kiss her so badly. Instead, he gave her a tight hug and a light kiss on the cheek.

"Have a safe flight in the morning," he said.

CHAPTER SIX

-----CRIMINAL MINDED-----

Michelle waited at the Miami-Dade Correctional Institute for the guards to bring out James, her son's father. The smell of mildew and dirty diapers permeated the entire room. Women of all ages and races sat with their young children clinging to their bodies. The sounds of babies crying and women's chatter in different languages competed with the continuous buzzing from the electronic prison door, a signal that the guards were escorting an inmate into the visiting room.

"Mommy, I want to go home," J.J. whined.

"J.J., Mommy wants you to meet someone," Michelle replied.

"But I want to see Nana and Big Pa."

"If you can be patient for just a little longer, I promise to buy you a toy."

"If I behave, Mommy?"

"Yes, baby," she said as she gently kissed him on the forehead.

J.J. saw a boy his age and gestured that he wanted to play. She pulled J.J. closer to her. "No, J.J."

Her son began to cry. Michelle calmed J.J. and walked over to the vending machine to buy a candy bar, hoping it would distract him while they waited for James. She wiped away J.J.'s tears and handed him a piece of candy. While J.J. was engaged with eating the candy bar, he rested his head on her bosom, and Michelle kept checking her watch, hoping James would come out soon.

"Mommy, I'm finished."

"Good boy."

The loud buzzer caught her attention as she wiped traces of chocolate from J.J.'s face, and she turned to see James being led into the room.

Michelle and James dated throughout high school, against her parent's wishes. James was the polar opposite of Michelle, who had been an honor roll student and a track star in high school, while James was constantly in trouble and eventually expelled from school for brandishing a gun at a teacher. While the two of them shared nothing in common, they believed they were meant for each other, and nothing could tear them apart.

One rainy afternoon, James and his friends went joyriding in a stolen car and robbed a convenience store with a gun. The owner of the store fought with James as he tried to take away the gun, and during the struggle, the store owner was killed. James and his co-defendants were tried and convicted. During the sentencing, the courtroom was crowded with anxious family members from both sides, as well as onlookers. Michelle had consoled his crying mother while James stood impassively. His lips twitched, but otherwise, his face remained a mask of indifference as the judge handed down a sentence of life in prison on first-degree felony murder and nearly twenty-four to fifty years on aggravated robbery and conspiracy charges.

Michelle had to be restrained; she sobbed and screamed out, "No!" as James was ushered out of the courtroom.

Determined to move on with her life, Michelle left for Florida A&M University in Tallahassee. While in school, she discovered that she was pregnant. After completing a semester, she returned home to give birth to her baby son, James McFarland, Junior.

Michelle never forgave James for his involvement in the robbery, and for a while, she refused to allow her son to see him. However, her parents insisted that James meet his son. So, after four years, Michelle took J.J. to see his father.

"Hey, little man." James reached over to pick up his son, who looked exactly like him as a child. J.J. began to cry.

"Say hello to your daddy," Michelle insisted.

"My daddy?"

"Yes, baby, your daddy."

James was six feet tall and had a tawny-brown complexion. In high school, he wore his curly hair in neat cornrows that reached past the nape of his neck. His straight-edged nose, the warmth of his eyes, and round, full lips gave him a distinctive look.

Since his imprisonment, he grew taller and more muscular, with tattoos that were now visible everywhere, including his hands, knuckles, and the side of his neck, some with letters that signified his gang affiliation. James' hair was cut low, and he had no facial hair. It was clear that prison life had hardened him.

"How you doing?" James asked as he looked her up and down in a sexual manner.

"I'm fine."

"Yes, you *are* fine."

"Look, I'm here because of our son. I've moved on, and so should you."

"Yes, I heard. Some nigga from the church," James uttered under his breath.

"What did you say?" Before he could answer, Michelle said, "I'm done." She rose to leave, but James stopped her.

"I'm sorry, okay?" She hesitated but sat again.

After a brief pause, James said, "You never accepted any of my calls or letters. I thought you loved me."

"I did until you chose to put yourself in this hell hole." Michelle sighed. "Look. I don't want to get into it with you right now."

"Mommy, I want to go home," J.J. whined.

"Okay, baby, we're leaving now." Michelle rose again, and as she walked away with J.J. by her side, she looked back to see James watching her every move until he was taken away by the guards.

***

During a dinner party at her parents' home, Michelle's boyfriend, Antoine, was perspiring profusely and appeared unusually nervous. She took a napkin from the coffee table adorned with bowls of tortilla chips, peanuts, and mints for guests and began wiping the sweat from his forehead.

"Baby, are you okay?"

"Yes," he said awkwardly. Michelle saw him glance over at her dad and receive a nod. From that moment, everything seemed to be moving in slow motion as Antoine got down on one knee in front of friends and family.

"Will you marry me?" he asked.

Michelle placed her hand over her mouth and squealed, "Yes!" Everyone roared with cheers and raised their glasses, toasting for a long-lasting future.

Antoine was a great father to J.J. and their three children together. While they were married, Antoine gained a considerable amount of weight. He had several bouts of unemployment, which put a financial strain on their marriage. Over the years, her father made a few calls on his behalf to hook him up with a job. But once on the job, Antoine's work performance was less than favorable, and he often had excuses, including blaming racism for his dismissal.

***

As the years went by, James and Michelle grew closer as she continued to take J.J. to visit his father. She was James' only true friend on the outside, and they leaned on each other for support.

When Roger Williams was looking for someone to go after Jennifer, Michelle reached out to her son's father, James. Even from behind bars, he still wielded power on the streets, and Michelle knew James could get it done. When they were young, he was her protector, and she, his saving grace.

"I want someone to put the fear of God in her," Williams demanded.

James' network was so extensive he had people from important places working on his behalf. Anything he needed from the outside, he could get it done.

Michelle would receive wads of cash from random people sent by James. One Sunday, she was in church, and a woman dressed in a large, white floppy hat and a blue dress followed her into the restroom.

"Are you Michelle," the woman asked.

"Yes," Michelle answered. The woman looked around the restroom to see if they were alone and handed Michelle a stack of bills from her purse. She had never seen this woman in her life and never saw her again. Michelle knew it was from her son's father and placed the money in her purse. James had been sending money to her since J.J. was born, but she refused his support until it became apparent that Antoine could not deliver as a consistent provider for their family. No one in Michelle's family knew about James running one of the largest drug cartels in South Florida. From prison, he orchestrated the filtration of drugs from the housing projects throughout the streets of Miami. James took over The 8th Street Boys' gang after its leader and mentor died at the hands of a rival gang member.

It was rumored that Mr. Williams was growing fond of Michelle.

It was said that she reported to him on everything, including what other co-workers were saying about him. Everyone believed Michelle was his eyes and ears. No one really liked her at work but tolerated her because of Roger Williams. She attended meetings on his behalf but would never say anything unless Williams told her to speak.

Besides, the last time he had an affair with someone in his office, it nearly cost him his job. He was slapped with a three-million-dollar sexual harassment lawsuit, which he won. Antoine hated Mr. Williams. He didn't like that Michelle spent late hours in the office.

Mr. Williams trusted no one, not even his truest ally, Michelle. It was believed that he watched her every move in the office, and according to rumors, he even ordered IT to monitor her computer and laptop. She was the only person aside from Williams who had a company laptop, iPad, and two cell phones. No one was allowed to attend professional development conferences except for him and Michelle. When she traveled out of town on his behalf, it was believed she stayed in suites at the best hotels. Some even said Michelle and Mr. Williams often had closed-door marathon meetings that lasted for hours in his office. Most of their meetings about Jennifer, I was told, were held outside of the office.

"It's time to turn up the heat again on Jennifer," Williams told Michelle over lunch.

"No problem."

"I don't want anyone to get hurt," Williams warned. "You hear me?" He raised his voice, causing Michelle to jump. "That's the last thing I need right now."

"I'll get right on it."

"Let me know how much it's going to cost me. This shit is burning holes in my fucking pocket."

"It's working, right?"

"Well, not yet. Hopefully, this bitch will get the message."

It was said that there were no email or text messages exchanged between him and Michelle about Jennifer. Rachel had no doubt that Williams was fully aware that email and text messages from government-issued cell phones and computers were public records. No one was allowed to enter Williams' office when he wasn't there, not even the cleaning staff. When he left his office to use the restroom, he locked his door. If he left it open, he was either close by, or Claire was around to make certain no one entered. Michelle also kept her office locked at all times.

***

When James sat in front of Michelle, he immediately took hold of her hands. The touch brought so much warmth to her heart. She'd never stopped loving him and wished his circumstances were different. James grew up in Liberty Square, also known as the Pork "N" Beans housing projects in a Liberty City neighborhood in Miami. His white mother was a crack addict, and his black father spent most of James' life incarcerated. James was the oldest of seven children, five of which were removed from his home and placed in foster care by the time James reached high school.

During their visits, Michelle made sure she wore something tight and revealing and his favorite perfume. James had school photos of J.J. and a few of Michelle alone.

"I need your help; it's that time again," Michelle told James.

James looked around to see if anyone was listening. "I thought this nigga was done with her."

"No, he's not, and he's willing to pay more."

"It's going to cost him. Does he want us to take her out?"

"No."

"What's the deal with him and this bitch?"

"It's a long story."

During her drive home, Michelle thought about Jennifer and didn't feel good about what she was doing to her, although she did believe Jennifer had this coming to her because she should have kept her mouth shut. Besides, Michelle's loyalty was to Roger Williams, not Jennifer. Michelle was making a great salary for someone who didn't possess a college degree. She also loved the perks that came along with the job. Mr. Williams made sure no one bothered her. Staff and board members often complained to him about Michelle's costly mistakes. However, it didn't matter because she had proven beyond a doubt that she would be with him until the end.

Michelle dreaded going inside the house. She knew Antoine would drill her on her whereabouts. He was unaware that, at times, she met with James alone.

Michelle couldn't bear the thought of making love to Antoine again, but she had to go along with it. When she did, she thought about James; it was the only way she could have an orgasm. For her kids and parents' sake, she had to play the part.

Antoine was working for her dad and had taken more of a leadership role in her dad's church. Michelle and Antoine ran the couples' ministry and often participated in activities with the group. Everyone in the church, including their parents, believed they were madly in love with each other; they were the most admired couple in the church.

CHAPTER SEVEN

----- AMBIGUITY -----

With pillows propped behind her and reading glasses riding on the bridge of her nose, Jennifer placed the book she was reading to the side and leaned in toward her husband, who was slowly drifting off to sleep.

"Honey, I don't believe we need the police officer in front of the house anymore," Jennifer said. Things appeared to be back to normal for them. At least for now, it seemed, and Seth had returned to working full-time between Washington D.C. and Miami.

"Well, it has been several months since anything weird happened," Seth replied. "But we can never be sure."

"I don't want our kids to feel they aren't safe in their home. I think we will be fine with the new alarm system in place."

"Are you sure you want to do this?"

"Yes, I'm sure."

"I don't want anything to happen to you guys while I'm away in D.C."

"I know, honey, but we'll be fine. Now, you get some rest. You have an early flight to catch." She leaned close and gently kissed him.

Through the support of her husband, Jennifer started a consulting business at home. Despite Roger Williams' attempt to blackball her, she was able to secure clientele in the Washington D.C. area and several in Miami, including the former operator of the Empowerment Center in Little Haiti. Jennifer implemented a multi-year fundraising plan, which allowed the agency to solicit from new and existing donors. The organization operated under the new name Toussaint Louverture Family Center.

There were multiple streams of income coming in, and the organization was able to rehire most of the staff that had been laid off earlier in the year. Jennifer also incorporated some safety nets, including an outside accounting firm, which managed their funding supply.

Between juggling work and managing her kids' extra-curricular activities, she stayed busy, but in the back of her mind, she worried about the safety of her and the kids. The school administrators and teachers were aware of what took place several months before and knew to contact either her or Seth directly in case of an emergency.

Roger Williams was under a lot of pressure. Jennifer's attorney had moved forward with a lawsuit against the agency, and the feds were closing in on their investigation. The Ethics Commission initiated a probe with the federal government about expenses that were not associated with the grants issued, and the audits could not substantiate more than four hundred thousand in bills involving a number of programs.

Every day the feds were removing boxes of files from the office. Staff was under the impression that it was the State doing their routine audit. Only a few people from management were aware of the probe, and they were sworn to secrecy, or else they would be fired. Williams routinely met with those staff members in private to go over any requests made by the feds.

"Claire, get Rachel in here now," Williams yelled from inside his office. Every day he came into the office upset. He could be heard yelling at staff over frivolous stuff; anything seemed to trigger his screaming. The atmosphere in the office was like walking on landmines. He ordered Rachel to send out press releases every day on items that weren't newsworthy, mainly about him receiving an award that he more than likely paid for.

He never consulted with Rachel on developing a strategic communications plan. The outcome from the plan could have served as a diversion from the allegations. If anything, sending out press releases every day with no clear message supporting them only brought more attention to the fact that he was hiding something.

"Where is the press release about the award I told you to prepare?" Williams asked in an accusatory tone.

"I sent it to you yesterday at 4:00 pm." He searched through his inbox on his computer. When he found the press release, he began reading it to himself.

As he looked up at Rachel, he said, "I don't like the quote. That's not what I would say. I need you to redo the entire press release."

"Is there anything else that you don't like about it?"

"I don't like it, and I want you to redo it," he shouted, then slammed his fist on his desk. "You better stop rolling your eyes at me, or this conversation is going to end rather quickly. And you are not going to like the outcome."

"I'm not rolling my eyes," Rachel said on the verge of crying. This was not the first time Williams accused her of such a thing, and she had grown so tired of his accusations that she no longer looked him in the face.

Williams' antics and verbal abuse reminded Rachel of an ex-boyfriend and how he treated her. She had endured so much pain and hurt from his abuse. Now, she found herself back in a similar situation, but this time, it was with the man who signed her paycheck. There were so many days she wanted to quit, but in reality, she couldn't afford to. She wasn't putting money away consistently in savings as she had set out to do earlier in the year. And some of the money Rachel had saved was spent on clothes, dining out and entertainment. Retail therapy, as she would like to call it.

Rachel applied for dozens of positions, as Dr. Rosenblatt suggested, but she never received a call for an interview. It was evident the economy was slowly emerging from the recession, and leaving a good-paying salary job would not be in her best interest. So she was in survival mode until she could find something better.

Meanwhile, Richard and Rachel were becoming closer. He was a great distraction from work. They talked and texted each other several times a week. Though he was very understanding and supportive of her work situation, she trod lightly and avoided overloading him with her issues. She knew better and certainly wasn't going to make the same mistake twice. They often made fun of Williams by acting out a scene from the Tina Turner biopic *What's Love Got to Do with It*, where Ike Turner force-feeds Tina, who was born Anna Mae Bullock. "Eat the cake, Anna Mae, I mean, Rachel, I mean Anna Mae," she stuttered in a deep male-like voice, and Richard bellowed in laughter. They were making plans to see each other, and Rachel was looking forward to seeing him again.

***

Michelle dropped off an envelope filled with money and pictures of Jennifer to one of James' associates in an apartment in North Miami. When she pulled up to the building, there were men standing around the entryway. As she walked up, the chattering in

Haitian Creole abruptly stopped. Her pin-striped pantsuit, Louis Vuitton handbag, and the newer model Lexus she drove were dead giveaways that she was not from the neighborhood.

Michelle clutched her purse close to her body as she made her way inside. The second she crossed the threshold of the building, the smell of marijuana and urine invaded her. Graffiti was plastered everywhere. As she made her way through the dimly lit hallway, the pulsating bass from the Kompa music grew louder. As Michelle knocked on the door, she heard people talking.

A short Latina in her twenties answered.

"Is K-Dub here?" Michelle asked.

"K-Dub!" the woman shouted over her shoulder. It was surprising to see how K-Dub managed to hear the pint-size woman scream his name with the music blaring.

K-Dub's skin color was shiny and dark as tar. He had a long beard, and his dreadlocks stood on top of his head, woven into two big braids. He wore a white t-shirt and denim jeans with no belt, leaving his jeans to sag below his waist, exposing his plaid boxers. With her hands on her hip, the young Latina woman stood behind K-Dub the entire time, giving Michelle intimidating looks. When he smiled, the platinum crowns on his front teeth stood center stage.

Michelle handed him the envelope then waited to see if he would say anything to her, but he didn't. He simply took the envelope and walked away.

Everything was all set, thought Michelle as she made her way to the other side of town. She was excited about getting a raise and felt that she deserved it. Williams promised her that he would reward her with a twenty-thousand dollar increase in her annual salary. While she was excited, nervousness washed over her. She began to think about the consequences if the plan failed. Michelle knew her job and life were also on the line. If anything were to tragically happen to Jennifer, she could find herself in prison for a very long time. She didn't want to risk losing her children either, but she was confident that James had everything under control because he loved her.

She was so eager to let Williams know that everything was good on her end that she sent him a text. Williams made it very clear he did not want to receive any text messages relating to Jennifer on any of his cell phones, but she had momentarily forgotten. When Michelle realized what she had done, she quickly sent him a text apologizing. It was too late, though, and she knew Williams was going to be pissed at work tomorrow.

***

Williams knew things were not looking good for him in the investigation. The Feds were almost done. He stood to lose everything and get prison time. He was determined to fight to the very end. The Williamses were no punks, and he was not going to allow some bitch to get in his way.

He couldn't believe Michelle sent him a text when he had explicitly told her not to. He couldn't afford any mistakes. During the management meetings, he avoided eye contact with Michelle and said nothing to her the entire day. Other than her attendance at the meetings, she remained in her office and didn't know what was going on with him. He called a meeting and chose not to invite her. When Roger Williams was mad at someone in the office, everyone knew about it. He would avoid the person and make them feel isolated. As he did with Jennifer, he began to call other staff members in Michelle's unit to his office for one-on-one meetings. He wanted to teach Michelle a lesson. He never wanted to give one person too much power, and he wanted to get his message across to Michelle. Besides, he didn't trust her because she knew too much.

***

During an early morning jog through her neighborhood in Miami Shores, Michelle thought about Mr. Williams and didn't know what was going on with him. The last thing she wanted to do was disappoint him. During the previous two weeks of him not speaking to her, Michelle left the office feeling like she had done something wrong, and it showed at home. Antoine lay in bed with Michelle, the kinky hair on his chest untamed and his stomach protruding over his underwear. He could sense that Michelle was not herself.

"Is everything okay at the office?"

"Yes, everything is good," she said absently.

"Are you sure," he asked.

"Yes, baby." She pasted on a smile she couldn't feel for his benefit. "I'm just a little tired, that's all."

He nodded. "I spoke to Brian."

"Who, your cousin?"

"Yes, he just opened up a trucking company in Detroit. He could use my help in the accounting area, and I was thinking that maybe we could move to Detroit. There are many opportunities for us out there. My cousin also said there are good schools."

"Honey, I'm not moving, and neither are the kids. We have the support of our families here."

"I don't like depending on your dad for help. I'm a man."

"This is not the time for us to move. Besides, I'm in line for a promotion."

"Okay, so more hours at work?"

"No, more money and fewer hours because I'll have more staff to divide up the work. You don't like working for my dad?"

"I want my independence back."

"My dad said you're doing a great job."

"Still, I want a job making more money so that I can provide for our family."

"Baby, I appreciate everything you do for our family."

"Well, I'm thinking about checking the job out for a few weeks. It never hurts to try."

"What are we going to do about daycare while you're gone?"

"My mama can pick them up from daycare."

"Your mom can't handle our children. She's up in age." Michelle was frustrated with Antoine and thought he was being selfish for wanting to leave for Detroit. She raised herself up in the bed and looked directly into his eyes.

"If you leave us, don't expect to come back." Then she slid from the bed and stormed out of the bedroom.

With pillows and a blanket in tow, Michelle headed toward the kitchen. She poured herself a glass of wine, pulled some chips from a cabinet, and set to camp out in the living room watching TV, where she remained for the next couple of nights.

CHAPTER EIGHT

----- ESCAPE FROM REALITY-----

Roger Williams received a call from his attorney requesting a meeting with him to discuss the investigation with the feds. As he walked into his attorney's office in Brickell City Centre, he wasn't quite himself.

"Roger, thanks for coming by on such short notice."

"How does it look so far with the investigation?"

"Not so good, Roger. The feds want to set up a time to talk to you and a few of your staff members. I can be present for your interview, and the good news is, they're cooperating with us. While two hundred thousand dollars has been recovered since the investigation, they want to know about the rest of the money and how it was spent."

"And if the money can't be accounted for, what will happen?"

"The Feds may want to take it to a grand jury for an indictment. But we're getting ahead of ourselves. The investigation isn't complete. As for the lawsuit involving your former employee, Jennifer, I'm working on a response. Before I send it out, I'll have my secretary send you a copy for approval."

Frustrated by the entire situation, Roger decided to stop at his favorite tavern for a few drinks. "Let me get a double McClelland on the rocks."

Everything was coming down at him all at once. He was under a lot of pressure from everyone, including his boss, who made it clear that if there was any wrongdoing on his part, he would be out of a job.

Roger feared if word got out that his agency was under a federal probe, he would land himself on the front pages of the *Miami Herald* or Bob Norman, an investigative reporter from a local news station, would seek answers and expose the truth.

After several rounds of drinks, Roger made his way to an area north of downtown frequented by prostitutes. He noticed there were a few missed calls from his wife and one from Claire at the office. The last person he wanted to hear from right now was his wife. She would only nag him. She meant well, but he didn't want to worry her. Besides, the less she knew, the better.

Since his arrival in Miami, Mr. Williams had been a habitual customer of a prostitute named Cindy. One of his frat brothers referred him to her. "Man, she'll take real good care of you. The best head I've ever had."

Cindy was a Latina in her early twenties, who looked a lot like Mel B. She wasn't the average prostitute; she was young and very beautiful. Her girl-next-door charm, dancer's body, and oral skills were popular among businessmen and also NBA and NFL players.

"What can I do for you tonight, *Papi*?" she asked.

"The usual," Roger replied, then handed her forty dollars. "I need you to work it real good for me, okay?" he whispered as he caressed her long loose curls. Williams reclined his seat while Cindy leaned forward and unzipped his pants. She gently pulled his penis out and held on to it before sucking and maneuvering her tongue up and down from the head to the base of his testicles. She pursed her lips and bobbed in a rhythmic way.

Roger moaned, "Oh shit." Before he could ejaculate, he quickly maneuvered her until she straddled his lap, then he thrust against her. She gyrated until he came all over the place. As Roger gained his composure, Cindy climbed off him, opened the door, and hurried away.

***

The relationship between Antoine and Michelle was strained. She said very little to him at home while they continued their charade of a happy and loving couple in front of their parents and fellow parishioners. Antoine led discussions in bible study and often gave suggestions on how couples could recover from marital issues.

Michelle sat in the front pew gazing at Antoine as he recalled being in the delivery room when she gave birth to their children. As he spoke, Michelle thought about James and the letter she received from him pledging his love.

She received his letters at a post office box which she picked up on Saturday mornings. She would sit in her car for hours reading them with the children in the backseat eating McDonald's. When she finished reading, she immediately discarded the letters to avoid any risk of Antoine finding out. Although she was aware that James would never see the outside world, she imagined the two of them together again as a happy family.

Michelle and Antoine held hands as they left the church, smiling and waving goodbye to some parishioners who were also heading toward their cars. Once they pulled out of the parking lot, Michelle resumed her silence the entire ride home.

***

Jennifer arranged to have one of the guest rooms in her house renovated into a home office. As she took phone calls and kept busy on the computer, workers came in and out with materials. She was excited about the renovation project because she was one step away from fulfilling her goals. She was making progress and hoping to expand her business to other areas. Jennifer and Seth talked about having another child. However, Jennifer wanted to wait until she had a good handle on her business. Seth was making contacts with several people throughout the South Florida area in hopes of landing a full-time gig in Miami. Things were looking promising with the Jorge Perez Museum, a modern and contemporary art museum owned by a wealthy Cuban developer. Seth planned on remaining with the National Jewish Museum as a consultant. His partners in the tech company were also hoping he could come on board full-time.

Little did Jennifer know that while things were moving forward for her at home, K-Dub and his crew were surveying her every move.

***

Rachel met with Richard in the lobby of the Delano Hotel, where he was staying during his visit to Miami. As she walked into the lobby, Rachel saw Richard smiling away. They hugged and walked over to the Bianca Restaurant inside the hotel, where they had reservations for dinner.

"You look amazing," he said.

"Thank you. I'm so happy to see you."

"How are you holding up over there with Roger Rabbit?"

"It's going. Thanks for asking." I smiled. "Actually, it's been pretty stressful. He's been in a rotten mood, and his tone with me at times can be unbearable."

"I think you should say something to him. It's just going to get worse."

"Everyone tells me that. Well, enough about me. How are things coming along with the foundation?"

He grinned and took Rachel's hand. "Rather well. I met with the board, and we just completed a five-year strategic plan. The future of the foundation looks promising. We're fundraising to build a state-of-the-art youth center, and our plan is to break ground in two years. We want to offer mentoring and all sorts of other classes, including coding."

"Wow, that's wonderful. I'll have to introduce you to my friend Jennifer, who consults with foundations. We haven't spoken in a while, but maybe I can reach out to her before you leave."

"I would love to meet her. We could use her help."

They proceeded to make small talk over the next few minutes, then he reached for her hand. "And I'm hoping to see you tomorrow evening. I'm so happy to be here with you."

After dinner, they walked along Collins Avenue holding hands as tourists and club-goers passed them by. When they made it back to his hotel, the valet pulled up with her car, and Richard kissed her goodbye. This was the first night in a long time that Rachel went to bed not thinking about the office, Williams, or his antics, and she slept through the night.

When Rachel arrived in the office the next morning, she received a call and an email from a reporter with the *Miami Herald* requesting information on the senior program. They wanted to know how many people currently served in the program, how much money was allocated toward the program, how much money had been spent, and how many people had completed the program? The reporter had an afternoon deadline and needed the information immediately. Before responding, Rachel sent the request to Roger Williams, knowing that depending on what he deemed important determined whether he would respond to the request or not, so she was more than surprised to hear from him about a half-hour later.

"I want you to tell the reporter that we're gathering the information, and we'll get back to him on Monday."

"Mr. Williams, the reporter's deadline is this afternoon."

"What did I just tell you?"

Rachel bit her tongue. "You want me to tell the reporter he'll have the information by Monday."

"Exactly," he said and slammed the phone down in her ear.

When she returned the reporter's call, he mentioned that he had contacted Williams a few days ago and never heard back from him. Rachel explained that IT was extracting the data from their system, and they wouldn't be able to have it to him until noon on Monday.

She suspected Williams wanted to buy more time so the attorney could review the information before it was released.

"I received a call from the *Herald* asking questions about the senior program. Did any of you tell anyone about the investigation?"

Rachel could have heard a pin drop in the conference room; no one uttered a word. Williams had so many enemies inside the office and out that the possibilities were endless. Anyone could have leaked the information.

"Rachel, I need you to write a press release on the scholarships we gave out to undocumented children in Homestead. It needs to go out today," he demanded.

She was so afraid to tell him that the press release should go out on Monday and not late on a Friday afternoon. Besides, she didn't want to get into it with him and knew he wouldn't listen to her in any case, so why bother? Plus, she just wanted this day to end. So, she simply nodded and left it at that.

As she left the meeting, Claire smiled and said, "You have a package waiting for you on Elizabeth's desk."

Curious, Rachel headed straight to reception to retrieve the package and found that someone had sent her a huge bouquet of long-stemmed roses. The moment she returned to the privacy of her office, Rachel opened the card to discover it was from Richard. She was so happy that she cried and didn't wait another moment to send him a text thanking him for the beautiful roses.

She responded, *No, thank you for being in my life.* He followed up with a picture of him playing golf.

Rachel didn't want her workday to turn into a late night, so she wrote the press release and sent it over to Williams, hoping he would respond to her in a timely manner. He sent the press release back with minor corrections, which meant errors. Williams didn't like when she corrected his mistakes, but what choice did she have? Before the press release could be sent out, she had to send him another email with the revised copy, requesting his permission. Often, this meant another lengthy wait, so, in the meantime, she attended to other business.

After making some follow-up calls to the press about the scholarships, she saw it was almost five o'clock, and not wanting her entire evening ruined, she went by Claire's desk, pretending that she needed office supplies, just to see if Williams was even still in the office. She saw his office door was closed, and a garbage basket sat in front of the door, which meant he'd already left for the evening.

***

Richard and Rachel went out on a yacht and had dinner with another couple. They laughed and drank throughout the evening and enjoyed each other's company. The couple, Marc and Janet, went inside the cabin while she and Richard stood outside mesmerizing over the beautiful skyline.

"So, Rachel, what are we going to do about us?"

"Richard, we live in two separate states."

"You're right," he started, "but I don't mind coming to see you."

"I would love to be with you."

"But...?"

"I just had a nasty break-up not too long ago."

"Do you still have feelings for him?"

"No, not really."

"What do you mean, 'not really?'"

"I care about him, but no, I'm not in love with him anymore."

"How do you feel about me?"

"I enjoy being with you. I haven't felt this way in a long time."

"You sound like you have some reservations."

"I do." She hesitated and turned to face him. "I don't want to get hurt again. But, I'm willing to give it a try."

Richard leaned in and kissed her passionately. When the evening ended, they headed back to his hotel room for the night.

CHAPTER NINE

-----TRUST NO ONE-----

"*Agency Embroiled in Federal Probe*" was the caption that appeared on the front page of the *Miami Herald*. The office was in an uproar. Copies of the article circulated around the office. Staff appeared anxious and could be seen huddled around each other's desks, speculating whether the agency would shut down or if Williams would be hauled off in handcuffs. Rachel fielded calls all day from reporters requesting information about the investigation. In the meantime, Williams was nowhere in sight, and she wasn't given any information on what to brief the reporters, and there was no crisis communication plan in place, as Rachel suggested when she first came on board.

Rachel sent Williams an email asking if he wanted to issue a statement or hold a press conference, and she received no response. Claire claimed to have no clue when he would next appear in the office. Rachel received text messages from practically everyone in her personal circle, including Courtney, Anita, Alice, Jennifer, and Richard. Rachel told them all that she would give them a call later on. "*Stay strong,*" Courtney texted. Most of the day, Rachel sat at her desk, wondering if this was a sign from God that it was time for her to leave this job.

Despite how horribly Williams treated his staff, he was recognized mainly for his work. Over the years, he built a stellar career with very few blemishes on his record. However, this was by far the worst that could have happened to him. An investigator close to the case spoke to the *Herald* on the condition of anonymity that impropriety in the agency dated back several years. The man everyone trusted and valued was now the focus of a major federal case and could be facing time in prison.

***

Who leaked it to the press? Roger wondered as he paced his home office with his wife badgered him from the doorway. "Honey, everything will be fine," he assured her.

"But I need some answers," Sloan begged.

"Well, I don't have any to give you right now." Infuriated by the media attention, he snatched up his briefcase and headed for the door.

As he pushed past his wife, she said, "Walk out now, and the kids and I won't be here when you come back."

He narrowed his eyes and turned to point a stiff finger in her face. "You're not going anywhere with my kids. You hear me?" He gritted his teeth and raised his hand, ready to take his frustration and fear out on her, but retreated and turned again, heading for the garage.

"I have no choice," she cried, following behind him. "Do you see the reporters that are camped out on our fucking lawn? Our children are being taunted at school. Tell me what you've done, Roger. You owe me some answers." She wrapped her fingers around his forearm, but Roger pulled away and stomped out, slamming the car door after he slid behind the wheel.

As he pulled out of the garage, reporters swarmed his car with microphones in hand. Of course, he ignored them completely.

He needed more time, and the media was a major distraction. He thought about Michelle and wondered if she had anything to do with it, although he knew it could have been anyone on the management staff. But he had a feeling...

There were staff members who pretended to be his ally, but behind doors, they plotted against him. He was sure of it.

Little did Michelle know, she was going to be his scapegoat.

His attorney had been trying to reach him all morning to discuss his legal options, but instead of answering, Roger avoided his calls and stopped off at a neighborhood bar in the hopes of drinking away his problems.

A small television above the bar aired a news report about the case. Roger watched intently as his colleagues and customers provided their opinions, some demanding his resignation.

He handed the bartender a fifty-dollar bill and stumbled out of the bar. He sat in his car and contemplated ending his life.

"All that I've worked for is down the fucking drain." He loosened his tie as sweat and tears streamed down his face. His cell phone buzzed. He took out a .45 semi-automatic from the compartment in his armrest and positioned it against his temple. He shut his eyes tight, gritted his teeth, and pulled the trigger, but the bullet jammed in the chamber. He dropped the gun and began crying uncontrollably.

***

Richard and Rachel had grown closer and even talked about marriage and having a baby. She was in love again, and it felt good to be loved by him. He flew down to Miami a few times a month. Their weekends were filled with endless lovemaking, romantic dinners, and walks on the beach.

While their relationship appeared to have blossomed into a storybook romance, she was still uneasy about its future.

Rachel had been back a few times to visit him in Little Rock as well. Their nights together were mostly spent in hotels, not at his home. In all this time, she had been to Richard's home only once, and it was brief and in passing.

At Alice and Anita's urgings, she decided to do a background check on Richard. The result left her shaken and devastated. Richard was married and had been for many years. Courtney said there must be a reasonable explanation and begged her not to throw in the towel just yet. But what excuse could he possibly have for dating while being married?

"Hear him out," Courtney urged.

Rachel didn't know how to approach him about his wife. A part of her was afraid of losing him, but she refused to go down this lane again.

"Baby, what's wrong?" Richard asked.

"Nothing," she said.

"Are you not enjoying your breakfast?"

"Yes," she lied. The food tasted like sawdust in her mouth as she tried to swallow past the hurt and pain lodged in her throat. Placing her silverware on the table, she knew she couldn't hold what she had discovered inside any longer.

"Richard, we need to talk. I need you to be honest with me."

"What's up?" he asked, wiping his mouth with a napkin.

"Why didn't you tell me that you were still married?"

Richard sighed, and after a moment, he sat forward and took her hand in his. "I wanted to tell you, Rachel, but I didn't want to lose you."

Rachel struggled to hold back the tears. "I'm not dealing with another married man again."

"My wife and I are not romantically together."

"So, why is she living with you?"

"She fell on hard times. I couldn't allow the mother of my child to be homeless. My son was worried about her, and his grades were suffering. As his dad, I had to do something about it."

Rachel wanted to believe him. "So, why not just lend her the money to get her own place?"

"Rachel, the reason she fell on hard times is that she's battling pancreatic cancer. I take her to chemo, and a nurse comes by the house to care for her."

"Oh. I see. Are you still in love with her?"

"No, but I worry about her. She's my son's mother. Look, this is why I didn't want to tell you. I didn't think you would understand."

"I do understand, but... Do you guys ever plan on getting a divorce?"

"Before she became ill, we talked about getting a divorce. But right now just isn't the time. She knows I'm seeing someone. And, when the time is right, I'd like to introduce you two."

"How awkward will that be, me meeting your wife?"

"Vanessa and I have become great friends. She'll love you."

"If we're going to be in a relationship, I expect you to be honest with me.

"Rachel, I love you, and I don't want to lose you."

***

When James sat down, Michelle noticed he had a bruise on his hands. "Are you okay," Michelle asked.

"I'm good. My crew and I had to take care of a few things."

"Just be careful."

He chuckled and, in what she took as his effort to change the subject, said, "You look beautiful."

"Thank you, baby."

"I saw your boss on the news."

"Yes, that's nothing serious."

"Baby, when the feds are involved, it's serious. I hope you ain't down with that bullshit."

"Of course not."

"Wait a minute, is that why he's fucking with that chick?"

"Yes. She snitched on him."

"You need to stay out of it. Word on the street is that he's bad news. I don't trust that nigga, and you shouldn't either."

"He's been good to me, James."

"I don't care. Watch out for him. If he does anything stupid to you, trust me, he'll be done."

All too soon, the hour was up, and her visit was over. Michelle watched as James was escorted out of the visiting room, and the moment he was gone from her sight, she lowered her guard. In front of James, she had to appear strong, but she was hurting inside. She yearned for his touch. She wanted so badly for her and James to be together as a couple, living under the same roof.

Her marriage was on its last limb; she could no longer stomach being around Antoine and pretending she was in love with him. Besides, James was her protector; he always had been.

When she was in high school, her mother's youngest brother, Uncle Mitch was staying with the family until he could find a place of his own. Uncle Mitch had been in and out of prison since he was fourteen years old. At the age of forty, he was finally out and trying to reacclimate to society.

Since she was a child, he always made her uncomfortable with the suggestive looks he would give her. Then, one evening when her parents were out, Uncle Mitch made his way into her room while she slept. She woke up abruptly when she felt him trying to remove her nightgown.

"What are you doing in my room, Uncle Mitch?"

"I want to show you how a real man feels," he said, standing back to pull out his erect penis.

"Get out of here!" she screamed.

"Baby, calm down."

She threw a lamp at him but missed. Pieces of the lamp shattered everywhere. He forcefully grabbed her and held her down.

"Lay still," he demanded.

As he lay on top of her, Michelle could smell a mixture of dark liquor on his breath and cheap cologne on his body. He tried to penetrate her, but she managed to get away from him and ran outside for help.

James and a friend were walking up the street toward her house when they heard Michelle screaming for help.

"What's wrong?" James asked.

"My uncle just tried to rape me," Michelle cried, barely able to get the words out. James and his friend ran into Michelle's house just as Uncle Mitch was trying to slip out the back.

James' friend caught him, and James punched him several times in the face. Uncle Mitch fell to the ground as James and his friend stomped on his head. Afraid that James would kill her uncle, Michelle pulled James off of him.

Blood flowed from Uncle Mitch's face to his shirt and pants. He could barely move as James demanded he leave, which he did.

She later told her parents what took place while they were out. The police were called, and Uncle Mitch was found and arrested. He was never allowed back in their home. Michelle's parents' saw James in a different light after that.

On her way home from visiting James in prison, Michelle thought about her boss and how their working relationship had recently changed. He had become distant and said very little to her anymore. Most days, it appeared as if he was trying to avoid her.

She couldn't understand why, although she assumed it was simply because he was under a lot of stress and frustrated about the investigation.

She worried about Williams, especially now that everyone knew about the case the FBI was building against him. She tried calling him several times on both his personal and work cell, but he never answered.

She loved how James acted jealous of her relationship with Williams. Michelle just laughed it off. She trusted her boss and knew he would never go against her.

***

It had been a busy morning for Jennifer, but a good one, and she hadn't even left to take the kids to school yet. She hung up the phone with a smile and sighed with relief. Her client load had expanded, and Seth had been offered a position with one of the largest art galleries in South Florida, although he was still in D.C. wrapping things up as he transitioned back to being in Miami full-time with his family. He would be home in just a few hours. And learning that things were finally moving forward with the investigation against Roger Williams gave both her and Seth some relief. Things were finally moving forward in a positive way.

She prayed that justice would prevail and Roger Williams would soon be behind prison bars.

After dropping the kids at school, Jennifer stopped off at Starbucks before heading back home for a client meeting. She noticed she had a few missed calls from her assistant Jan, so she checked in.

"Are you on your way home?" Jan asked.

"Yes, I'm about five minutes away. Is everything okay?"

"Yes, but please get here right away. There's something you need to see."

Jennifer made it home to a baffled Jan, who pointed to the computer. "This came up on Google alert."

Jennifer followed Jan's gaze to see nude photos posted of Jennifer on at least a dozen porn sites. Jennifer's mouth dropped as she stared at lewd photos of naked bodies with her face superimposed on them. She clapped a hand to her mouth to keep from crying out. Jan placed an arm around her shoulders.

"I can't believe this is happening to me." She immediately called Seth, who was already at the airport in D.C. on his way home to Miami. Seth was seething mad and immediately notified their attorney about the situation. Seth had no doubt that Williams had something to do with this harassment, and he was going to get to the bottom of it once and for all.

CHAPTER TEN

-----THE NAKED TRUTH-----

It had been a few weeks since Williams had been seen in the office, and there were so many rumors flying around about his whereabouts. Of course, it wasn't unusual for staff to speculate about his downfall. In fact, in the past, whenever he was out of the office for more than two days, the rumors would begin circulating. One had him traveling out of state for an interview. Another rumor had him on the brink of death and under treatment. One thing for sure, whenever he was out of the office, there was peace. The atmosphere was usually calm, and everyone appeared to be in a better mood. This time, however, it was different; we all wondered how this story was going to play out.

***

Roger's wife and children were gone. There were no remnants of his family anywhere in his house; his wife had taken all of their personal belongings. Even the family photos that once covered the walls of their home were gone. He wanted so badly to reach out to her and the kids but didn't have it in him to fight to get them back.

He missed his family. His children meant the world to him, and the thought of him not being with them was eating him alive.

The inside of their home was in complete disarray; there were empty scotch bottles, takeout meal containers, and clothes piled everywhere. Most days, he camped out on his couch, disheveled and despondent. While he experienced moments of fear, a part of him refused to go down like a punk.

"I'm about to lose every fucking thing!" he screamed from the top of his lungs as he sat tilted over on his coach, clinging to a bottle of scotch, hoping it would help the pain go away.

His personal cell phone rang and broke him out of his stupor. He looked down at the screen to see it was his childhood friend and fraternity brother calling. Roger fought to gain his composure so he could answer. It had been two weeks since he'd accepted anyone's calls, even those from the office.

"Hello," Roger murmured into the phone.

"Man, it's me, Gerald." "I've been trying to reach your ass for a week. Where the hell have you been?"

When Roger didn't reply, Gerald said, "Man, get up and go see your attorney. Call me later."

After a brief hesitation, Roger agreed and paid his attorney a visit later that day. Dressed in a black suit, wrinkled white shirt, and gray tie, he knew the gray stubble on his cheeks and chin and the dark circles under his eyes made him look a lot older than he was. He sat befuddled as the attorney spoke about a potential indictment.

"The feds are wrapping up their investigation and will decide soon whether to take the case to a grand jury. Witnesses may be called to testify, and evidence will be presented to the grand jury to determine whether there's enough to charge you."

"What's the likelihood that I would be indicted?"

"You never know. Again, it's based on evidence and testimony. I suggest you keep your sexy staffer, Michelle, happy. Her testimony could make or break the case." Rest assured, if you're charged, our firm will fight vigorously on your behalf."

The attorney hesitated, then said, "On the other matter, I heard from Jennifer's attorney about photos from her computer transposed onto porn sites. Do you know anything about this?"

"Not sure what she's talking about. I'm not even in contact with her."

"Well, they're claiming you had everything to do with it."

Roger pounded a fist on the man's desk. "That's slanderous and meritless. What proof do they have?"

"Calm down, Roger. If they continue with their outlandish threats, we'll have no choice but to counter sue. I'll take care of it."

Roger wanted so badly for Jennifer to disappear for good. He made a vow to himself that if he ended up getting indicted, she was going to catch a bullet to the head from his gun. In the meantime, he would focus on Michelle.

Determined, he cleaned himself up and got back in the office. While he spent most days in meetings, he made sure his presence was known.

There was a somber mood in the office, and he gave the staff hell. He wanted everyone to know he was still in charge, even though his fate was lurking over his shoulder.

He no longer invited Michelle into his meetings, and when he did meet with her, he made sure to criticize her work and blame her for anything that didn't go his way. When she tried to update him about Jennifer, he pretended not to know what she was talking about.

He arranged for IT to monitor Michelle's computer, saying he suspected she might be behind some of the things the FBI was investigating him for, and randomly checked the access card report to observe her activity in the building. He couldn't take any chances with Michelle, so he also hired a private investigator to follow her.

"So, what do you have for me?" he asked the private investigator late one night as he handed over a wad of bills, then looked around to see if anyone was watching them as they sat in Roger's car parked in the lot of a local bar.

"Your church girl is super clean. She leaves work and goes home to her four children and husband. Every Saturday, she goes to the post office to pick up letters from her oldest son's father, James Duperville. She visits him about twice a month in the pen."

In a New Jersey Italian accent, the investigator began to laugh at how Michelle's attire changes when she visits her oldest son's father, an indication that she still may have feelings for him. "Church girl wears red lipstick and tight skirts or dresses for her son's father."

"What about her husband," Roger asked.

"He's fucking the church secretary, and from what I can tell, doesn't appear to know what his wife's up to."

"Good job, Frank."

Roger didn't like how Michelle had a close relationship with her son's father, but it would explain how she had arranged for his dirty work to get done.

This didn't deter him from believing he could control her, however, as the information gave him something he could use as blackmail. He would soon reel her back in and make Michelle feel special again since she was apparently not getting any love at home.

He was an expert on how to deal with women, after all, which was why he hired them, particularly black women. He felt they were the most loyal but also the most naive. *No matter the circumstances, they will always remain loyal*, he thought.

***

Since Williams' return to the office, his attitude toward Michelle had changed, and he was becoming unbearable to deal with. He assigned her busy work, which forced her to stay late, and caused even more stress at home. Williams never gave her the raise he promised her for helping him retaliate against Jennifer, either, even though she was already earning less than everyone else on the management team.

Michelle should have taken James' warning about Williams more seriously. Obviously, Williams couldn't be trusted. But for now, she didn't want James to know that she was having problems at work, so on her next visit, she straightened her shoulders and plastered on a smile.

Michelle had lost a lot of weight since her last visit, and there were bags under her eyes. She seemed worried and was being evasive. James knew something was wrong.

"So, what's up with your boss?" he asked after a few minutes of their time together.

"He's okay. But, baby, let's talk about us."

"How's Antoine?"

"He's been working with my dad at the church. My father keeps him busy." She smiled.

"That nigga ain't put his hands on you, has he?"

"Of course not. baby, everything is fine."

"Well, K-Dub told me everything is good on their end. How's James Junior?"

"He's getting big and looking more like you," said Michelle. "I'll bring him with me next time."

James nodded, and they continued to talk about James Junior. A while later, an awkward silence ensued between them. The feeling that something wasn't right continued to bother James. He was going to get to the bottom of it.

Soon after, the visit was over, and Michelle stared deeply into his eyes as he stood. But James was too upset to speak, so he simply turned toward the guards and left her there. It was moments like this that made him feel powerless; he couldn't be there for Michelle like he should. He considered it his job to protector her, and he wasn't going to allow anyone to mess with her.

It reminded him of when he and Michelle were in high school. She was always in the middle of some drama at school because of him. Her light skin, long, pretty tresses, and beautiful figure caused many girls to envy her. And the fact that James, the most popular kid in school, just happened to be her boyfriend made everything more difficult for her.

He remembered when a group of girls plotted to fight Michelle after school and joked about ruining her face. James had been under suspension from school at the time, and his boys alerted him about what was planned to take place that afternoon. James stole his mother's car and drove quickly to the school to warn Michelle. One of the guards stopped him as he made his way inside, but James gave him twenty dollars and was allowed to enter the building. He ran through the hallway and saw Michelle at her locker, gathering her belongings.

"What are you doing here?" she asked as she looked around.

"Why are you still here?"

"I was studying in the library," she responded. "You know if Mr. Rodriguez sees you here, you're going to be in serious trouble."

"Don't worry about that. I need you to come with me."

"What's going on?"

"Just follow me."

Tugging her along, they ran through the hallway and downstairs toward the boiler room, where there was a door that led to the outside, then quickly jumped into the car and drove off.

"Keep your head down," he said, driving by about forty girls standing around the school grounds.

Thanks to his urging, Michelle transferred to their rival school, where she was less of a distraction to the female students.

***

Richard and Rachel had been making love all morning with the Isley Brothers' song "Between The Sheets" on repeat. It had been two months since they last saw each other, and they were making up for lost time. They even ignored the knocks at the door from housekeeping. Rachel lay lifelessly, moaned, and a few times belted out his name and God's, while she held tightly to his sculpted back. Richard kissed between her legs, which caused her body to quiver. One thing for sure, Richard knew how to please her. Their lovemaking was so intense that, at times, Rachel felt like a dancer in an encore performance.

Vanessa's health had taken a turn for the worse, so Richard had taken her to her doctors' appointments and stood by her side to make sure she was comfortable. The doctor gave her six months to live. Rachel could tell Richard was worried about how his son would take losing his mother; they were very close. She listened intently in bed as Richard proudly recalled when Vanessa gave birth to their son.

"I received a call from Vanessa that she was heading into the hospital. Thankfully, it was a home game, and the coaching staff arranged a police escort for me so I could beat the crowd and get to the hospital on time. With one good push, Vanessa gave birth to our baby boy. He was the most beautiful baby I had ever seen," he boasted.

"So, what happened? How did your marriage fall apart?" Rachel asked.

"I was young and stupid. I just got in the league, and women were everywhere. After Vanessa gave birth, she no longer wanted to make love to me, her focus became our son, and I began spending more time in the nightclubs. It got to the point where we couldn't talk to each other without her crying and throwing things. I loved her, but I wasn't ready or mature enough to handle having a family and being in the league. I never meant to hurt her. The first ten years of our marriage were terrible, and we both were unfaithful. Eventually, Vanessa and I stopped communicating at all.

"A few times, I left her, but I always came back because I missed my family. I wanted a better life for my son. I grew up without a father, and I didn't want that for him. Besides, I didn't want any other man disciplining him. Since then, Vanessa and I have grown closer and become great friends. We put our differences aside and chose to raise our son as a team.

Right before she was diagnosed with cancer, I had planned to ask her for a divorce, but when she became ill, I couldn't find it in myself to ask. She was so weak, I owed it to her to be there for her. Especially when I saw how it affected our son."

"What about us?"

"What do you mean?"

"I don't feel comfortable sleeping with a married man. What we're doing isn't right."

"What do you suggest that I do? Ask Vanessa for a divorce when she's on her deathbed?"

Rachel didn't know what else to say, so she offered, "How about we stop seeing each other until she gets better or..." Richard sat up and held her.

"Baby, I told you that Vanessa and I have been dating other people for years. Besides, I'm not sure if I could handle not seeing you."

Later that evening, Rachel told Richard that she could no longer be with him. He refused to accept her decision that she wanted to move on with her life without him. While she loved him, she could no longer be involved with a married man."

While sitting at her desk, thinking about her intense weekend with Richard, Rachel became startled by the sound of the office phone ringing and looked down at the caller ID to see it was Mr. Williams. She closed her eyes, cleared her throat, and answered, "Yes, Mr. Williams."

"Rachel, swing by my office," he demanded.

"Why me, God?" Rachel whined after hanging up the phone. She didn't want to see him today. Since he came back, he had been treating everyone like shit, non-stop.

When she walked to his office, he was on the phone and gestured for her to come in. As Rachel waited, she noticed he had gained weight and looked like he had not shaved in weeks. She began panicking and wondered if she had made all her deadlines. She didn't want him to have any excuse to harass her.

"Hello, Rachel. How are you?"

"I'm fine," she said nervously. The phone rang, and he picked it up. This time he talked for at least twenty minutes. Once that call was complete, he took another from his cell phone. It was now after five o'clock, which meant Rachel was going to be in his office for a while. Mr. Williams would often do this to staff. It was obvious he didn't want her to leave at 5:00 pm, and it had been a while since he'd called Rachel into his office. He probably wanted to make sure she remembered who was in charge.

"I have to take this call," he said with a smile. "Go to your office. I'll call you when I'm ready."

It was now 7:00 pm and no word from Mr. Williams. Rachel wondered what he wanted from her. She was afraid to leave because she knew if she left, he would call her on her cell phone and demand that she return to the office. So she waited for another thirty minutes before deciding to check back with him.

There was no one around, except for her. It was scary. With the exception of the light from the exit sign, the corridor leading to his office was dark, and his office door was closed. She was startled by the cell phone ringing. It was Richard.

"We need to talk."

"Not right now, Richard."

"What's wrong?"

Rachel explained to him what happened, and he urged her to go home. He stayed with her on the phone while she went back to her office to shut down her computer and gather her belongings. As she walked toward the elevator, her phone call with Richard dropped. A moment later, Rachel thought she heard someone walking behind her. When the elevator opened, she saw Hilda, the lady who cleaned the offices. She greeted Rachel with a kiss on the cheek.

"Que *tal*, Hilda? *Vistes mi jefe?*" Rachel asked.

"*El se fue como dos horas y pico,*" she said in a Cuban accent.

Mr. Williams had left a while ago but never told her he was leaving. He never mentioned why he wanted to meet with Rachel either. She saw it as a good thing and kept moving. The less interaction she had with him, the better she felt.

CHAPTER ELEVEN

-----KING'S GAMBIT-----

"We reached out to the proprietors of the websites, and the photos have been removed." Seth's attorney explained. "Unfortunately, this doesn't guarantee the photos won't appear elsewhere on the Internet. I've assembled my entire team on this matter, and they're closely monitoring the Internet for any sightings of the photos."

"How can we go after Williams? Seth asked. We know he's responsible for all of this. Jennifer and I have changed our mobile and home telephone numbers. We've added security to all of our computers. But what can we do to put an end to this?"

"Unless he's caught in the act or the person he's hired to do these horrible things is caught, there's very little we can do. The only consolation I can offer you right now is that Roger Williams will be in jail soon, and hopefully for a very long time. These days, he's not a happy camper. The authorities have discovered that expenses were improperly paid with federal funds. Now, the agency's access to those funds has been restricted. Until then, both of you will have to remain careful. Seth, you may need to arm yourself. The good news I can report is that the law will allow for damages and statutory penalties."

As he left the attorney's office, Seth assured himself that Roger Williams would be convicted of a crime soon. He had to be. Jennifer had been distraught for several weeks now, and unless Williams was taken care of, that wasn't going to change.

There were days she couldn't leave her bed, and if it wasn't for her assistant, Jan, Jennifer wouldn't have been able to maintain her business. It had gotten so bad that Seth took it upon himself to reach out to her mother to help out with the kids. He did everything he could to help bring her spirits up, but she couldn't seem to shake herself out of it.

Until Williams was taken care of, Jennifer would continue to feel their lives were under constant threat. Seth couldn't imagine losing his family, and he would do anything to protect them.

The attorney was right; it was time to purchase a gun.

***

At the penitentiary, Michelle shared with James that she was shocked how Mr. Williams commended her in the management meeting for a project she worked on. She was suspicious of his actions. It didn't make any sense after he'd spent weeks before ignoring her. And now, all of a sudden, he was praising her work.

Michelle leaned in closer to James and looked around to see if anyone was listening. "Williams has been treating me differently ever since that article came out," she told James. "Some of the files stored on my computer are missing, and IT says they can't account for them. A couple of times, when I've come into the office in the morning, I'd swear some of the things on my desk have been moved.

"What do you think is wrong with him."

"I thinking it may be because he knows I might have to testify."

"You mean snitch on him?"

"His attorney says my testimony is crucial to the case against him."

"I told you, he can't be trusted."

"So, what am I to do?"

"Play him at his own game."

"What about Jennifer?"

"Unless he pays up again, we're done. Just be careful."

"I will."

The guards arrived a few moments later to escort him out of the room. James gave Michelle one last look before he left. "I love you. Watch your back, okay?"

***

Inside her car, Michelle placed her head on the steering wheel and began to weep. She didn't want to leave without James; she needed him now more than ever. Her visits were becoming difficult for both of them, and every visit was a reminder that the man she loved would never be free. Her life was falling apart. Her marriage to Antoine was non-existent; they barely spoke outside of church, and she no longer had any interest in working for Roger Williams. She didn't trust him at all.

On her way home, she decided to stop by the church to see her dad. As she walked in, Antoine and her father's secretary, Monica, were leaving the building. They appeared startled when they saw her.

"Hey, what are you doing here?" Antoine asked.

"I thought I'd stop by to see my dad. Where are you guys off to?"

Antoine and Monica began speaking at the same time. "We're heading to Office Depot to pick up some supplies."

Monica smiled awkwardly at Michelle and looked away. Antoine had been working late at the church for the last several months and had been late picking the kids up from his parent's home, something he rarely did. He often took calls at night and would walk away to speak to the person on the phone. Michelle never imagined Antoine would cheat on her, but something didn't feel right between those two. The last thing Michelle wanted to do was worry about Antoine and be threatened by a secretary, who obviously ate far too many cheeseburgers.

As they drove away, the thought immediately escaped Michelle's mind, and she began thinking about James. What he said about Williams was right; she had to play him at his own game. And she was up for the challenge.

Michelle didn't want her dad to worry about her, so she pretended like everything was going well in her life. "How's Mom doing?"

"She just left about an hour ago," her father replied. "How are things at work?"

"Everything's going okay."

"How's Roger coping with the investigation?"

"He's keeping busy."

Her father nodded. "Roger has done so much for the community. It would be a travesty if he was removed from his position. You let him know that the community is pulling for him."

"I certainly will, Dad. I'm sure he'll appreciate your support. Well, I have to go," Michelle said as she stood. "I have to pick up the kids from daycare."

He leaned in to give her a hug. "Did you happen to see Antoine on your way in?"

"Yes, he and Monica were leaving for Office Depot."

"Oh. Okay. I'll see you on Sunday."

Williams had everyone in the community believing he was some dark knight who came to town to save Black Miami, which couldn't have been any farther from the truth. While her father received thousands of dollars from the agency for community programs, Michelle knew how Williams really felt about the community. Everything he did was a facade. He gave money as a way to control the neighborhoods. If anyone spoke badly about him or did something he didn't like, he would strip away their funding. He didn't care how much of an impact it would have on the community.

The Ministerial Alliance, which was comprised mainly of African-American pastors from the greater Miami community, was one of his biggest supporters. Even though the article exposed Williams, the Ministerial Alliance hosted prayer vigils for him. He could do no wrong in their eyes. For them, Roger Williams was another black man the system was trying to destroy.

Michelle was preparing dinner when Antoine came in from work. After dinner, he tucked the kids in bed and sat on the couch with his cell phone in hand. Michelle lay in bed, reading a book. Her thoughts drifted to her childhood with James. He had been a freshmen when he arrived at her high school.

***

His reputation preceded him; the teachers were afraid of James. The girls were enamored by him, and the boys emulated him. James was smart but rarely showed it in class. One afternoon, James was being disruptive, and Mr. Pierre, the math teacher, called him to the front of the class. Everyone began to laugh. Mr. Pierre was trying to make an example out of James, but his plan backfired. Instead, Mr. Pierre was amazed at how James was able to do the math problem. He began to call on James more often. When everyone started teasing James about it, he began to lash out at the teacher. He was eventually kicked out of class.

Michelle was the only girl in school who paid no attention to James. He made every attempt to talk to her in the hallways and at lunch, but Michelle was not impressed.

"I think you like me, but you're playing hard to get," James said to Michelle.

When he realized he was getting nowhere with Michelle, he chose to be her friend instead. The friendship blossomed into a relationship. Her parents were against the relationship in the beginning but realized they loved each other and nothing was going to tear them apart.

James' mother, stricken by drug abuse, was in and out of jail for prostitution, and James often had nowhere to go. He spent most nights sleeping on the floor of Michelle's bedroom. During those times, they would dream about their future. Michelle dreamed big, but James didn't imagine he'd live that long.

"What do you want to be when you grow up?" Michelle asked him one night.

"Not sure. I just hope to live past eighteen and not be in jail."

She looked down from her bed toward the floor where James was wrapped in blankets. "James, you have to dream big."

When her parents left for work, James would shower and ride to school with her. And even though they were in love, it didn't stop other girls and his poor decisions from tearing them apart. James started selling drugs in the tenth grade and was arrested a few times, landing him in Juvenile Detention. Michelle begged him to stop, but James loved the fast life enough to choose it over Michelle. Their on-and-off relationship at times became volatile. Michelle tried to date other guys, but James wasn't having it. When he discovered Michelle was in a relationship, he would beat up the guy.

Antoine and his mom became members of Michelle's parents' church. Michelle and Antoine had a budding relationship. Antoine was the guy in church that everyone looked up to. He had academic and athletic scholarship offers from several schools, he played football and had aspirations to play in the NFL.

Unfortunately, in his sophomore year of college, he ruptured his ACL and would never make it to the NFL. While Antoine caught the attention of a lot of girls, he only had eyes for Michelle.

James knew very little about Antoine because church was the last place James would attend, not even at the urging from Michelle.

She and Antoine remained friends until she came home from college, and while they shared similar interests, her heart was with James even though by this time, he was in prison for life. Still, she never imagined life without him.

Antoine came to bed, and Michelle pretended that she was fast asleep, but she was still in deep thought. The life she was living was not what she had planned. She considered asking Antoine for a divorce but didn't want to disappoint her children, parents, or the congregation.

***

Seth drove to the seediest place in town to purchase a gun. The shop was located in a dilapidated strip mall where a pawn shop, liquor store, beauty supply, and a Chinese restaurant with homeless people hanging around were the backdrop of the area. Definitely not a safe place for a white man in a business suit. But Seth was determined to protect his family, and he wasn't willing to wait around while the government conducted their background check on him. He knew Jennifer would be upset if she found out he was purchasing a gun, but it had to be done.

"I want to buy a handgun," Seth told the clerk behind the counter.

"What type of handgun are you interested in?"

"I need something powerful."

"What are you planning to do with the pistol?"

"It's to protect my family at home."

The clerk went to the back of the store and brought out a stainless-steel handgun. "The SIG Sauer 1911 is a full-size, .45 caliber pistol that carries a capacity of seven to eight rounds. It's powerful, yet small enough to be stored away safely in a lockbox."

"I'll take it."

When Seth arrived home, Jennifer was lying out near the pool with her mom and the kids. He placed the gun in a safety box stored away in the closet, high enough that the kids couldn't reach it. He didn't want to scare Jennifer and decided that it was best not to tell her right now. She seemed to be doing better today, and he didn't want to dampen her mood.

After storing the gun away, he joined his family outside. Seth's family meant the world to him, and he couldn't imagine life without them. He vowed that if there was no conviction of Roger Williams, he would take matters into his own hands.

CHAPTER TWELVE

----- FALLACY-----

Michelle logged into her computer, and this time, all of her files were gone. Once again, IT could not provide her with any answers about the whereabouts of her files. She became even more frustrated when Stephanie, who was recently hired to her unit, walked into her office and began giving her orders.

"I need your monthly report."

"I sent my report to Mr. Williams," Michelle explained.

"Well, from now on, you'll have to send your report to me. I need it by the close of business today," Stephanie said as she walked away.

Stephanie was a petite, rotund, and talkative white woman from Vermont. She had been hired to fill Jennifer's position. Rumor had it that she knew Williams from college, but no one knew for sure if that was true.

Stephanie's no-nonsense attitude infected the entire office. Her staff had to sign in and out to use the restroom, and eating at your desk was no longer allowed.

Michelle got the impression Stephanie had it in for her right from the start. Stephanie kept tabs on her and would brief Williams on her activities in the office.

An hour later, Michelle gathered her belongings and headed for the elevator. Just as she reached out to press the call button, Stephanie came up behind her.

"Where do you think you're going?" Stephanie asked.

"I have to take my son to his doctor's appointment."

"I wasn't aware of this doctor's appointment."

"I sent in my request to Mr. Williams several weeks ago," Michelle replied, ignoring Stephanie's demanding posture and stepping into the elevator as it arrived.

***

As Michelle waited for her son to come out of school, she gave Jennifer a call, but the call went straight to voicemail. She wanted to come clean with her. She knew Jennifer deserved to know the truth about Roger Williams.

"Hi, Jennifer, this is Michelle. I hope all is well. You and I really need to talk. There are some important things I need to share with you about Mr. Williams. Please, please call me back."

James Junior came running out of school with his book bag in tow. As he hurried toward her car, Michelle realized how much he was growing. He was no longer her baby. James Junior was a popular eighth-grade honor roll student and the spitting image of his dad. And like his father, he was well-liked by the girls. James was so proud of his son. He often boasted about him to other inmates and the guards.

"My son is going to grow up to be a doctor," James would say proudly.

James told Michelle how he kept photos of James Junior and his report cards all over the walls of his prison cell. He didn't want James Junior to be anything like him. During visits with James Senior, their son would always beat his dad at chess.

When James Junior opened the car door, he saw the McDonald's bag on the seat.

"Mom, you bought me McDonald's," he gushed with excitement, taking the cheeseburger and fries from the bag.

"Put your seatbelt on," Michelle said. Her son complied then tore into the burger. "How did you do on your science test?"

"I think I did well on it."

Michelle reached over and planted a huge kiss on his cheek.

"Mom, don't embarrass me."

While heading to the doctor's office from the interstate, Michelle thought about how she would tell Jennifer about Williams' revenge against her and how she had played a part in his plans. She wasn't sure how well Jennifer would receive the news. She was also concerned about her safety. Roger Williams was a dangerous man.

***

Michelle and James Junior were leaving the doctor's office when Michelle noticed she had a flat tire. She tried reaching Antoine several times at work and on his cell, but her calls went straight to voicemail.

"Mom, is Dad on his way?"

"I can't reach him, but I'm calling Popop, so sit tight."

Just as Michelle began calling her dad, a tall, slender Latino man in a suit approached her.

"You need me to change that tire for you?"

"Yes, please." She smiled. "You're a life savior."

James Junior sat on the steps with his headphones on while the good samaritan changed her tire. "How much do I owe you?" she asked when the job was complete.

"Nothing. A beautiful woman like you shouldn't have to pay anyone to fix your tire," the guy said.

"Thanks."

Michelle continued home and merged onto I-95. She turned up the volume on the car radio when she heard Whitney Houston belt out, "I'm Your Baby Tonight." She immediately thought of James and couldn't wait to see him that weekend.

She approached her exit and suddenly began to lose control of her car. She pressed the brakes to slow down, but nothing happened. The car maintained its speed. Frantically, she pumped the brakes, praying for her car to stop. As she rounded a curve, she lost control of her vehicle.

The car careened off the highway and flipped over a few times before landing upside down on the opposite side of the highway in oncoming traffic.

Barely conscious in the mangled car with the deflated airbags draped across both her and James, Junior, Michelle heard someone yell, "The woman is alive!"

Pastor Covington was in his office when he received the news that Michelle had been in a serious car accident. Michelle's parents immediately rushed to the hospital to be by her side. When they arrived at the hospital, they received the news that Michelle had been rushed into surgery, and James Junior had been pronounced dead upon arrival.

Michelle's mom screamed, "Oh God," and fell in her husband's arms as he consoled her. Pastor Covington made frantic calls to Antoine and Monica, but there was no answer. Antoine's parents came to the hospital immediately to join other family members, friends, and congregants.

***

Monica was on top of Antoine, holding tightly to the headboard and moaned as he entered her. He caressed her plumpish body and held on to her round breasts as they flopped up and down. After an hour of lovemaking, Monica and Antoine held each other and dozed off to sleep. Monica woke up and went into the bathroom that Antoine shared with his wife. There was an assortment of lotions and perfumes lined up on the counter of the bathroom sink. Monica showered and lathered her body with Michelle's shower gel. The entire bathroom smelled like Michelle. Monica went into Michelle's closet, perusing through her clothes and tried on Michelle's shoes. Monica gave herself a tour of the house and walked into the kid's room, where she saw family photos. Monica thought she heard Antoine wake up and immediately hurried back into the bedroom, where Antoine was still fast asleep. Monica returned Michelle's size too small robe, where she found it hanging on the bathroom door. When she finished getting dressed, she picked up her purse and noticed there were several missed calls from the pastor.

She listened to a voice message from Pastor Covington crying that Michelle and James Jr. had been in a terrible accident.

"Antoine, wake up! Wake up," she said.

"What's wrong?" he asked nervously.

"Oh, God! Michelle and James Junior have been in a car accident. We have to get to the hospital right away."

Monica and Antoine arrived at the hospital and were greeted by a nurse who escorted them to the family waiting room. Ms. Covington sat reading her Bible, her eyes sullen. Pastor Covington stood up, and when Antoine walked into the room, he couldn't contain himself when he shared the awful news about James Junior and how Michelle was clinging to life. Antoine broke down crying. Monica tried to comfort him, but he walked away from her.

Antoine went into the dark and cold sanctuary in the hospital. He got on his knees and made the sign of the cross, then began to pray for Michelle. He begged for mercy. Although he and Michelle had said very little to each other for several months, he still loved her, and especially James Junior. He considered him as his son. When James Junior came into his life, Antoine accepted fatherhood with open arms.

Antoine didn't know how he could go on with life without him. He promised God that if he kept Michelle alive, he would be a better husband and father to her and the kids. He knew he had to break off his affair with Monica. Antoine didn't know how he was going to tell his other children about their mom and brother.

Monica came into the sanctuary as Antoine was praying, walked over and placed her hand on his shoulder. Antoine stood up and brushed her hand off.

"I'm sorry, but we can't do this anymore. My wife is fighting for her life. I love her and will be by her side."

He walked out of the sanctuary, leaving Monica to wonder if he would ultimately change his mind. She loved Antoine but wanted to respect his space.

When the doctor walked into the waiting room, everyone rose to their feet and gathered around to hear what he had to say.

"Michelle is in critical condition. She suffered a traumatic brain injury. Fortunately we were able to stop the hemorrhaging."

"Thank you, God," said a family friend.

"However," the doctor continued, "time will tell if she will recover fully from this injury. We will continue to monitor her condition."

"Can we go in to see her?" asked her father.

"I would say in about an hour. The nurse will let you know when you can come in."

***

While Antoine sat at Michelle's bedside, Roger quietly walked into the hospital room bearing flowers. Michelle had an IV and tubes that ran from her body and hooked to a machine. Her eyes were swollen shut, and gauze covered the crown of her head. Antoine turned and nodded to Roger but said nothing as he stood silent in the doorway.

After a few minutes, Roger left without saying goodbye to Antoine. Once in the lobby, he hugged Pastor Covington and his wife. "I'll be in touch."

As he sat in his car in the hospital parking lot, Roger thought about Michelle and her condition. Everything was spiraling out of control. While he felt bad about Michelle's son dying, he still believed he'd had no choice. He had done the right thing by setting up the accident. He had to think of saving himself first.

***

While Jennifer prepared for bed, Seth came into the room after putting the children to bed.

"I received a few frantic messages from Michelle wanting to talk to me about Roger Williams," Jennifer told Seth.

"Did you call her back?"

"I tried—a few times, actually—but there was no answer. I figure Williams probably put her up to it. I don't trust her."

"Wonder what that's all about."

Jennifer shrugged. "Well, if it were really important, she would have called back by now."

***

James was excited that he was going to see Michelle today. The thought of her made his penis hard. He remembered how he and Michelle almost got caught having sex in her parent's home. When James heard the car door shut, Michelle pushed him off of her and quickly grabbed her clothes while James scurried around the room, trying to figure out how he was going to hide from her parents.

"Get in the closet," she demanded. James believed his son was conceived that night. He laughed to himself as he rubbed his hard penis. He missed everything about Michelle, including her sensual touch.

He waited and waited for Michelle to arrive. Eventually, visiting hours were over. At first, he was upset with Michelle and couldn't understand why she would choose to miss a visit with him. But knowing how much it was unlike her, he began to worry. She had promised him she would bring James Junior's eighth-grade prom pictures to the visit.

As he lay in his cell with thoughts of Michelle and his son going through his mind, a guard came by and handed James a cell phone, so he could call Michelle. There was no answer at her home, so he tried her parent's home but still got no response.

The next morning, James received a message from Pastor Covington that Michelle and James Junior had been in a serious car accident. He told him that Michelle was in the hospital in critical condition, and James Junior had died.

James' scream reverberated throughout the prison walls. He threw his mattress on the floor and destroyed everything he could get his hands on. It took several guards to restrain him, and James was later placed on suicide watch.

***

Seth ran into the bathroom. "Honey, Michelle and her oldest son were in a car accident. They just showed her picture on the news."

"Oh my goodness," Jennifer exclaimed as she turned off the water and quickly put on her robe.

"That's probably why she didn't return your phone call."

"Did they say what caused the accident? Are she and her son okay?"

"No, the cause hasn't been determined yet. Michelle's listed in critical condition, and her son was killed." Jennifer couldn't imagine life without her children and began to cry.

She had a gut feeling that Roger Williams had something to do with Michelle's accident and was determined to get to the bottom of it.

CHAPTER THIRTEEN

----- SINS OF HIS PAST-----

Overcome with emotion, Jennifer walked through the busy ICU in the hospital. Sweat beads formed around her face, and unwelcomed thoughts raced through her mind as doctors and nurses scurried back and forth from the nurse's station to the patient rooms. Everything moved in slow motion for Jennifer, even the somber faces of the families of patients waiting for encouraging news.

Michelle fighting for her life and the untimely death of her son was a reminder to Jennifer that something had to be done about Roger Williams. She was convinced he was responsible for Michelle's accident; she just wasn't sure how she could go about proving it. She could no longer sit back and watch another person fall victim to his crimes.

She stepped into Michelle's room and stood by the door for several long moments before approaching her bedside. Michelle showed very little movement. Her eyes were closed, and a deep reddish-pink color covered her eyelids. A tube connected from a machine to her mouth helped her breathe as an IV slowly dispensed fluids in her frail body. Jennifer fought back the tears as she stepped forward and held Michelle's hand.

"It's me, Jennifer. I'm so sorry I didn't answer your call. I believe you meant to warn me about something."

Antoine came into the room as Jennifer spoke to Michelle. The nurse followed after him and began to check Michelle's vitals. Antoine and Jennifer gradually made their way out into the hall to allow the nurse time with Michelle.

Jennifer took Antoine's hand. "I am so sorry for your loss. If there is anything we can do for you and Michelle, please let me know."

"Thank you," Antoine mumbled. "The funeral services will be this Saturday at 9:00 am at my father-in-law's church."

Grief and torment flooded Antoine's eyes, making Jennifer's heart ache all the more for this family. She desperately wanted to talk to him about her suspicion but felt it wasn't a good time.

After spending a few more moments with Michelle, Jennifer left the hospital, anxious to go home to be with her husband and children. Seeing Michelle in the hospital made her reflect on her life, and how in a blink of a moment, things could change drastically. Despite all that she had endured, she had a lot to be grateful for.

***

James was transported to the funeral outfitted with shackles on his feet and wrists. He was nervous and anxious to see his son for what would be the last time.

He grappled over the loss of his son and spent most days leading up to the funeral in his cell, staring at his son's photos and reflecting on the fateful night of the robbery. The sins of his past caused his son to die; James was certain this was all his fault.

He often replayed that night in his head as it was with that whirlwind of events that his life took a turn for the worse.

It was a rainy night, and Michelle was at home studying. Things were not going so well with her and James. It was Michelle's senior year in high school, and she had been accepted to several universities, most being out-of-state. Michelle had made up her mind that she was leaving Miami and chose Florida Agriculture and Mechanical University, a historically black college, in Tallahassee. James was upset and didn't want her to leave, and most days, they argued over her decision.

"Are you coming over?" asked Michelle.

"I'm stepping out with my boys."

"We need to talk about us."

"There's nothing to talk about. You've made up your mind, and I need to go; my ride is here," he said, then hung up the phone.

James jumped into the passenger seat of his friend's Porsche and was handed weed and alcohol as hip-hop music blared through the speakers. They drove for hours and in between, made a stop in South Beach, picked up food, and flirted with girls.

"Damn, man, we don't have any more blunts to roll," said Curtis.

"Pull over to old man Stewart's store," said James.

He entered the small convenience store and walked along the aisles beside his friend. Behind him, he heard Curtis run, followed by, "Hand me the money. All of it, now!"

James turned around to see Curtis brandishing a gun at the clerk, who struggled to get the drawer open. Tears streamed down the store employee's face as he cried. James rushed over to Curtis, not knowing what was happening.

"Man, what the hell?" James asked.

"Naw, nigga, we need some more cash," Curtis said laughingly. "Bitch, you better get that fucking money out, or else your folks are going to be wiping your blood off this damn floor."

"Man, I got it. Let's go," James said. As he looked back in the direction he just came from, he saw the owner of the store emerge from the back, then run behind Curtis and pointed a gun at his head.

"Drop the gun," the owner said. James tackled the owner from behind, and a fight ensued. Curtis jumped over the counter and snatched the money from the drawer.

"Lay down on the floor, bitch," Curtis ordered the clerk. Several shots rang out through the small store, and the owner fell to the ground. James stood over the owner.

"Ah shit, I think he's dead," said James. Curtis walked over and shot the man in the chest a few times to make sure.

"Come on, man, let's go," said James.

They drove away, and about two miles down the busy street, police sirens could be heard in the distance. Curtis sped through the streets, dodging in and out of traffic as the police swarmed the area. The car crashed into another vehicle, and Curtis and James jumped out and began running away from the scene. However, the police were already on their tails with their guns drawn. They demanded that they stop. With no other place to run, Curtis and James obeyed and were arrested and booked.

He had missed so many precious moments with his son, and because of his own failings, another man had to assume his role.

James had been banned by a judge from attending the service and was escorted into the sanctuary before the guests arrived. At the mahogany coffin, James scanned his boy's face, desperate to chronicle every last feature, even if they were made surreal by the mortician's makeup.

James Junior appeared to be sleeping. He wore a black suit and a blue tie, his body surrounded by white lilies and a large photo of him dressed in his soccer uniform and smiling. James gripped the casket, ignoring the soft satin beneath his fingers and sobbed. His only son was dead—his "mini-me," as Michelle would often refer to James, Junior.

James spent the allotted fifteen minutes talking to his son, begging for his forgiveness. Once his time was up, James leaned down and pressed a kiss to his son's cool, lifeless forehead.

"I love you, lil man," he said one last time, squeezing his shoulder as if to comfort him on his journey into eternity. James brought his handcuffed hands up to his face and wiped the tears with his knuckles. Taking one last moment to compose himself, he allowed the guards to escort him to the van to report back to prison.

**

During the service, a soloist, accompanied by a choir, sang a stirring rendition of Mahalia Jackson's "Precious Lord Take My Hand." Mourners in the large sanctuary gave praise as the song moved over them. Afterward, friends and classmates shared stories of their time with James, Junior. Toward the end of the service, Pastor Covington delivered a powerful sermon about seeking compassion in the midst of grief.

Jennifer sat stoically, trying to make sense of it all, while Seth appeared dumbfounded by the intensity of emotion displayed in the predominately black congregation. It was nothing like his Jewish faith, where the services were fairly simple and aimed at the deceased, not the mourners.

She glanced over at Antoine, who looked to be struggling to hold it together. His children sat on each side of him, and throughout the service, they buried their heads in his chest to avoid looking at their older brother lying in the casket.

When the casket was closed, family and friends could be seen fainting and heard weeping out loud. At times, some mourners began engaging in spirit-filled dancing by their seats.

Jennifer couldn't believe her eyes when Roger Williams made his grand entrance a moment later and was directed by the ushers to the front of the church, where elected officials and dignitaries sat. When Pastor Covington introduced Williams, he spoke about a man of faith committed to giving back to the community. He denounced the federal investigation by referencing David and Goliath, a scripture in the Bible.

Pastor Covington's voice grew louder and huskier as he pointed out that Roger Williams was up against a giant. "You come against me with sword and spear and javelin, but I come against you in the name of the Lord Almighty."

Some of the mourners shouted, "Amen," in agreement. The uncanny support Williams had in the church sickened Jennifer. Seth could obviously tell that the whole scene was affecting Jennifer, as he held her tightly while the pastor went on.

Jennifer couldn't keep her eyes off Williams as he pranced along the pulpit, boasting how wonderful a mother Michelle was to her kids. He mentioned the few times he met James Junior and how he was taken aback by his intelligence and wit and that James Junior had reminded him of himself as a child.

"While James Junior was only here for a short while," Williams intoned, "he made an impact on the people he met and the friends he made."

Williams closed his speech by announcing his plans to open a computer center at the church in honor of James Junior. "The agency will fund the program and provide the supplies."

Pastor Covington stood, closed his eyes, and held his hands together as a gesture of thanks.

"Let the church say amen," Pastor Covington called out as Williams made his way to his seat.

Afterward, the funeral procession carried James Junior's casket to a horse-drawn carriage, making its way to Miami Memorial

Park Cemetery, a few miles from the church. Few were in attendance as they lowered his coffin into the ground.

On the ride home from the cemetery, Jennifer shared with Seth her suspicion about Mr. Williams being responsible for Michelle's accident.

"Why else would Michelle be calling me?" she asked Seth. "Something is strange about this entire situation."

"Honey, the attorneys are confident that Roger Williams will be behind bars, where he deserves to be. Let's just wait and see what happens."

"Do you think I should share my suspicion with Pastor Covington?"

"Not unless you have solid proof. Williams is weirdly a god-like figure around here. You saw how they treated him in there. Not only do I think the pastor wouldn't believe you, but I wouldn't want to take that chance of Williams getting wind of your accusations."

***

The entire office was abuzz with the news of Michelle's accident and the death of her son. A few of Rachel's colleagues attended the service, but Rachel chose not to attend because she knew Williams would be there and very likely put on a show. She was not in the mood for his theatrics.

Oddly enough, in meetings following those first days and weeks after the funeral, Williams voiced how extremely disappointed he was with some of Michelle's reports. He even talked about wanting to hire someone else with better skills. His behavior didn't surprise Rachel. Williams could turn the switch on and off at a moment's notice.

Meanwhile, he had everyone believing he was developing a computer center in her son's name. Most of the office staff didn't believe he would go through with it. He would undoubtedly come up with some nebulous plan to keep Pastor Covington at bay and later give him all sorts of excuses as to why he was unable to fund the project.

Claire, Williams' personal secretary, gave Rachel the keys to Michelle's office to obtain statistics from her reports to add to the annual report. But what really surprised Rachel was that Claire had done so without Mr. William's permission. Rachel figured Claire was buried in work and probably didn't realize what she had done. In that office, no one could move without Mr. Williams' permission.

It felt odd entering Michelle's office knowing that she was in the hospital gravely injured, fighting for her life. Still, Rachel went through the files looking for what she needed, and as she did, Rachel noticed that a good many of Michelle's files seemed to be missing.

While she searched Michelle's desk, Rachel found a Post-it Note with a scribbled reminder to call Jennifer on the floor next to Michelle's wastebasket. Thinking quickly, she stuck the note in her pocket, then conducted a hasty search of Michelle's desk drawers. Once she found what she needed, she closed the door to Michelle's office and headed back to her own, where she contacted Jennifer and made arrangements to meet for lunch.

***

Jennifer looked as beautiful as ever and appeared well-rested. As the small talk commenced, she pulled out her cell phone to show Rachel some family photos and talked about her children and how much progress Mathew had made in school.

"The funeral service was beautiful, and Pastor Covington gave a wonderful sermon. There wasn't a dry eye in the church," Jennifer went on.

Rachel nodded. "I would have come if I wasn't so sure Williams would be there. You saw him, didn't you?"

"Unfortunately, yes, I saw Jim Bakker. I mean Mr. Williams." Jennifer chuckled.

"Who's Jim Bakker?" Rachel asked.

"You know, Jim Bakker, the televangelist and convicted fraudster who was married to Tammy Faye."

"Oh yes, and his wife was the one who wore long fake eyelashes and a ton of makeup."

Jennifer shook her head in disgust. "Right. Well, Williams made his appearance in just that style. Like the grand fraud, he is."

They both laughed.

Jennifer hesitated, then said, "I visited Michelle, and her prognosis is grim. But the family isn't giving up hope. She tried contacting me the day of the accident, but I didn't take the calls. It had been well over a year since we last spoke, and we didn't quite end on good terms."

"Actually, that's what promoted me to call you. I found a sticky note in Michelle's office, reminding her to call you."

"I tried calling her back after I thought about it, but not in time."

"Why do you think she wanted to talk to you?"

"I'm not sure. But I have a sneaking suspicion it had something to do with the affairs in the office. The voicemail she left me sounded urgent. Rachel, I have an awful feeling Mr. Williams was responsible for her accident."

"You really think so?"

"Yes, well, I don't have any proof, of course. But Williams is so feral that I would be surprised if he didn't. Michelle is a key witness in his case, and her testimony could be damaging."

Rachel leaned forward and lowered her voice. "How's the investigation going? You probably know more than I do."

"The federal investigation is basically complete. Now we're just waiting to see if the feds are going to request a grand jury."

"Williams wasn't in a good mood this morning. He complained about Michelle's reports and how they were prepared improperly. It was strange, especially so soon after her son's funeral."

Jennifer sat back and took a sip of her cooling coffee. "Well, I plan to invite a few of Seth's detective friend's over for dinner. I'm hoping after a few glasses of wine, I'll be able to pick their brain about the accident."

"Most of her files are gone from the office."

"They were probably used as evidence for the investigation."

"Maybe." Rachel reached into her purse and pulled out a thick envelope. "I found a few note pads tucked deep into Michelle's desk while getting what I was sent in there for. I thought maybe you could gain some insight from something in them."

"Thanks. I'll make sure you get them back."

"Oh, don't worry about that. In fact, I'd rather not risk being caught with them."

***

Rachel left lunch feeling sick to her stomach. She couldn't believe what she had just heard. *Could he really have done something so egregious?*

She then pulled out her phone and notified the office that she was going home because she wasn't feeling well. She knew Williams would have something negative to say the next day about her leaving early when there was something due for him, but Rachel didn't care. She just wanted to be home, away from work.

CHAPTER FOURTEEN

----- GHOSTLY-----

Haunted, images of Michelle's accident played out in Roger's nightmares. He saw himself lying in a coffin and became paralyzed by fear. He would wake up drenched in sweat. He downed some scotch and watched CNN to kill time, hoping he could escape his fears, but they only intensified.

He yearned to be with his family. He knew his wife and kids loved him, and he missed coming home to his wife's cooked meals and the kids running amok. They were the only people on this earth he could trust.

A few times, he tried calling his wife, but she ignored his calls. He often went by his children's school, hoping he could catch a glimpse of them on the playground. While it had been only a few months, it felt like years had passed since he held his children in his arms.

He felt compelled to make amends by following through with his promise to open a computer center in James Junior's honor, and in a panic, ordered staff to have the computer center up and running at Pastor Covington's church by the end of the week.

But he also felt at ease, knowing that Michelle was still in a coma and not fit to testify against him. His lawyer advised him that without Michelle's testimony, the feds didn't have much of a case.

***

"I'm confident you all can get the job done," Mr. Williams announced during a staff meeting after ordering them to get the center operating before the end of the week. Williams' sudden sense of urgency to have the center operating at such short notice sent astonished glances around the room.

Rachel went back to her office, wondering if she could possibly pull off a ribbon-cutting without a hitch in less than a week. She immediately began making phone calls inviting dignitaries and hoping to secure some media coverage, but there were no guarantees, which was something Mr. Williams had trouble understanding.

She and Richard had been in contact since he buried his wife. He grieved her death and was concerned about his son's welfare, who was having a difficult time coping with the loss of his mother. She wanted to be there for Richard as a friend, but it was hard since she was still madly in love with him and wasn't sure where she stood.

But not seeing Richard, coupled with the stress from work, was definitely taking a toll. It was best for both of them that they give each other space, but many nights she longed for his touch and late-night talks.

***

White chairs lined the plush green grass of the church grounds as blue and white balloons swayed back and forth on a balmy Friday afternoon. A welcoming poster with a picture of James Junior was displayed in front of the church. Fifty spectators, mainly family members, parishioners, and supporters of the church, and a few reporters braved the searing high temperatures by waving paper fans handed out by the ushers.

Mr. Williams arrived shortly before the ceremony began, strutting around and ordering his attending staff members to get things going. Pastor Covington opened the ceremony with a prayer, and later a soloist performed a gospel song in acapella.

Looking haggard and not his usual upbeat self during public events, Mr. Williams approached the podium with the speech Rachel had prepared for him in hand.

At times, he forgot parts of his speech, even though Rachel provided him with talking points.

Williams cleared his throat. "I'm sorry, everyone. I'm asking you all to please pray for my family and me. The last couple of months have been extremely difficult for us. I'm unsure of my fate, but I trust that God will see me through this storm," he said, visibly fighting back tears.

"Please join me in prayer," Pastor Covington intoned to the audience.

After the prayer, the mood and the atmosphere slightly changed. Everyone roared in applause as Williams presented a check to Pastor Covington in the amount of five thousand dollars toward a scholarship fund in honor of James Junior.

Following the ceremony, Williams disappeared while the rest of the staff returned to the office. When he didn't show up at the office the following day either, Claire told the staff that he was out of town attending a conference.

Rumors started up again. Some of the staff suggested he turn himself in to the feds, and others believed he was on the run, while some simply believed he was down on his luck and had checked into a rehab center of some sort. With all the different theories floating around, Rachel wasn't sure what to think, but whatever was going on with Williams, she knew it wasn't anything good.

***

Antoine was dismal at work and no longer his buoyant self. He didn't say much to anyone, including Monica, who he avoided as much as possible. He wasn't taking the news well about Michelle's failing health. The family gathered at the hospital to meet with the doctor to discuss her recent setback.

"Her condition isn't improving, and the longer she remains in a coma, the bleaker her chances of fully recovering," the doctor said.

Antoine held his mother-in-law as the family searched for answers. He struggled with knowing that he could end up raising his children as a single dad. His kids often asked him when their mommy was coming home and if James Junior was ever coming home from heaven. Antoine tried to answer their questions the best he possibly could but always came up short.

He also carried the burden of his affair with Monica. He hadn't loved her but never meant to hurt her either. And now, he had ignored her for so long that she was making threats to expose their affair to the entire congregation.

"I love you, Antoine, and I can help you with the kids," Monica begged.

"Monica, I don't think it would be a good idea if we continued to see each other. Let's just keep this friendly."

But Monica wasn't taking no for an answer. She was relentless in continuing their affair. She believed that God wanted them to be together and tried to lure Antoine with sex. She even began dropping off dinner unannounced at his home.

Antoine was notified by his kids' school that a woman tried to impersonate Michelle and attempted to sign the kids out one day. He also discovered that she had stolen a few pieces of Michelle's jewelry when he saw her wearing it at work. Of course, she denied taking it from his home, even though it was obvious she was lying.

It wasn't long after that Antoine realized Monica was not well and needed help. He wanted no part of her. And the more she pushed the issue, the more he wanted to tell Pastor Covington everything, but he feared hurting Michelle's family, and especially Pastor Covington. *It's just not the right time.*

***

Jennifer and Seth invited their close friends, Jim and Maria, over for dinner at their home. Jim was a veteran cop for the police department, so Jennifer didn't waste any time asking him questions about Michelle's accident.

"Any updates on the car accident on the I-95 exit ramp involving a mother and child?"

The puzzled look on Jim's face suggested he wasn't quite sure what Jennifer was talking about, so she continued to probe for answers. "The accident involving a son who died and the mother who remains in a coma," Jennifer continued.

Seth looked over at Jennifer, signaling her to stop, but she waited for Jim to respond.

"Yes, I do remember," Jim replied. "It was determined that the cause was a tire that came loose because lug nuts were missing from the car's right front and rear tire rims. It's also believed that the driver was going slightly above the speed limit and lost control."

"Do you think someone may have tampered with the tires?" Jennifer asked.

"Possibly. Or the mechanic may not have tightened them properly. Mechanics do it all the time."

"I find it odd that two tires would have been missing lugs. Don't you?"

"Are you guys up for some dessert?" Seth asked after giving Jennifer a look.

Jim chuckled. "I'd love some."

"Great. We have some homemade Crème Brule that Jennifer's mom made."

Later while cleaning up the dishes, Maria came in and offered to help while Seth and Jim sat out on the patio, smoking cigars.

"Is everything okay?" asked Maria asked.

"Yes, I'm fine," Jennifer replied. "I just have a lot on my mind."

"Are you worried about Michelle?"

"I am. I believe someone meant to hurt her."

"Do you believe it's the same person who was harassing you?"

"Yes, Maria. I really do."

***

Later in the evening, Seth expressed his concerns with Jennifer about her burning desire to solve Michelle's accident.

"Honey, I think you should leave the investigating to the police. You heard Jim. It's likely that her mechanic didn't tighten the lug nuts."

Jennifer sighed. "How could you think it's merely an accident when I've had so many strange things happened to me?"

"I just want you to be careful. This man is dangerous."

"Well, I'm not going to be able to sleep well, knowing that her son died because of this man. You need to support me on this, Seth."

"I do. I'll just say again, I want you to be careful."

"Of course. You know I will."

***

Jennifer called Antoine the following day but didn't want to alarm him with her suspicions. Instead, she asked for the name of Michelle's mechanic to gain some insight on the last time Michelle had her car checked.

"It's been close to a year since she took her car in for any type of service," Antoine said. Before the conversation ended, he told Jennifer that Michelle had left him a message that she had a flat tire and a passerby helped her replace it.

The passerby could have been anyone, Jennifer thought. And could have been responsible for loosening the lugs on the tires.

After hanging up, Jennifer sat mulling over her conversation with Antoine when Seth came in. "How was your day?" he asked as he leaned over and kissed her on the lips.

"I'm exhausted, honey," she said before rising and slowly disrobing to get in the shower. "But I did find out from Michelle's husband that she had a flat tire when she came out of the doctor's office, and a stranger changed it for her."

"Well, there goes your theory."

"Maybe. But what if the person who changed the tire intentionally flattened it so they could loosen the lugs?"

Seth smirked. "Are you a detective now?"

"Honey, this is serious. I don't believe for one minute that Michelle lying in a hospital bed, fighting for her life, is an accident."

"I know, and I don't either," he replied, going to her and rubbing her shoulders. "I'm just concerned that you're meddling in someone else's business. Don't forget that our lives are at risk as well. Let's not do anything to stir more trouble for us."

Jennifer's shoulders slumped in defeat and disappointment at the direction of the conversation.

She nodded and headed for the bathroom without another word, but after climbing in the shower, she called out to Seth, "I didn't realize I brought trouble to our family!"

A moment later, Seth spoke through the door, "I'm sorry, honey. I just don't know what I would do if I lost you and the kids."

Even though she knew Seth had a point, Jennifer remained upset throughout the evening. It was time she focused on family and expanding her business. Still, something in her wouldn't let it go. She simply couldn't let Michelle go out like that.

***

James continued to mourn the loss of his son. He often dreamed about the three of them together as a family. His dreams felt so real that he would catch himself talking in his sleep. Pastor Covington had been to visit James since Michelle had been in the hospital. He told him how the police had not yet relinquished the report determining the cause of the accident.

"I can't accept that she's in the hospital fighting for her life," James mumbled.

"Son, you keep your head up and remember God is in control."

James wanted so badly to believe that Michelle would fully recover from the accident, so he began praying, something he had never done before. He started thinking about his life and, after the urging of an older inmate, he began reading more, immersing himself in all types of literature to broaden his mind.

James admired Malcolm X, who later became El-Hajj Malik El-Shabazz, and was able to transform his life not once but three times, and read his autobiography. His radical readings of racial divisiveness evolved after embarking on a spiritual pilgrimage to Mecca, to a calling of peace between people of all races.

James wondered if he could change his life for the better. He knew he couldn't remove his past, but moving forward, he could make an effort to better himself. He enrolled in a GED class, and while he sought a path of transformation, he couldn't commit to not killing Roger Williams if he found even the slightest evidence that the man was connected to the accident.

CHAPTER FIFTEEN

-----REVELATION-----

Antoine dropped the kids off at school and headed to the hospital to be with his wife.

When he entered Michelle's room, shock reverberated through him, seeing his former mistress sitting with his wife. Fear and anger raged inside him, and he struggled with which emotion to deal with first. But knowing what Monica was capable of, he decided it was time to talk to her.

"We need to talk, Monica," he said, careful not to disturb his wife. The nurse walked into the room before Monica could respond, but they later met in a quiet corner in the cafeteria, where they could have some privacy.

Antoine looked around to see if he knew anyone, and seeing he was in the clear, began to chastise her. "Let me be clear. I don't want to have anything to do with you."

"You said you loved me," Monica cried.

"I can't be with you. I'm a married man, and I love my wife. Don't you understand? I need to be with my family now." When she didn't respond, he rose from his seat and walked away, hoping to end any desire she had for him once and for all.

***

Antoine stood in front of the door leading to his father-in-law's office. His hand hovered above the doorknob as he gathered his courage to confess everything.

He had spent the weekend contemplating what he would say to the man who had been a father figure to him most of his life. He never meant to hurt Michelle, but at times, he felt prayers couldn't erase their problems.

Taking a deep breath, he firmly rapped his knuckles against the window frame. "Pastor Covington, sir. It's me. Antoine."

"Come in, son. Have a seat. You look like you've got the weight of the world on your shoulders."

"It feels like it," Antoine admitted, rubbing his sweating palms against his pants.

"What's on your mind?"

There was no gentle way to tell the father of his wife that he had cheated on her. But Antoine figured it was best to grab the bull by the horns and just tell it from the beginning.

He took a seat. "A few months ago, Michelle and I were having problems in our marriage."

"I wasn't aware," the pastor said.

"I found love letters written from James to Michelle. It was apparent they were having an emotional affair. Every time she came home from a visit with James, she would be in a spellbinding trance for days that I couldn't break. Nor could I compete with those feelings. She shut me out completely, and Monica gave me her undivided attention. I fell for the temptation," Antoine cried.

Pastor Covington appeared stunned by the admission. He also didn't look happy.

"Earlier in my marriage, I had an affair with another woman, and it almost cost me my marriage and family. An affair, young man, is not worth losing your family over; your family is depending on you. Do you understand?"

"Yes, sir."

"I'm going to transfer Monica to the youth center. If I were you, I would limit your interactions with her."

Relieved that he had spoken with the pastor, Antoine made a promise to God that he would be a better man.

****

As Jennifer left her client, she decided to stop by the pediatrician's office. Michelle's kids used the same pediatrician as Jennifer's, and even though she promised Seth she wouldn't focus on the accident, she was compelled to see what she could discover. And something told her the answer lay at the doctor's office.

It was located in a busy strip mall, and she wondered if anyone had seen anything. Inside the pediatrician's waiting room, parents were in deep conversations while they struggled to gain control of their busy toddlers. Jennifer could barely hear the receptionist, but no one in the office could offer much information. As she departed another doctor's office in the same strip mall, a clerk suggested Jennifer speak with the manager of the mall and view footage from the outdoor cameras. While she wasn't sure she would find anything, Jennifer believed it was worth a try.

***

James kept himself busy by delving into stories like *Down These Mean Streets* by Piri Thomas, *Dopefiend*, and *Never Die Alone* by Donald Goines. He enjoyed reading these types of stories because they closely mirrored his life. He felt connected to the characters, and most of all, it kept him from thinking about his terrible loss.

The guards often dropped off copies of the *Miami Herald* to his cell. Reading the paper kept James abreast of the outside world, especially the metro section, where he could check out the latest arrests in the neighborhood.

James learned about the cause of Michelle's accident in the newspaper, and the news didn't sit well with him. It didn't make any sense, and the more he thought about it, the more he was convinced that Roger Williams was tied to the accident.

An inmate and a childhood friend of James reminded him about a similar fatal car accident involving a rival gang member's relative.

News had traveled fast, and it was only a matter of days after that when James found the person responsible for causing the accident that killed his son. He ordered his boys to torture him until he gave up some answers. His friends thought it was odd that James didn't want the man killed, but James knew Williams was the real culprit behind the accident. Killing the man who had taken the job would be too easy, and James wanted him to suffer the consequences.

****

Rachel was excited to see Alice and Anita, and it meant a lot to Rachel that they came to see her. They had a lot to catch up on.

Rachel took Thursday off to get her house in order for her upcoming guests. After settling down from a busy day, she sat on her patio drinking a glass of Chardonnay while thinking about Richard. As if telepathically speaking to him, the phone rang, and it was him.

She couldn't believe how lonely she felt after hearing his voice. They talked through most of the night about how he was ready to move forward with the relationship. While she loved him, Rachel was afraid of getting hurt again.

"I love you, Rachel. You have to trust me that I'm not going to hurt you."

"This just isn't a good time for me. I'm so ready to walk off my job—"

"I understand, and if you need some time, then I'll give you some space."

"It's getting late, and tomorrow I have a long day ahead of me. We'll talk again. I love you," she said.

"I love you too."

***

She was so happy to see her friends. Being together seemed to help her forget all the pressing issues of the moment. Alice and Anita were her sources of strength.

They were all so excited to see each other. Alice decided to go natural and did the big chop. She showed off her cropped curly afro that complimented her facial structure. She wore dangling wood earrings to accentuate her hairstyle and a long flowing green maxi dress. Anita donned some fitted jeans and heels with a t-shirt that read, "I'm a proud mom of a Howard University Bison."

After a long day of shopping, we ended the day sitting by the pool, talking and drinking wine.

"How are things with you and Richard?" Anita asked.

"We're giving each other space, but it's really hard."

"What's the reason behind the space?" Alice asked.

Anita looked over at Alice.

"What?" Alice asked as she glared back. "I know she's horny as hell," Alice said with a giggle.

"Sex isn't everything," Rachel replied.

Alice laughed. "Girl, please. You're talking to your friends of twenty-plus years."

"Look, his emotions are everywhere. I need to know for sure that I'm not jumping into a relationship with someone who's confused about how he feels. Besides, I'm afraid. I've been down this road before, and I need to know I'm making the right decision."

"Has he given you any reason to believe otherwise?" Alice asked.

"No, not really."

"I get that you're afraid of getting hurt—"

"Yes, I am afraid. And I'm not ready to make a commitment to him right now."

"How long do you expect him to wait around?" Alice asked.

"Until I'm ready. What about you and Clarke?"

Alice grinned. "We're just friends."

"More like friends with benefits," Rachel said.

Alice burst out in laughter. "No, we really are just friends."

Rachel turned to Anita. "You're awfully quiet," she said while pouring more wine into each glass.

"Well, ladies, I have some news to share with you all."

"Are you pregnant?" Alice asked.

"Of course not. My shop has been closed since the mid-nineties. But I am dating someone new."

"Tell us about him."

"Well, Tim is a divorcee. He works for a software company, and he has two teenage girls. We met online, and I've already done a background check on him. He's clean. But, there's just one more thing." Anita hesitated, then announced, "He's white."

Alice spit out her wine, and we all burst out in laughter.

Anita stood with her wine glass in one hand. "You guys can wait on your dark knight. I'm not limiting myself to dating only black men. Besides, white men have been hitting on me for years. I'm tired of staying at home on a Friday night watching Netflix." After her declaration, Anita stumbled back into her seat.

"Well, I love chocolate," Alice replied.

"Let the church say Amen," Rachel said.

Anita frowned. "I do too."

Rachel reached over and patted her knee. "You're just trying something new."

"Until she gets tired of him," Alice interjected, then took another sip of her wine. "Like she does with all the men she dates."

Anita laughed. "Well, he's all right in my book. Not only is he well endowed..." she began, then paused to clear her throat, "...but he knows what to do with it."

"Ain't nothing wrong with that," Rachel cheered as they gave each other high-fives.

"Seriously, guys, he's so sweet. We have so much fun together, and I think he might be the one." We raised our wine glasses and cheered for Anita.

"So, when do we get to meet him?" Rachel asked.

"Soon."

Alice asked, "Well, does he have a brother?" We fell out laughing.

Once Anita caught her breath, she said, "No, he has a sister."

"Uh, no, thank you," Alice returned.

They finished three bottles of wine and laughed until the wee hours of the morning. And as Rachel straightened up before turning in, she said to herself, "I am so happy that I scheduled that spa appointment for us late in the day tomorrow."

CHAPTER SIXTEEN

-----INDICTMENT-----

An indictment was handed down by a grand jury along with a warrant for Williams' arrest. With his attorney by his side, reporters swarmed around him like bees to honey, seeking answers as he made his way into the police station. He was fingerprinted and processed in the county jail and released two hours later on his own recognizance.

Crammed into the small kitchenette, Rachel stood with the rest of the office staff, staring at the TV screen with disbelief. His face flushed with anger, Williams ignored the reporters' shouted questions as his attorney hustled him through the crowd, and they drove away from the chaos.

Later that morning, staff was called into the conference room, where a meeting was held to discuss his tenure at the agency. Some staff cried, which Rachel thought was odd, considering he tormented each and every one of them. Rachel was beyond relieved, screaming for joy inside.

The assistant director informed the staff that he would assume Mr. Williams' responsibilities. He also mentioned that if Williams was ultimately cleared of all charges, there was a chance he would return to his position.

After the meeting, Rachel went back to her office and sent texts to Courtney, Alice, and Anita with the good news of Roger Williams' arrest. They were all happy for her.

Rachel was eager to talk to Richard that evening. After much convincing from her friends, she decided she would give it a try and pursue a relationship with him. She loved him and didn't want to lose him because of fear.

***

After much convincing, Jennifer was able to meet with the manager of the strip mall to review tapes from the outdoor cameras. Seeing Michelle and James Junior leaving the doctor's office hand in hand was heartbreaking. In the video, a Latino male in his mid-thirties appeared to be walking toward his car as Michelle hovered over her flat tire with cell phone in hand. As the young man changed her tire, Michelle walked away from the car and made a few phone calls. The camera caught the stranger quickly loosening the lug nuts on other tires as Michelle and James Junior stood by, their attention diverted. When he finished changing the tire, Michelle returned and offered him a few dollars, which he appeared to decline.

Jennifer was excited to find a video showing someone tampering with Michelle's car before her accident. While the video was grainy, Jennifer believed she had something tangible that the authorities could use to identify this mystery man in the video. She wondered how she was going to break the news to Seth about the video. She knew he would be upset, but she didn't like withholding information from him.

Jennifer met with Jim at the police station. "We may be able to identify this man by using facial recognition software," Jim told her. "If there's a match, we'll bring him in for questioning. But I'm going to be honest with you, Jennifer. This video doesn't show him flattening her tires, nor can we see him clearly tampering with the other tires. Without additional information, this video alone probably won't hold up in a court of law. Still, I'll check into this and do whatever I can.

Jennifer gripped his hand enthusiastically. "Thank you, Jim."

A few days later, she received a call from Jim telling her that the police had identified Juan "Bud" Garcia as the man in the video. He had a criminal rap sheet dating back to 2000, stemming from aggravated assault to possession of a controlled substance with intent to sell. He was a career criminal. While the police didn't have a warrant for his arrest, they wanted to bring him in for questioning about the accident.

***

The doctor informed the family that Michelle was brain dead, and her other organs were failing. A machine was keeping her alive. The news of her condition shrouded the family in turmoil.

Pastor Covington believed that God would be able to heal her in time. However, Antoine felt there was little hope of her recovering. Each day, family members sat by her bedside and prayed, hoping she would regain consciousness. But as the days went by, it became apparent she was not going to survive.

Days following the accident, the family decided to remove the machine and allow Michelle to go freely.

Antoine grew distant and, at times, wanted to end his life, but he knew he had his children to raise. He spent most days preparing his children for the death of their mother. He regularly brought them to see her in the hospital.

"Daddy, when can mommy come home with us," his oldest asked.

"The doctors are taking care of Mommy."

His youngest offered to care for her instead. Most nights, when he put the kids to bed, he would cry himself to sleep.

***

With tears streaming down his face, Pastor Covington held Michelle in his arms and cradled her as though he was rocking a newborn baby.

Hundreds of family members and friends bid their final farewells to Michelle. The cemetery was damped from the rain showers the night before. The casket sat on a device over the grave as Pastor Covington blessed the body.

"Please remain prayerful for our family as we mourn the loss of Michelle." Family members began to cry as her body was lowered into the ground, and roses were thrown on top of her casket.

***

James had men on the streets looking for a guy named Bud, who he believed was responsible for tampering with Michelle's car. Bud was well-known in the streets of Miami and said to have done this type of crime before. But Bud was nowhere to be found, not even at the places he was said to frequent.

James was determined to get some answers. He was convinced Roger Williams had something to do with the accident, and time was running out for him as well. If Bud couldn't be found, Williams would be next, whether James had proof of his culpability or not.

When James was informed that Michelle had died, he grew even angrier and urged his men to take out his entire family until Bud reappeared.

Losing James Junior and Michelle ripped James' world apart. He often wondered now if his life was worth living at all. The first few years in jail, he slept with her photo and pleasured himself by thinking about her. At times, he had to refrain from his thoughts because he had to remain focused.

He constantly had to look over his shoulder. Not even someone you thought was your best friend could be trusted in a place like this.

During the first three years in prison, he took his frustration out on rival gang members and landed himself in solitary confinement. While he had been in prison for nearly a decade now, prison life was something he could never get used to.

Seeing Michelle an hour a week was like having steak for dinner. He spent hours doing sit-ups in his cell.

Michelle's visits were the only thing he could look forward to, and now, both she and his only son were gone.

Since Michelle died, his mom had been to visit. The petite fifty-four-year-old white woman with piercing blue eyes had been estranged from him for a few years.

Drugs took a toll on her once strikingly beautiful looks. Her almond-shaped eyes had sunken, her teeth were stained, and some were missing. The fine lines around her eyes and mouth had grown deeper and told a story of neglect and abuse.

Despite his mother's many flaws, James loved her with all his heart.

"Honey, I'm so happy to see you. I've been worried about you. I heard about James Junior and Michelle," his mother said. "Are you alright?"

"I'm doing okay." Knowing full well that he wasn't, James quickly changed the subject. "Ma, you've put on some weight."

"You'll be proud of me. I've been clean for a year now," she told him. Her eyes welled up with tears. "Baby, I fell on hard times. I lost my job and have been living in and out of shelters for a year."

"Mom, stop crying."

James had been down this shaky road of sobriety with his mother. She'd struggled to stay off drugs and alcohol for as long as he could remember. His mother moved to Miami in the early eighties from Kansas and met his dad in a nightclub. Their whirlwind romance was complex and often turbulent. His father introduced his mother to crack and spent most of James' life in and out of prison.

James made sure his mother had money after he went away to prison, but she used it to support her habit, so he stopped supporting her when James Junior was born.

"Have you talked with your dad?" she asked.

"No. I don't want to talk about him." James never forgave his father and blamed him for the problems they inherited when he went to prison.

She shared with James how she was working as a cashier at a local department store. The visit ended with his mother promising she would stay clean.

Seeing his mother walk past the guards was a stark reminder to James of his volatile childhood. His mom often left him and his siblings behind to fend for themselves. James did everything he could to erase those awful memories, but somehow, they would always come back to haunt him.

***

While eating breakfast, Roger perused the newspaper. His attorney assured him that he would be vindicated of all charges. He spent most days indoors, reading books and drinking booze. He avoided going to places where he could run into people he knew.

Pastor Covington contacted him and informed Roger of Michelle's death. Roger offered his condolences then began to share his concerns about his impending trial.

"I'm afraid," he told the pastor. "I miss my wife and children."

"Roger, you need to be around your wife and kids. Call her. Talk to her."

Roger took Pastor Covington's advice and reached out to his wife, who agreed to meet him at Starbucks. He was anxious to see her. Nervous, he drank three cups of coffee as raindrops pummeled the streets. When she walked in, his wife appeared uneasy about their meeting. It had been nearly six months since they last saw each other.

Roger offered to buy her a coffee, but she politely declined.

"You look so beautiful," he said.

"Thank you," she said as she sighed.

"Honey, I miss you and the kids so much. I want you guys to come home."

"For several months, the kids and I tried reaching you. You never returned our calls."

"I didn't know what to say."

"I'm sorry. I can't be with you anymore."

Roger couldn't believe what he was hearing.

"I love you, Roger, but I can no longer be married to you. I've been a good wife to you and have dealt with all that comes with loving you—the infidelities, the lies, and making me feel insignificant."

"Please hear me out," he begged. "I know I haven't been good to you. The last couple of months have been terrible. I want to do better for you and the kids."

"When you're in prison?"

Roger became furious. "How dare you talk to me that way? I've made a good life for you and the kids. That's why you're able to drive a brand-new Lexus, wear designer clothes, and trot around with expensive purses and take lavish trips."

"The material things mean absolutely nothing to me." She paused, then said, "Wow, for a second there, I thought you had changed. But I see you're still up to your no-good ways. You're a power-hungry bastard who feels entitled. You desperately need help, Roger."

She agreed to let him see the kids but no longer wanted to have anything to do with him. A few minutes later, from the store window, Roger watched his wife drive off.

CHAPTER SEVENTEEN
-----THE SMOKING GUN-----

Juan "Bud" Garcia had been in and out of prison since he was a teenager and raised primarily by his ailing maternal grandmother until her death. His mother died from a drug overdose, and he was estranged from his father. When he turned eighteen, he enlisted in the Army. After two years, he went AWOL. He returned home and began selling drugs, and went to prison for five years. When he was released, he couldn't find work and eventually landed back on the streets doing what he knew best. He was nicknamed Bud for his love for smoking weed, and the name never left him.

The police had been by his sister's house, asking questions about his whereabouts, and word on the street was that some guys were looking for him. He was constantly looking over his shoulder. Most nights, he didn't leave the efficiency he rented in Little Haiti until the wee hours of the morning. He would grab a quick bite to eat and head back to the apartment or roam the streets. He was never in one place. Things were getting so hot in the neighborhood that he contemplated heading west to Tampa to visit his cousin until things calmed down.

One evening, as he headed back to the apartment to gather his belongings, he made a quick stop at the corner store to buy some cigarettes. As he entered the store, the barrel of a gun pressed to the back of his head.

"Don't move motherfucker, or I'm gonna blow your fucking head off." A man wearing dark clothing and a hoodie that covered his head forcefully threw Bud in the back of a van.

Bud couldn't figure out where they were traveling to in the windowless van. The trip was bumpy and uncomfortable. He was afraid they were taking him somewhere to kill him. When they arrived at a destination, two men pulled him out of the van with guns pointing toward his face.

"Where the fuck are you taking me?"

"None of your fucking business," one of the men replied.

They entered a dark and damp warehouse, where puddles of blood and carnage were everywhere. The two men tore Bud's clothes from his body, leaving him naked and exposed. They tied a length of rope around his bare ankles and hoisted him to the ceiling, leaving him hanging upside down for hours. Bud tried to sway his body back and forth to loosen his legs from the tight shackles, but nothing worked.

The men laughed at his struggles. They refused to identify themselves, but Bud was confident the men were working with Papo. He didn't doubt for one minute that it could be the Miami police, even though he knew they were as crooked as the thugs on the streets.

The men began pummeling him with their fists, pipes, and whatever else they had handy. Bud began to doubt he would survive the torment.

"Who ordered you to kill Michelle and her son?" a short, stocky white dude with a distinct northeast accent asked.

"I don't know what you're talking about."

"You want to play games, motherfucker?" the man yelled. "We're going to be here all fucking night until you start talking."

For several hours, the men continued to beat him to a bloody pulp. His eyes were swollen shut, and the sweat that formed on his chest dripped down to mingle with the blood from his bruised face causing an agonizing burning sensation.

"I didn't do shit to her. I just helped with her car. She had a flat tire," Bud cried.

He couldn't bear the pain any longer and begged the men to take him out of his misery. The men left, and this time didn't return for hours. Though for Bad, it felt like days.

This time, they returned with chainsaws and threatened to sever his limbs if he didn't start talking. The men finally lowered him to the floor and shoved him into a chair. They wasted no time securing his wrists to the armrests and his ankles to the legs of the chair, where they left him to sit for hours.

The stocky white thug brandished a menacing knife and stabbed Bud in his right thigh. He yelled out in pain, and the man twisted the blade in his flesh.

"Okay, okay, okay!" Bud screamed. "I'll tell you. I'll tell you everything," he cried.

He breathed heavily against the wrenching pain of the knife still stuck in his leg. "I was in a bar on Seventy-Ninth Street having some drinks, and a man in a suit approached me about doing a hit for him. I had never seen him before in my life. I thought he was Five-O. I told him to get the fuck out of my face, and I began to walk away. He handed me a hundred-dollar bill just to hear him out and told me he needed a favor. He showed me a picture of her and said he wanted her killed. He asked if I could do the job. Man, I needed the money. Shit was getting rough for me. He paid me five Gs to get the job done.

"For several weeks, I followed her to work, home, and back to church. Most of the time, she was with her kids. Once I realized she was Papo's baby's mother, I didn't want any part of it.

"I met with the guy again and told him I didn't want to get involved. I knew about Papo from back in the day. He was ruthless, and I didn't want any part of him. But the dude pressured me to get it done.

"One afternoon, she was with her son, and she went into an office building. I quickly flattened her tire. When she came out, she noticed her flat, and I offered to help. When she walked away, I loosened the lugs on two tires in the front."

"Did the nigga tell you his name?"

"Naw, but I saw him on the news not too long ago about stealing some money from the feds."

The two men walked away from Bud and began whispering. They came back a moment later, and the white dude pulled out a shotgun and shot Bud twice in the head. They discarded his body and reported back to James that Bud was dead.

***

Jennifer sat in silence while the kids ate their breakfast. Jim informed her how human remains were discovered in the Everglades, and the police believed the remains were those of an adult male, possibly Juan "Bud" Garcia. The remains were sent to the Criminal Investigation Department to be examined. Jennifer wondered why anyone would kill him.

"This guy was trouble. It could have been anyone who wanted him dead," Jim said.

The police later confirmed the body was indeed Garcia. Jennifer thought maybe Mr. Williams had something to do with his death. Did he want him dead because he feared Garcia would confess to the police?

Jennifer dropped the kids off at school and decided that she would spend the remainder of the day cleaning out her closet. She discovered a gun in a box hidden under some clothes. She was so upset with Seth because he promised her that he wouldn't ever bring a gun into their home. Jennifer's anger spilled over into the night, and she confronted Seth about it.

"Honey, why would you bring a gun into our home? I thought we agreed that we would never do that."

"I'm sorry. I felt I had to do whatever necessary to protect my family. I bought it several months ago," Seth explained.

"And you were never planning to tell me about it."

"Were you ever going to tell me about the police investigation?" Seth shot back.

Jennifer began to cry. "I'm sorry I didn't share with you that I had been talking with Jim about the case. I just feel like I have to do something. This man cannot get away with murder."

"Hun, I just want you to be careful. I know how much this investigation means to you, and I'll support you every step of the way."

****

The attorneys were preparing for pre-trial and spent several hours a day drilling Roger on what to say in court. They even made recommendations on his attire. He couldn't appear aloof or as someone with money. But the thought of wearing a non-designer suit in court sounded foolish to Roger. He believed his tailored-made suits were a symbol of his success.

"Hard work pays off," he often said in the office. Still, the attorneys didn't want the jurors to form a negative opinion of Roger, so he reluctantly agreed to tone it down.

Roger left the attorney's office feeling emotionally drained. The thought of going to prison terrified him, and he wanted so badly for his life to return to the way it was a few years ago. He recognized that his life had changed rapidly, but he didn't know how to get that former life back.

When he arrived home, a sheriff handed him papers to sign; his wife had filed for divorce.

This was too much for him to handle all at once. He wanted to work things out with her, but she wasn't having it and wanted out of the marriage.

The lawyers urged Roger to try to make amends with his wife. They didn't want to give the impression to the public that she wasn't supporting him. Roger doubted it would be possible to convince her to change her mind. Still, he sent her flowers at home and at work. He left love notes on her car and offered to take her to dinner at the same restaurant where he proposed to her.

After several weeks of rejecting him, she finally agreed to go out with him. He planned the entire day. He arranged for a sitter and made an appointment for her at the spa. Later in the evening, they had dinner together.

Roger was good at charming women. His wife seemed elated that the man she loved had returned. He had courted her for several years before she accepted his marriage proposal.

The night ended with Roger dropping her off at the apartment she had been renting since their separation. He wanted to spend the night, but his wife believed it was too soon and didn't want the kids to believe they were getting back together.

"I had a wonderful time tonight," she said.

"Baby, I miss being with you. I'll do anything for you to be back in my life again."

"We have children together, and we'll always be emotionally tied to one another," she explained.

"That's different. I need you and the kids to be with me."

"Well, we have a lot to work on, and it's going to take time." She kissed him goodbye and entered her apartment.

For several minutes, Roger sat in the car at the curb, staring at her window. He was growing impatient with his wife. The longer it took to convince her to come home, the more distraught he became, and her failure to stand by his side was jeopardizing his case.

Even though he assured his attorney that his wife would support him and attend the trial, he was losing hope and began drinking heavily. He believed she wanted to reconcile their relationship but was being influenced by her parents and friends, who had been against their relationship from the start.

Roger continued to sit in his car outside his wife's apartment until he saw the babysitter leave. Frustrated, he decided to head back to his empty home, where he retreated to the couch for the night.

With his foot planted on the leather ottoman, he began flipping the channels, hoping he could find something worth watching. During a commercial break, he went into the kitchen to get some popcorn. With a glass of bourbon in tow, he opened the refrigerator and discovered what appeared to be a severed head that looked very similar to the man he paid to kill Michelle. He jumped, dropping the glass in his hand, which shattered everywhere, then began vomiting uncontrollably.

The minute he got himself under control, he slammed the refrigerator door and ran back into the living room to retrieve his cell.

"911, what's your emergency."

Thoughts raced in his head like who could've done this and how would he explain to the police why someone would leave this thug's head in his house. Roger hung up in fear that he would have way too much explaining to do.

He decided to discard the head himself. The stench of decomposing flesh emanated throughout the entire house as blood dripped on the kitchen floor. He placed the head in a huge black garbage bag. The phone rang, and he saw it was 911 calling back. Trying desperately to control his breathing, Roger answered.

"Yes, everything is okay. I'm sorry. I accidentally dialed 911. Yes, I'm sure. Thanks."

He placed the bagged, severed head in the trunk of his car and drove fifty miles away from his home, his thoughts spinning the whole time. Someone was on to him. Who killed Bud, and who could have entered his home?

He found a remote area off the highway and drove as far as he could into the brush. The location was damp and muddy from a rain shower the night before. The pitch-black location made it difficult for him to see. He dimmed his car lights, dug a hole, and buried the head, driving away with the hopes of putting the ordeal behind him.

CHAPTER EIGHTEEN

----- MALFEASANCE -----

During the pre-trial, Roger's attorney argued that the grand jury process that led to the initial indictment was soiled from the intense media exposure the case had garnered.

"Your honor, there was no way for Mr. William to have an impartial grand jury process; it's been tainted."

The U.S. District Attorney countered his argument by stating, "The jurors were not influenced by the publicity and had been asked whether they had heard of Mr. Williams and the allegations. No one had."

After an hour of intense arguments, the judge denied the motion to dismiss the indictment against Roger and set the trial for October.

Roger was overwhelmed by this legal setback. His attorney assured him that everything was under control, but Roger not only had his impending trial to worry about. He was also terrified that someone wanted him dead.

A few nights later, he awakened to gunshots fired in front of his home. The neighbors in the quaint, gated community called the police. Roger refused to say much when questioned.

"Please give us a call if you see anything suspicious," the officer advised him.

Roger took the business card and went back inside. The rest of the night was spent drinking and watching CNN. He turned on the local news and saw how during a morning run, a jogger with her dog discovered what was believed to be a human head near a wooded area off the highway.

Roger couldn't believe what he was seeing. The entire night he tossed and turned in his sleep.

The next day, the agony over the ordeal the night before lingered into his meeting with his attorney. Roger was distracted and could barely keep up with what the attorney was saying. He was worried about being connected to Garcia's murder. The bags under his eyes were a dead giveaway that something was wrong.

"Are you okay, Roger?"

"Yes, I'm fine. I didn't get much sleep last night."

"Well, we won't be long," the attorney assured him. "My staff is working around the clock to make certain we're prepared for trial. I want you to get some rest, and we'll resume on Monday."

Roger lost his cool. He stood and began shouting, "Look, I'm okay. You need to focus on doing whatever you can for us to win this case. I don't want to go to prison."

"Lower your voice, Roger. As I've told you before, we're doing all we can to make certain that doesn't happen."

Without another word, Roger stormed out of the attorney's office.

***

Jennifer was busy with her clients and taking her kids to and from music lessons and sports activities, but her mind could not escape the death of Garcia.

Who killed him and why? she pondered. Over dinner, Jennifer gave Seth a breakdown of the case and shared her thoughts. "Honey, can you believe someone killed Garcia?" she asked her husband.

"I'm not surprised. He was a drifter and a career criminal."

He sighed, then said, "Babe, let's just move on from this whole mess. Why don't we talk about taking a family vacation?"

Jennifer shook her head. "It's not a good time for me. The district attorney will likely call me to testify in Mr. Williams' case. I also have work that has to get done by the end of the year."

"Well, how about we go away for Christmas leading into the New Year? We'll go to the Bahamas."

Jennifer knew the mere mention of Roger Williams set Seth in a frenzy. So, for his sake, she was prepared to put the subject to rest, at least for now. A trip to their oceanfront villa in the Bahamas overlooking the sandy white beaches and tranquil blue water was just what her marriage desperately needed.

***

Rachel and Richard spent most of their first day together in months lounging on the beach in a cabana drinking mojitos, and that night, their bodies became one. Not even a classic love song could fully divulge the intensity of their passion and what it meant to Rachel.

Everything seemed perfect, and life was beginning to feel normal again. Williams was no longer in the office, and the atmosphere at work was improving. Never in a million years did Rachel believe she would find a man who would make her feel special.

Worried she would jinx the relationship by sharing every intricate detail of their love affair, she refused to discuss it with her friends. She also promised herself that she wouldn't lash out at Richard for what the last man chose not to do. She was done carrying that extra baggage and was prepared to give Richard her heart.

After a night of salsa dancing, they went back to her place and the only evidence of them ever leaving was the trail of clothes left behind at the door. Rachel couldn't help but be high on the endless possibilities of how far their relationship could go. They talked about their future, and it was clear that neither wanted this to end.

"I love you," Richard proclaimed, "and I haven't felt this way in years. I need you to be in my life."

The idea of living together and him moving to Miami was something they both wanted to happen. He had some reservations, though, and so did Rachel. He didn't want to leave his son behind nor the network of friends and colleagues in Little Rock. They talked and laughed until the sun came up, and the desire for sleep took over.

The next morning, the aroma of bacon and maple syrup permeated the entire house. Richard smiled from ear to ear as he walked into her bedroom with a tray of scrambled eggs, bacon, and fluffy pancakes piled high, two glasses of orange juice, and a hibiscus flower he'd picked from her yard.

"Good morning, baby. Did you sleep well?" he asked as he placed the tray on the bed. He leaned over and kissed her.

"I did."

They sat in bed like two old lovers made for each other, ate, laughed, and reminisced about their romantic time together. When they had their fill of breakfast, Richard placed the tray with empty plates on the floor. They exchanged caresses, and the heat quickly rose between them. He pulled her hips toward him and placed her legs on his shoulders. Once inside, he moved in a steady, deep, and methodically grinding rhythm.

For a while, they ignored the annoying buzzing sound from Rachel's cell phone on the night table, but eventually, it disrupted their rhythm.

Richard stopped. "You want to answer it?"

"No," she moaned as she wiped the sweat from his face and began kissing him.

"It may be urgent."

Rachel sighed and reached over for the cell phone. After glancing at the screen, she was surprised to see it was Bernard, whom she hadn't heard from in two years. She ignored the call, but it was clear that Richard could sense something had changed in her mood.

"Oh, it's nothing. It's just work."

Their romantic weekend ended with Richard surprising Rachel with a beautiful bouquet of roses and promising to see her next month.

She stood by her car outside of the airport with tears in her eyes as she watched Richard fade into a sea of travelers heading to their flights.

All week she avoided Bernard's repeated calls. In his messages, he apologized for all the pain he'd caused her and said he desperately wanted to clear the air. Eventually, she replied by telling him she couldn't promise to meet with him because she was busy at work.

Then, suddenly, she had a change of heart and arranged to meet with him. She didn't tell Richard about her meeting, though, because she didn't want him to get the impression that she had any unresolved feelings for Bernard.

She was so anxious about the meeting that she changed clothes five times and decided at the last minute to go with the first outfit she'd selected. Rachel didn't want to wear anything too revealing, but she did want to look sexy as a reminder of what he'd missed.

She didn't know what to expect from their meeting but was definitely going to let Bernard know that she was in a committed relationship.

She arrived ten minutes late and found parking a few restaurants down from the café. When she entered the restaurant, the hostess directed her to a table. She spotted Bernard from a distance, gauging her every move as she made her way toward him. When she reached the table, he stood, and they embraced.

"You look amazing," he said.

"Thank you." It was apparent Bernard had been working out.

Over drinks, he boasted about how his business was doing well after he parted ways with his former business partner.

"How is life treating you?" he asked.

"It's better. Things are much better at work. Thanks."

"Yes, I read that your boss had been indicted."

Rachel glanced at her watch.

"Look, I'm sorry for how I treated you," he said. "I knew you weren't happy, and I didn't know how to help you."

"Bernard, I was going through hell at work."

"That's why I'm here to tell you I'm sorry. I know I did wrong by you, and I regret not reaching out. I wanted to let you know that Max and I ended our marriage.

"I'm sorry to hear that.

"Don't be sorry. We stayed together longer than expected. It was time that we moved on with our lives. Our daughter is our number one priority. Are you seeing anyone?"

"Yes, I am happily in love," Rachel announced with a smile. "Well, Bernard, I have a meeting to attend, and it's a twenty-minute commute from here. So, I need to get going."

"I'm happy we had this conversation."

"Me too."

Bernard walked Rachel to her car and gave her a big hug. She drove away with a sense of pride that she did not come off as a jilted ex-lover but a woman who had closure and had finally moved on with her life.

****

James was pleased with how things were coming along with Roger Williams. James' men were watching the jerk's every move.

Meanwhile, James was stunned to receive a letter from his estranged father. He hadn't heard from his dad in over fifteen years. His father was going to be released from prison soon and wanted to mend their relationship. But James refused to have anything to do with him. James attributed his life of misfortune to his father abandoning their family.

Then, during another visit, his mom begged him to forgive his father. "James, it's time to let go of the past. I know you're upset with your daddy, but you need him."

"What can he offer me? I told you I don't want to have anything to do with him. Do you think I can forget how he used to beat the shit out of you? I guess you forgot, but I haven't. He's about to be released now, and he's telling you everything you want to hear. You're falling for the bullshit again. Let me remind you. We never stayed in one place because he would always use the rent money to buy crack.

"Where was he when the social worker snatched my baby brother out of your hands and took my other siblings away? Or the times when you came to my parent-teacher meetings held at night wearing sunglasses? He was never a father to me as a child, and I don't need him to be one up in here," James spat.

His mother sobbed as James recounted the horrible memories of his father. From her reaction, James knew those painful experiences were hard to swallow for Carol. Over the years, she expressed to James how her co-dependency for his father played a role in their family's demise. Despite the toxic nature of their relationship, she still loved him with all her heart. She really believed he had changed for the better.

"Mom, stop crying. I know when he comes out of prison, you're going to take him back. I don't want to see you get hurt again."

Shortly after being released from prison, James' father reunited with his mother. James learned from his contacts on the outside that it wasn't long before the physical abuse started up again. He dislocated her arm and gave her two black eyes within weeks of his release. When his mother stopped showing up for her visits, James knew something had gone terribly wrong.

James heard his father was back on drugs again and had stolen a family heirloom that was passed on to his mom from her great-grandparents. It was the only thing she had managed to keep over the years.

His mom later told him that when she discovered it was gone, she confronted his dad about it. "Eugene, where are my candle holders," she demanded.

She said he refused to tell her, and when she pressed for answers, he slapped and dragged her by her hair across the apartment floor like a rag doll. A neighbor later found her lying unconscious in the hallway and called 911. James found out what had happened to his mother and ordered his men to find his father and kill him.

It tore James up that he couldn't be there to help her. While over the years, his mother had struggled with her own demons, James never stopped loving her.

Within weeks, his father was found dead in a crack house, where he'd reportedly overdosed on crack cocaine laced with rat poison.

James acted as though his father's death was news to him as his mom recanted the violent altercations leading to her hospitalization. She grieved over the man she'd loved for over thirty-five years but said she found relief in knowing that turbulent chapter of her life was finally over.

CHAPTER NINETEEN

----- CONSEQUENCES -----

It was a never-ending tug war in the courtroom between the two attorneys, who had opposed each other's choice for prospective jurors. They drilled each juror about their backgrounds and beliefs for hours.

"Is there anything that would prevent you from being fair and impartial in the trial. "the judge asked.

"No," replied a prospective juror. The entire process made Roger uncomfortable. During jury selection, he kept himself busy by jotting down notes, affairs he needed to get in order.

His house had been on the market for several months now. While the feds had seized most of his accounts and mounting legal fees had wiped out his savings, he still had money stashed away for a rainy day. He wanted to make sure his kids were taken care of.

When he saw them that evening, his wife urged him to have a conversation with his children about the possibility of him going away for a while.

"Daddy, I want to go home with you," his son whined.

"Soon, baby."

When Roger gave his wife a look to convey how uncomfortable his son's comment made him, she quickly intervened.

"Okay, guys, it's time for bed."

He kissed his son goodnight.

"Don't forget to wash your face and brush your teeth," his wife told the children.

Roger and his wife began talking when the sounds of the kids became a distant chatter.

"Are you planning to have a talk with the kids about your legal situation?" she asked.

"No, it's too soon. I don't want the kids worrying about me. Besides, they have more important things to worry about, like school."

"If you haven't noticed, your case is all over the news. I don't want our kids to be teased in school. They deserve to know, Roger."

"I'm not ready to talk about it."

"Well, can I get some answers?"

Roger became agitated by her sarcasm. He didn't feel he needed to explain to anyone about his legal woes, including his wife. "What is it that you want to know? No, wait," he said, holding up a hand to stop her. "Let me start by saying that I've been subpoenaed by the prosecutor. My attorney will be in contact with you about it."

"Of course, like everything else, you want to conveniently sweep it under the rug. You just don't get it, do you? I'm so tired of you being emotionally unavailable to the kids and me. I devoted most of my adult life to being a good wife and a good mother to your kids. I gave up a thriving career so that I could support your dreams. Yet you still don't feel I'm worthy enough to know what's going on? I have to piece everything together from gossip and the news."

"If I'm convicted, you and the kids will be fine. I'm confident everything will go in my favor. You have to trust me."

She shook her head and walked away. As he headed toward the door, Roger said, "I'll pick you up around 8:00 am for court. I love you."

He left the apartment feeling anxious about court in the morning. Roger wasn't so sure everything would go in his favor. Plus, his life was in danger. He had been receiving threatening phone calls around the clock and was being followed. He had avoided the person a few times by dodging in between delivery trucks with his car, and on more than one night, he saw a dark SUV parked outside his home. It was clear the person who killed Garcia was watching his every move, and Roger wasn't taking any chances. He installed cameras throughout his home and kept a gun on him at all times.

***

The criminal investigation was still underway. The lab determined the head discovered near the highway was Garcia. While there were no significant leads in the case, the police believed the murder stemmed from a rival gang dispute. The DNA found at the scene could not be traced to anyone linked to a gang. The detectives were in limbo as they combed through evidence and questioned anyone who knew Garcia.

"My brother was a loner and never really hung out with anyone," said his sister, Yvonne.

The detectives questioned Yvonne for several hours in her tiny cramped apartment. With a baby clinging to her bosom, Yvonne talked passionately about her younger brother.

"My brother had no enemies and would never do anything to hurt anyone," she said. She shared early childhood photos. Yvonne gave the detectives a set of matches and a napkin she found in her brother's pants pocket.

The detectives visited the bar, whose name was inscribed on the matches and napkin showed the bartender a photo of Garcia.

"Yes, he used to come in here all the time. He never said much. He would always order a gin and tonic," said the bartender.

"Did he ever meet anyone here," asked the detective.

"Yes, I do recall him meeting someone a couple of months ago."

"Male or female."

"It was a nicely dressed African-American man in his early fifties."

"Did their meeting appear tense?" asked Jim.

"Not really sure, I was busy working. I can tell you he didn't know the guy very well because of their interaction with each other," said the bartender. The detectives had very little to go on but were inclined to find out the identity of the man who met with Garcia shortly before he was killed.

Jennifer expressed to her husband how she was anxious about testifying at Roger Williams' trial but prepared to share all she knew under oath. And she desperately wanted to have a conversation with Pastor Covington on how she believed Roger Williams was involved in Michelle's death. She didn't know how to approach him about it, though, especially with no evidence linking Williams to the accident.

"It's all speculation," Seth remaindered her. "Remember, Pastor Covington isn't only a close friend of Williams but a spiritual advisor to him as well. Unless you have some concrete evidence, which you don't, I suggest that you stay out of it."

Jennifer tried to believe it was only a matter of time before it surfaced that Williams was linked to Michelle's accident. But since she wasn't so sure, her need to uncover the truth just wouldn't go away.

After giving it more thought, Jennifer decided she had a better chance of getting someone to listen by talking with Antoine, so later that day, she sought him out.

As he walked toward her, he began to tug on his shirt, which looked way too tight. He had noticeably gained a lot of weight. Jennifer didn't want to react because she could sense he was uncomfortable with his appearance.

Just as Antoine took a seat, his phone began ringing. It was his daughter wanting to know where he placed the television remote. His daughter also took the opportunity to complain to him about her brother, who she said was nagging her.

"Honey, you guys need to stop fussing. I'll be home shortly, and be sure to listen to Grandma."

While Antoine had put on several pounds, he appeared to be in better spirits.

"Thanks for meeting with me," Jennifer said when she gained his full attention.

"It's good to see you," he replied. "These past couple of months have been difficult, but the kids and I are managing well. Thanks to my parents, the in-laws, and the church members. It's made my life easier. How about you?"

"Seth and I are doing well. The kids are growing too fast, as you can imagine. I'm busy shuffling them between school and extra-curricular activities. Needless to say, we have a busy schedule in our household." She laughed then asked, "How are you coping?"

He shrugged. "There are days when I don't want to face the world, but I live for my kids."

"Please know that whatever I can do to help, I'm here for you and the kids. I know how much Michelle loved you and them." Jennifer hesitated, then said, "Antoine, I'm not sure if you were aware that my relationship with Michelle had suffered a great deal before I left the agency. In fact, we weren't speaking at all by that time."

He shook his head. "I didn't know that. Michelle kept me in the dark about a lot of things that happened in the office."

"Out of the blue, I received a phone message from Michelle a few hours before the accident."

"What do you think she wanted?"

"I'm not sure. It seemed urgent, and I believe it involved Mr. Williams."

"Well, he's not my favorite person," Antoine scoffed. "I wanted to have a talk with him about Michelle working late hours, but Michelle was against it."

While talking with Antoine, Jennifer decided to take Seth's advice and not disclose her thoughts on Williams' possible connection to the accident.

But after seeing Antoine's expression when she mentioned Williams, Jennifer couldn't help wondering if Antoine's dislike for his wife's former boss caused problems with Michelle's working relationship with Mr. Williams.

The most surprising news of the day came when Jennifer returned home to find a message from Jim informing her that Roger Williams had been named a person of interest in the Garcia murder investigation. He may have met with Garcia a few times in a bar, and the authorities wanted to know why this unlikely pair had met. Jennifer prayed the police would be able to uncover the truth.

***

Roger was entering the dry cleaners when someone from behind him asked, "Roger, do you have a few minutes to spare?" He turned, and two detectives now stood in front of him. One flashed his badge, identifying him as Jim McKeon.

"How can I help you, men?"

"Let's chat for a few," Detective McKeon said.

"Where were you on July sixteenth?"

"I was at my daughter's birthday party."

The detectives showed Roger a photo of Garcia.

"Do you know this guy?" the detective asked.

"No, he doesn't look familiar."

"Are you sure?"

The second detective nodded toward the photo. "Take another good look."

Roger shrugged. "Never seen him in my life."

"Let's the cut through the bullshit, Roger," McKeon said. "We have witnesses who saw you meeting with him at a bar on Seventy-Ninth Street."

"Okay, I met him twice. He wanted me to help him find housing, and I told him that I would see what I could do."

"Were you aware he was murdered a few months ago?" McKeon asked.

"Yes, I heard about it on the news."

The second detective asked, "When you met with him, did he mention that someone wanted him dead?"

"No. He told me he wanted to get his life back in order."

When the detectives remained silent for several beats, Roger took control of the situation. "Well, gentlemen, I need to be on my way. Do you have any more questions for me?"

"No, we're done here," McKeon replied. "We'll be in touch, Roger."

***

The atmosphere in the office was tense; everyone was walking on eggshells. A sense of concern was written on everyone's faces, the exact fear Mr. Williams inflicted on staff when he was a daily fixture in the office. Rumor had it that some of Rachel's colleagues were called to testify in his trial. Some were subpoenaed by the prosecutor, and others for the defense.

Most staff wanted to see him go down but would never admit their disdain for him publicly. The ones that were vocal about their support weren't sincere. Rachel was among the former and kept her opinion to herself. While Williams was no longer physically in the office, he still had his spies. He was notorious for blackballing those he believed were against him, and she had to play it safe.

Her focus was on Richard now. He was looking for property in Miami. The idea of both of them living in the same city was both exciting and frightening at the same time. Everything seemed to be happening so quickly. Both the changes at work and in her personal life.

She needed some distraction and decided retail therapy was exactly what the doctor ordered. So after work, she headed over to the mall to catch some sales. She spent two hours going through clothing racks and trying on clothes, hoping to find the right attire for her hot date with Richard this coming weekend.

CHAPTER TWENTY

----- A DOUBLE LIFE -----

Reporters covering the case and curious onlookers packed the courtroom. The judge, a white man approaching sixty and wearing molasses rimmed glasses at the edge of his nose, had been stoic as the attorneys presented their opening arguments.

Inside, Roger was nervous, but outside, he remained calm and tried not to squirm in what he believed to be a less-than-flattering navy suit and white shirt. He scoffed at the thought of wearing a suit bought at a local department store. It made him feel regular and mediocre at best.

His wife and Pastor Covington sat a few rows behind him. As the proceedings began, Roger found solace staring at a black and white clock in the front of the courtroom and made very little eye contact with anyone, not even the mostly white jurors who held his fate.

The prosecutor stood in front of the jurors and locked eyes with each one as he divulged how Roger used government-issued funds as his own personal ATM and mastered how to cover his tracks. When a person leads a double life, sooner or later, those lives will collide, and the person will forget which one is real. The prosecutor's harsh opening arguments were jarring as he emphasized how Roger Williams was a crook and guilty and should be behind bars, where he belongs.

"The man thinks he knows me," Roger whispered to his attorney.

The prosecutor pointed to Roger as he spoke directly to the six men and six women jurors. "This is a case about greed," he declared. "Roger Williams is a narcissist who craves power and would do anything to achieve it, even at the expense of taxpayers. He uses money to silence his critics. It is my sincere hope that in the interest of justice, at the conclusion of this trial, you will find that the defendant, Mr. Roger Williams, is guilty of stealing millions of dollars to fund his lavish lifestyle."

When the defense's turn came, Roger's attorney stood before the jurors. "Ladies and Gentlemen of the Jury, we will present a case that will show Roger Williams has done nothing wrong and the only guilt prevalent here is shoddy record keeping. Over the course of this trial, the defense will introduce forensic accountants and individuals that will attest to how Mr. Williams is a man of integrity and has done tremendous work in the community. At the closing of this case, we will prove that Roger Williams is innocent of these charges."

***

As Jennifer took her seat on the stand, anxiety began to take over. Several times, she caught herself biting her lip or rubbing her hands together. Before she began talking, she quickly scanned the room to see any familiar faces. She saw a woman who easily could have been mistaken as her twin or sister but soon realized it was Mr. Williams' wife sitting close to Pastor Covington. She had freckles and a curvaceous body. Jennifer had never seen his wife in the five years of working at the agency, not even at the agency's holiday banquets. Mr. Williams was so private, not even photos of his family were seen anywhere in his office.

Jennifer spoke so softly that at times her voice came out barely more than a whisper.

"Please speak up, ma'am," the judge ordered.

A few times, she broke down and cried as she described the intense working environment in the office. She looked over to her husband for reassurance, and he gestured with a slight reassuring nod to continue.

She inadvertently locked eyes with Mr. Williams, who shot her a deadly stare as she spoke about her suspicion, and the prosecutor drilled her about her dysfunctional working relationship.

"Mr. Williams began to sabotage my work and pit others against me. He stopped answering my emails and would only respond to me through my assistant Michelle Porter."

"Michelle Porter was your assistant. The one who died in a freak car accident along with her son a few months ago. Is that right?"

"Yes," Jennifer replied as she began to sob. The judge handed her a tissue.

"Please take your time," the prosecutor said.

The defense attorney slammed his notepad on the desk. "Your honor, I object to this testimony on the grounds that the nature of Mrs. Porter's death is irrelevant to this case."

"Overruled," the judge replied. "Please answer the question, Mrs. Rosen."

When Jennifer hesitated, the prosecutor continued. "Your assistant Michelle Porter recently died in a car accident, correct?"

"Yes, she died a few months ago in a car accident. She and her oldest son."

"Can you describe for us the working relationship between Michelle Porter and Roger Williams?"

"They were very close. Michelle became his confidant almost immediately when she came onboard. Per Mr. Williams, I was no longer allowed to speak to our benefactors, and Michelle became their point of contact with the agency.

"I object," the defense attorney shouted.

"Sustained," the judge replied.

The prosecutor frowned. "No further questioning, Your Honor."

Jennifer spent the next several hours on the stand, battling her way through intense questioning by the defense during the cross-examination aimed at discrediting her. The makeup on her face slowly faded as the hours went by, and her ruby-red lipstick became a partially stained lip. Jennifer testified how Mr. Williams knowingly submitted false, inflated, and duplicate invoices. After she brought it to his attention, he made her life a living hell.

"At times, I feared for my life and my family. We received threatening phone calls, and someone broke into our home," Jennifer cried.

The defense painted her as a woman scorned by Mr. Williams' rejection of her advances. But then, everyone gasped at the chilling sound of Michelle's voicemail message to Jennifer.

"I believe she was calling me to warn me about Mr. Williams," Jennifer testified.

Pastor Covington became visibly distraught, and Mr. Williams' wife had to console him during the testimony about his deceased daughter.

The defense sought to dismantle the government's case by describing it as an elaborate scheme orchestrated by Jennifer. Following her testimony, several of Jennifer's colleagues and her ex-fiancé testified of their own negative experiences with her, which added to the drama.

Jennifer was nearly inconsolable by the time she and Seth returned home. She couldn't believe how the defense had tried to destroy her reputation.

"I felt like I was the one on trial. I worked with those people for five years, and they painted me out to be some nut case. I've never had any sexual interest in that man, and he's never expressed interest in me. In fact, I'm repulsed by him. They defended Roger Williams even though they know I'm telling the truth."

Jennifer placed her head in her husband's chest and cried.

"Look at me," Seth whispered in a soothing voice.

Jennifer reluctantly lifted her head, fearing her eyes were bloodshot and her mascara had run down her face.

"I am so proud of you. You did a great job," Seth assured her as he leaned over to kiss her. "You've testified, and your part is over."

"Do you think the jurors believed me?"

"Of course, they did. And we've done all we can. Now we need to move on with our lives."

***

Richard had most of his stuff moved into his new condo on the Intracoastal in Miami Beach. The tranquil breeze and calming blue water were the perfect backdrops for their love. Rachel didn't realize how much she was missing in their relationship by living in separate cities. Richard had become the rainbow of her cloud. The best thing about it all, they were together yet lived separately. The only possessions he kept at her place were a toothbrush and a few shirts and underwear, and the same with her at his. Being around each other more made a huge difference. They met for lunch a few times a week and were together most nights for dinner. By Friday, she was packing a bag heading to his place for the weekend.

Richard healed the pain caused by Bernard.

It felt great to finally have someone Rachel could lean on for support. Most days, she was a nervous wreck about the outcome of the trial, as were many of the others in her office. The prosecution and defense had finally rested their case, so now they waited to see what verdict the jury would return. It was hard to avoid the subject everyone was talking about it.

In the mornings, when Rachel bought coffee, someone either had the paper spread out on a table, or a group of employees could be heard rehashing the drama that had unfolded in the courtroom. Many of her colleagues expressed that they were afraid Williams would be acquitted and return to the office to terrorize them once more. Those who testified against him were terrified they would lose their jobs, and whispers in the halls revealed that many staff members were sending out resumes and interviewing for other jobs on off days and in between working on assignments.

Everyone believed he was guilty, but Williams always seemed to have a streak of luck on his side. Some even joked that he had nine lives. Sadly, everyone knew about his misdeeds, some had known for years, but everyone chose to ignore it. Until now.

Rachel was anxious as well. But things were going well with her and Richard, and she refused to allow the stress to come between their relationship.

"Honey, what's wrong?" Richard asked over dinner.

"Nothing, I'm fine."

"No, there's something wrong. You're usually more upbeat. Besides, you're guzzling down the wine like it's the last bottle you're ever going to drink." They both laughed. "Let me guess. You're nervous about the verdict?"

"There's no way I could ever work for that man again. The working environment is so much better without him, but even the thought that he might return has everyone on edge."

Richard leaned over and took Rachel's hand. "Baby, don't worry. He's guilty, and the defense did not present a solid case in his favor. There will definitely be a conviction."

"You're right, baby." Rachel wanted to believe Richard so badly, but her gut feeling wouldn't allow it.

CHAPTER TWENTY-ONE

----- DELIBERATIONS-----

Roger's full lips locked tightly onto Shawn's mouth but to no avail. His manhood fell weak, a stark contrast from the night before. Roger was no longer in control and on the winning end. The dark clouds that loomed over his fate had seized his ability to function.

He couldn't imagine spending twenty years in prison. Everything he'd worked hard for would be taken away from him.

After failing to become aroused, he rolled over to the side of the bed.

"It's okay, I'll help you," Shawn cooed. He pulled the white sheets away from their naked bodies and began to pleasure him, but Roger forcefully pushed him away.

"What's wrong with you?" Shawn yelled.

"Get dressed. I need to get some stuff done today."

Roger reached for a small mirror on his nightstand and, with a razor blade in hand, formed two white lines from the white powdery substance. He placed his nose close to the mirror and began snorting.

"Hey, give me some," Shawn complained.

Roger nudged Shawn away, then pulled a twenty-dollar bill from his wallet and left it on the bed.

"Call Uber to take you home," Roger said.

"Are you serious?"

Roger ignored him and walked out of the room.

A minute later, hastily dressed, Shawn came out of the bedroom, his alabaster skin now beet-red. "You are a fucking bastard," he yelled and slammed the door.

***

After hearing three weeks of testimony, jurors had begun deliberations. The process was even more terrifying than the actual trial for Roger. His attorneys believed they had done the best they could in defending him, and now it was up to the jurors to decide whether he would go to prison.

Roger made frantic calls to his attorney several times the first two days, wondering if the jurors had come back with a verdict. "Any news yet?"

"Not since the jurors requested copies of the forensic accounting report and the recording of Michelle's voicemail."

"What does this mean?"

"It could be a number of things, Roger. I don't want to assume. It appears that the jurors may be undecided about something, and they want clarification."

"Does this mean a not guilty verdict?"

"We won't know until the verdict is read in court. Hang tight, Roger."

***

To calm himself, Roger spent time with his children. He couldn't believe how much they had grown since they living apart from him. He wished he could have spent more time with them and felt bad about all the times he had failed to attend one of their recitals or other school event. He had instead chosen to spend time with a street hooker in the back of his car.

His children were so smart and driven, a perfect blend of him and his wife. They no longer depended on him for stuff like tying a shoelace. They even corrected him when he misspoke. His biggest fear was that his kids would grow resentful of him for being incarcerated.

Since the trial started, his wife refused to talk to him and still wanted out of the marriage. "Roger, I have nothing to say to you. I told you, don't call me. Text if you need to ask something about the kids. Yes, you can pick them up from school, but please have them home before dinner time." She then ended the call before he could say another word.

Roger snapped. He continued the conversation by text, threatening to leave the country with their kids. When she responded that she was planning to show the police his threats, he immediately wrote back and apologized.

***

Sloan was distraught by what she heard in court. She met with friends at a nearby café to get some things off her chest.

"Thanks for meeting with me.

"Give me a hug," said Cheryl as she reached to embrace her.

"Tosha sent me a text, and she's stuck in traffic. Lisa was called to an emergency meeting and won't be able to make it," said Sloan.

"Okay, No problem. Traffic is terrible. How are you?" Cheryl asked.

Sloan sighed, and tears began to roll down her face. "I don't know where to begin. This has been the worse experience of my life." She became distracted in thought.

"There's Tosha pulling up," said Sloan.

Tosha joined Cheryl and Sloan; they sat for hours discussing the trial.

"What freaked me out was how much that woman looked so much like you," Tosha said.

"You mean Jennifer?" asked Cheryl.

"You guys could go for sisters," said Tosha.

"My mama asked my daddy if he was sure he didn't have any children outside their marriage," said Sloan. They all burst out in laughter.

"The prosecutor was tough on you," said Tosha.

"He asked me everything under the sun, including how much my breast implants costs. I was so humiliated," said Sloan.

"Do you believe anything that was said in court?" asked Cheryl. "The finance director said Roger was the only person who knew the actual figures in the budget."

"Yes, I know," said Sloan.

"Well, Roger has ferocity for going for the jugular; he doesn't stop until you're done. Jeff, my ex, was convinced that Roger had some vendetta against him and a hand in his business going under. He claimed that Roger notified all of his clients and concocted some story about him being some drug lord in his former life and had been involved in some Ponzi scheme," said Sloan.

"Did Roger feel threatened by him?" asked Tosha.

"Yes, and I'm not sure why. Roger met him once at a conference, and from one introduction, he had a disdain for him. It doesn't take much for Roger Williams not to like someone. Jeff and I ended our relationship a year before I met Roger. We never kept in touch. In fact, Jeff was dating another woman who would later become his wife. Things went bad to worse for Jeff. He filed for bankruptcy. His wife left him, and he moved back in with his elderly parents."

"I heard he had a really tough time," said Cheryl.

"He's doing much better now," said Sloan.

"Good," said Tosha and Cheryl.

"So, if Roger is convicted, what are you going to do for money? If he's found guilty, you know the courts will seek restitution from Roger," said Tosha.

"As you guys know, my parents were not thrilled about me marrying Roger. They were so afraid that the relationship would end horribly; they began putting away money for me."

"Smart thinking by your parents," said Tosha.

"I'll downsize and practice law," said Sloan. "My children are my priority, and I've been thinking about moving back home to Georgia. My parents have offered to help out with the kids."

"Do you believe he's guilty?" asked Tosha.

"I don't know," she cried.

"We are praying for you and know that we are here for you," said Cheryl.

"Yes, let us know how we can help you," said Tosha.

Cheryl handed Sloan a tissue from her purse. The three friends hugged and parted ways. Sloan realized that the next time she saw her friends, her life would have completely changed. After spending time with them, Sloan was eager to move on with her life and had made peace with knowing that Roger could possibly head to prison.

***

Jim grew impatient with the investigation. He traveled to Tampa to see if he could gain some insight from Garcia's cousin Mark Joseph, known in the streets as Low. Jim knocked on a few apartment doors in a seedy neighborhood at the last address known for Low. The few people who were willing to talk to Jim claimed they didn't know his whereabouts.

"Have you seen this guy around?" asked Jim.

"Nah ain't never seen him around," said one man in his late twenties with coiffed locks in a neat bun.

Jim received a call from his office informing him that Low was working as a stock boy in a grocery store on the other side of town. Jim waited in his car checking emails on his cell phone until Low got off work. When Low appeared, Jim quickly got out of the car and approached him.

He pulled out his badge. "Mark Joseph," he said.

Low took off running for about two blocks. Jim ran behind and caught up to him until Low darted through a dead-end alley knocking over garbage cans. He attempted to scale a concrete wall that led to the next street over when Jim pointed his gun at him.

"Stop! I'll shoot," Jim yelled.

"Don't shoot," said Low as he slowly turned around and placed his work bag on the ground. He stood with his hands up facing Jim.

"I didn't do shit," said Low.

"Do you know this guy?" Jim asked.

"Yes, that's my fam.

"When did you speak to him last?"

"I spoke to him before he got clapped. He was thinking about moving up here."

"Did he say why?"

"He said some niggas was after him, and he needed to bounce for a minute."

"What did you tell him?"

"I told him he could crash at my crib," said Low. "I guess them niggas got to him before he could dip."

"Did he say why they were after him?"

"Nah, he didn't know."

"Did he ever mention a Roger Williams?"

"Naw," said Low. "Can I go?"

"Yeah, we're done here," said Jim. "By the way, why did you run off? You have no warrants."

"Man, when the po pulls up, you're either going downtown for some shit you didn't do or the morgue. I wasn't taking any chances."

"You want a ride?"

"Nah, I'm good." Low walked off with a suspicious look on his face.

On his third cup of coffee, Jim struggled to piece together what little information he had about the events leading up to Garcia's death.

"Any luck?" Detective Rodriguez.

"There may have been more than one person after him. Apparently, he never mentioned Roger to his cousin."

"So, we're back at square one again," said Rodriguez.

"I think we may have something here. I found out Michelle's childhood boyfriend is a member of a notorious gang in prison. He's also the father of her oldest son, who was killed in the car accident. He's in prison for armed robbery." He handed Detective Rodriguez a mug shot of James Senior.

"I don't get the connection," said Rodriguez.

"What if Roger Williams hired Garcia to kill Michelle."

"What would be his motive? That Michelle was prepared to testify against him?

"Yeah, so, he had her killed," Jim suggested.

"But James is in prison."

"Yes, but maybe James had one of his men kill Garcia in retaliation for killing his son."

"How would he know that Garcia killed his son? And why not go directly after Roger?"

"You're right."

"Good try though, Jim," said Rodriguez.

"There has to be to a connection here," said Jim.

Detective Rodriguez received a text message. "There's a verdict is in the Roger Williams' case."

"Hey, let's go check it out."

He grabbed his keys, turned off the lights behind him, and walked out with Detective Rodriguez.

CHAPTER TWENTY-TWO

----- CHICKENS COME HOME TO ROOST -----

The judge hit the gavel calling the court to silence. The twelve jurors sat with little or no expressions on their faces. Roger stood with his attorneys and quickly glanced back at his wife, hoping for some sign of encouragement.

The jury foreman stood and announced a return of not guilty on the first two charges, but they were deadlocked when it came to the third charge. Commotion erupted in the courtroom.

"Order in the court," the judge yelled as he pounded his gavel.

Roger abruptly fell into his sit and crumpled. He placed his head down on his hands and began to sob as his attorneys threw their arms around him. The prosecutor appeared visibly shaken.

Soon after, Roger left the courtroom with his legal team to address the reporters that awaited them outside. Surrounding the podium, reporters first drilled the prosecutor on his efforts to convict Roger Williams.

"Do you feel this was a fair trial?" one reporter asked.

"We prosecuted the case against Roger Williams based on facts and the law. While we respectfully disagree with the outcome, we are thankful for the jurors and their service."

A woman stepped behind the podium and said, "No further questions. Thank you."

The prosecutor walked away as reporters continued to hammer out more questions. Roger's legal team boasted to the reporters how the prosecutor never had a case against their client; it was merely a witch hunt that proved to have no legal merit.

Roger began to cry as a crowd of supporters cheered him on, and the reporters took notes on his tearful message. "I'm thankful to God for his continued protection over my family and me. I've been saying from the beginning that I was innocent of all the charges, and I'm relieved that we can put this to rest now."

"Are there any plans to return to the agency?" a reporter asked.

"Of course. My work in improving the lives of city residents is not over," he said and smiled.

As Sloan stood by her husband, she felt proud of him and believed he was a changed man. She couldn't believe that her prayers had been answered and was convinced that God had given her the answers she needed to get her family back together. She was prepared to do all she could to make it happen.

***

Seth had insisted they stay home to avoid the circus at the courthouse and instead received the news by way of the press conference held on the courthouse steps.

Within the hour, reporters began swarming their home, wanting to get Jennifer's reaction to the verdict, but Seth closed the blinds and shunned the reporters away that knocked on their door.

"How could he have gotten away with it?" she cried to her husband.

Seth paced and kept shaking his head. "I'm sorry, hun. I can't grasp the reasoning behind the jurors' decision."

Unable to eat, Jennifer went to bed early after putting the kids to sleep, but Seth couldn't settle his thoughts. He made a phone call and asked Jim to stop by. When he arrived, Seth invited Jim to the deck, where they smoked cigars and drank scotch while reflecting on the case.

"This guy is a fucking monster, and I'm going to put his ass behind bars, where he deserves to be," Jim said.

***

After the verdict was read, no one said a word in the office the rest of the day. Everyone stood huddled in front of the small television in the kitchenette, hoping to see Mr. Williams hauled off in handcuffs for good. Instead, they heard the opposite. From the expressions on the staff's faces, no one was happy. Not even the assistant director, who claimed to be one of Mr. Williams' biggest supporters.

Rachel was in complete shock. It was as if her heart had been snatched out of her body. She wanted to fall to her knees, but she couldn't show her anguish to the others; there was bound to be one snitch among them, mentally recording their every move to report back to Mr. Williams.

Nausea took hold of her body like a ghost creeping into the night. She ran out of the kitchenette, hoping to reach the bathroom before her breakfast spewed out and onto the floor. She stayed in the restroom to gather her emotions. She couldn't believe this son-of-a-bitch was not charged. Richard urged her to resign, but Rachel couldn't imagine relying on a man to take care of her; she was an independent woman. She was so eager to leave work.

At 4:45 pm , she stood waiting for the elevator. Rachel didn't care who saw her leave a few minutes early. When she arrived home, the smell of curry greeted her at the door; Richard had prepared a wonderful dinner. He bought roses and a card expressing his love. They talked and laughed as they ate over candlelight. She was so thankful to have found a man who truly loved her.

While the decision of whether to leave her job overwhelmed her, the thought of having a supportive man made things better.

Rachel's stomach began to churn, and she ran from the table and into the bathroom, where she began to vomit uncontrollably.

"Honey, are you okay?

"No, I'm not feeling well," she said. "The news of Mr. Williams coming back to work took a toll on me emotionally."

The vomiting persisted for several weeks, causing Rachel to drop a few pounds. It was the weight that she needed to lose anyway. Richard was concerned and had urged Rachel to see a doctor, but she assured him that she was fine. It was just Rachel's nerves getting the best of her.

The energy in the office was dead. Those who testified against Mr. Williams resigned from their positions. The remaining complained that they were doing the work of two.

Rachel applied for twenty jobs since he was acquitted and had only been on two interviews. She was overqualified for one and the other, she never heard back. Rachel believed that she was unlikely to find another job before Williams' return at the end of the month. She hoped to be in a position by the end of spring. Until then, she was going to make the best of it.

***

His plans on killing Roger Williams in prison had to change once there was no conviction, and James grew frustrated. The horror of losing Michelle and James Junior intensified even more when he heard the recording of Michelle's voice on the news. And hearing them talk about her was a reminder that she was gone.

His mother became distraught over the loss of her husband and suffered a relapse. Following another arrest, a judge ordered her to enter rehab.

James had not heard from or seen his mom in months. Word on the street was that she was either dead or strung out on drugs. While he was accustomed over the years to her disappearing or having extended stays in rehab, they had grown closer following the murders of his son and Michelle, and his mother became his confidant. He'd looked forward to her visits; his mom was his only connection to human touch.

After acting out on his frustrations, James was ordered to ninety days in solitary confinement. When the guards took him into confinement, he fought them until every ounce of energy was dissipated.

The echo from his screams reverberated throughout the cell block. Word had traveled fast among inmates that he was losing his mind or got hold of some bad drugs.

Solitary confinement was hard to adjust to. At night, fellow inmates shouted and banged on walls repeatedly until it became a normal occurrence. The veil of mental illness in his surroundings was apparent, and for James, it became his reality. Most nights, he cried and considered ending his life. While others, he dreamed of Michelle and James Junior by his side and would wake up screaming for them.

***

Sloan and the kids were moving back in by the end of the week, although, by this time, Roger wasn't so sure he was ready for his family to join him. Following the verdict, Roger had started enjoying his time alone. Then again, his wife had changed drastically since the verdict, and her willingness to give their marriage another try was a miracle he knew he shouldn't take for granted.

He had not seen this side of her in years. She began wearing lingerie when they were together and wore sexier outfits when they went out for dinner. Sloan made weekly visits to the hair salon and spoke less to her parents and friends. She even gave him oral sex in the car one evening after dinner, something she had not done since they were dating.

Clearly, she wanted things to work out between them, and Roger couldn't say she wasn't making one hell of an effort. Besides, he missed his kids and hated being restricted to when he could see them. He just didn't know what he was going to do with Shawn, who had become a nuisance.

Shawn had begun calling Roger's cell phone at all hours of the night from blocked numbers, threatening to show up at his house. Several times, he'd followed through on the threat, giving Roger no choice but to pull him inside to avoid the neighbors or anyone else getting wind of his latest affair. And now, with his wife and kids moving back in, Shawn was a problem Roger had to get rid of quickly.

Their first sexual encounter had been in an alley, where Roger stripped his pants down and entered Shawn from behind. They connected again when Shawn found him on social media and requested to be friends. Roger ignored him and even went further to block him. He later ran into Shawn at the same bar where he met him the first time, and after a few drinks, he took him home.

The chemistry between the two was undeniable. However, as that night ended, Roger realized it had been a bad idea to show Shawn where he lived. He had never brought anyone to his home before, not even a woman. But at the time, Roger had thought it was the safest place to conduct an illicit affair without the chance of anyone running into them.

But now, after the way Roger had treated him, Shawn seemed intent on taking full advantage of Roger's precarious situation. His latest threat was to expose their affair. "I want ten Gs in cash by tomorrow, or else I'm telling your wife."

Roger wanted him dead, but after being given a second chance, he thought it best to comply with Shawn's demand and made arrangements to meet with him.

"It's all there," Roger said, handing Shawn the money. "So, we're done here, right?"

"Yes, we are." Shawn grinned as he looked through the stack of bills. His expression changed, however, when he saw a bus ticket to Ohio in the envelope.

"You need to disappear for good," Roger told him. "If I see you around, I'm going to kill your fucking ass." He grabbed Shawn by the neck and began squeezing him hard, not releasing him until Shawn's face turned beet-red. Only one gasp of air could be heard from Shawn's mouth. "You hear me, you fucking punk?"

Shawn slid out of Roger's car in a hurry, and from what Roger could see, he didn't look back.

Later, with the help of his PI, Roger confirmed that Shawn moved out of the apartment he shared with his roommate and left the state the following day.

Roger was thrilled to be back at the office. Sloan and the kids were settled into the house, and everything was back to normal. When he arrived at work, he found his secretary had posted a welcome back poster with everyone's signatures and messages written all over it.

The first few days, he stayed mainly in his office behind closed doors meeting only with key staff members so they could brief him on everything that had taken place while he was away.

At the end of his first week back, he decided to address the entire staff in a meeting. When he walked into the conference room, the employees stood and greeted him with applause. Roger wasn't fooled. He knew the hugs and tears were fake, but he went along with it because soon, everyone would know he was back in charge again.

CHAPTER TWENTY-THREE

----- LOYALTY PAYS-------

Roger was busy framing his next plot. This time he would do things differently. The future ahead seemed promising for him. In a million years, no one would guess the type of year he'd had with all the good that was heading his way. He was confident he would get all he had coming to him one way or another. Just not without making a slight detour.

Spotting Pastor Covington already seated at a table and waiting for him, Roger made his way over. Noting the pastor had brought his son-in-law along, Roger frowned.

Antoine had put on a considerable amount of weight since Roger saw him last and looked haggard. From what Roger had heard, the pastor and his wife were doing all they could to support him in raising their grandchildren.

"Roger, it's good to see you," Pastor Covington greeted him.

"Good to see you both again, too," Roger replied, shaking both their hands. "So, tell me what's new since I saw you last."

"Antoine has been doing great work for the church," the pastor praised, "and has recently been promoted to Assistant of Operations. That's why I asked him to join us. I hope you don't mind?"

"That's fine," Roger replied. "Pastor, I invited you today to discuss an opportunity for developing a transitional shelter for women and children."

"Well, Roger, I think it's a wonderful idea." The pastor gestured to Antoine for his input.

"Yes, I think it's great," Antoine said.

"Our community could certainly benefit from a shelter," Pastor Covington added.

Roger nodded. "Good. And I wanted to save the best for last." He stood with a huge smile on his face and pulled out an architectural rendering of a building that read Michelle Porter's Transitional Shelter for women and children. "What do you think?"

"Praise God," the pastor cheered. "Michelle worked at a women's shelter in college and later became an advocate. My wife is going to be so happy to hear about this."

"Well, there's a lot of work to be done. But I believe we could break ground in a few months."

"I'm on board with the project, and you certainly have our support."

Roger glanced over at Antoine, who didn't comment, and something about the man's demeanor didn't feel quite right.

Things were moving ahead with the construction project, and with a week away to groundbreaking, Roger was in a panic. He wanted everything to be perfect. He went over the invitation list at least five times with the staff. Each time, he found a reason to eliminate someone, especially if they spoke out against him. Mr. Williams was becoming frustrated with what he believed to be Antoine's lack of vigor toward the project. His preferred point of contact with the church was with Pastor Covington or Antoine's assistant.

Antoine did not take it lightly that Roger Williams conveniently went over his head for some things he could have answered. Williams avoided Antoine's calls, and when he thought Antoine was near to missing a deadline, he complained to Pastor Covington.

On one occasion, Antoine happened to be in his father-in-law's office when Williams called, and the pastor had put the call on speaker without informing Williams that Antoine was present.

"Is everything okay with Antoine?" Williams asked.

"Good morning, Roger. Is there a problem?"

"Well, my staff has been trying to reach Antoine for a few weeks now for the executive summary."

When the pastor glanced up at Antoine for a reply, Antoine shook his head, indicating he'd received no such calls.

"Well, I'm sorry, Roger. I'll have a talk with him, and you'll have the executive summary tomorrow bright and early."

Williams seized that opportunity to engage in a discussion with the pastor about Antoine, asking if he believed his son-in-law was truly up for the job. The pastor assured Williams that although Antoine had suffered challenges since Michelle's death, they were optimistic things would get better. The pastor also assured Williams that he would personally make sure nothing slipped through the cracks.

"Be easy on him," Williams replied. "He's a great guy and trying to do his best, I'm sure."

"Yes, he's a great father, and my wife and I couldn't have asked for a better son-in-law."

***

While Williams pretended to be supportive, Antoine suspected the man saw this project as an opportunity to make matters worse for him.

His suspicions were confirmed when he agreed to meet with Williams one evening to go over questions relating to the grant's budget.

Antoine couldn't understand why Williams wanted to meet with him in the evening when his secretary had informed Antoine that Williams was available that same afternoon. But he didn't want to make a big deal about it, so Antoine had his sister watch the kids. The last thing he needed was Williams running back to his father-in-law and complaining about his unwillingness to meet with him at his convenience.

"Thanks for meeting with me this evening," Williams began, offering Antoine a seat. "I was booked solid all day, so this is the earliest I could manage. I meant to call you to tell you that you didn't have to come out after all because your assistant sent me the document that had everything we needed to complete the grant. But again, I was booked solid and just didn't find the time." He handed Antoine the document.

"No problem. I'm happy we were able to get the information over to you."

Williams nodded. "How are the kids?"

"They're doing much better. Thanks for asking."

"Michelle was a wonderful woman, and I miss her dearly," Williams commented.

"Yes, my wife was a great woman."

Williams began arranging things on his desk as he spoke. "She was a great support to me. You know, my wife and I separated for about six months. I asked God for strength and guidance. At one point, I thought she was cheating on me."

The conversation quickly became awkward. Antoine wasn't sure why Williams was discussing his personal life, but Antoine didn't want to hear it. He began gathering his things, hoping Williams would get the message that he wasn't interested in what he had to say about his marriage.

"I know you guys had a rough patch in your marriage shortly before Michelle died," Williams continued.

Antoine didn't respond.

Williams chuckled. "Michelle had a way of making everyone around her feel exceptionally good," he said as he stared into the distance and smiled. Then he glanced at his watch and stood. "Well, I'm running late, and my wife and I have reservations for dinner tonight."

Antoine didn't miss the implication and wasn't having it. He reached over and grabbed Williams by his shirt collar. "Roger, do me a favor, and stay the hell out of my business."

As Antoine stormed out of Williams' office, the bastard's laughter rang out from behind him.

Antoine struggled to believe his love had been enough for Michelle, and the thought of Williams and his wife engaging in an interoffice fling made him sick to his stomach.

He didn't want to disappoint his father-in-law, though, so he continued to work on the project but avoided interacting with Roger Williams personally.

Of course, this didn't stop Williams from trying to sabotage Antoine's work. A few times, he inadvertently omitted information and accused Antoine of the mistake. Fortunately, Antoine always kept his originals.

By the time they neared the end of the project, Antoine was beginning to feel overwhelmed. So, when Jennifer called to say she wanted to meet up for lunch, Antoine didn't hesitate.

***

Jennifer met Antoine at a local eatery. She was thrilled to see him but saddened to see he looked exhausted and overwhelmed.

"Nice to see you," she greeted him with a hug.

Antoine nodded. "It's good to get a break away from the office."

"Are you working on a new project?"

"Yes. Roger Williams and the pastor are developing a shelter for women and children. We break ground in two weeks."

Surprised, Jennifer hesitated to respond. "Wow. That's...wonderful."

"The shelter will be named after Michelle."

Jennifer couldn't believe what she was hearing. *How dare he!*

"What's wrong?" Antoine asked. Obviously, she hadn't kept her disdain from showing.

"Nothing," she said. "I'm surprised, that's all. Did Pastor Covington come up with the idea?"

"No. Roger called us in and told us about it."

"How has it been working on the project with him?"

"Roger's an asshole. I don't know how you and Michelle were able to work with him."

"Oh yeah, he's a piece of work, alright."

"Shortly before Michelle's accident, we began having marital problems. And for a while, we weren't even sleeping in the same bed. That's how bad the relationship got. I found letters between Michelle and her ex, James, the guy in prison. I didn't know what to do. It was clear that Michelle never stopped loving James."

Jennifer knew about his wife's unresolved feelings for her ex from a letter written in Michelle's notepad that Rachel had passed to her. Still, Jennifer pretended that she didn't know anything about it. Besides, she didn't want to hurt Antoine by confirming what she already knew. Instead, she continued to listen while he discussed his feelings.

"I began seeing someone from church," he said. "I don't believe Michelle knew about my affair. If she did, she never mentioned it. I ended the relationship the night of Michelle's accident. I feel terrible that I betrayed my wife's trust," he said, visibly fighting back the tears. "Do you believe Michelle cheated on me with Roger?"

"No, I don't. They had a close working relationship, but I don't believe they were having an affair. Why do you ask?"

"I met with Roger the other evening, and he insinuated they had a relationship."

"I have no doubt Williams was just trying to provoke you."

"Yes, I think so, too. Do you believe Roger committed those crimes?"

"Yes. And he got away it."

Jennifer told him more about the horror stories of working with Williams. "You have to be very careful with that man. I suggest that you make copies of everything and remember, don't sign anything without it being reviewed by an attorney."

Antoine assured Jennifer that he had everything under control. He also told her how he didn't trust Williams at all. "Something isn't right about this project."

"He can't be trusted."

"I agree. He's been on trial for stealing, after all. From the start, I've sensed Roger Williams was up to no good, but Pastor Covington constantly praises the guy, so I don't feel comfortable discussing my suspicions with him."

As they were saying their goodbyes, Antoine said, "It's time that I start getting rid of Michelle's belongings. I'm not looking forward to it, but I know a lot of women could use some of her things."

"I think you should have a garage sale. I have a few things that I can donate and add to the pile. I'd be happy to help you sort through everything."

"That would be great. Why don't you stop by this Saturday, say around 9:00 am?"

"That's a deal. I'll be sure to bring the kids so they can play," she said as they walked toward their vehicles.

***

Jennifer pulled up to the quaint cul-de-sac, where Antoine and the kids lived. The smell of fresh-cut grass filled the air as neighborhood kids stood behind a makeshift lemonade stand.

Antoine had everything mostly prepared. Jennifer helped with assembling Michelle's clothes and shoes. Within an hour, a small crowd of parishioners and neighbors began to gather around the tables. Pastor Covington and his wife came too and greeted everyone. Jennifer was the cashier, and as she exchanged money with an older woman, Williams walked by the table with an annoyed look on his face.

"Jennifer, do you have change for a twenty?" Antoine asked.

"Yes, I do."

Williams spoke with Pastor Covington and his wife, then made his way to his car and left. Jennifer could tell by everyone's glances her way that Williams had made it known to Pastor Covington that he was not happy with her presence. After Williams left, Pastor Covington and his wife said very little to her and acted a bit standoffish. Sensing the ensuing awkwardness, Jennifer decided to leave early. Over the next several days, she made repeated calls to Antoine but never heard back.

CHAPTER TWENTY-FOUR

----- WHO'S IN CHARGE-------

"Come in, Son."

Pastor Covington's office had become something of a shrine with photos and memorabilia of Michelle and James Junior adorning his walls and desk. Antoine entered, and his mind began to race. *What is it now?* he wondered. *Did Roger Williams complain again to his father-in-law about something he supposedly did or did not do?*

Antoine was prepared to walk away from the project, even if it meant him being demoted. Williams had become a thorn in his side, but he was a strong ally to his father-in-law.

Not knowing what to expect but eager to hear what his father-in-law had to tell him, Antoine took a seat.

"Were you able to sell a lot of stuff at the yard sale?" Pastor Covington asked.

"Yes, we sold everything."

"Well, that's great, Son. By the way, did you invite Jennifer to the yard sale?"

"Yes. It was her idea, actually, We had lunch earlier in the week, and she suggested that I host a yard sale."

"Well, Roger wasn't happy. It's probably not a good time to bring her around. We don't want to offend the hand that's been good to us."

Antoine wasn't about to say what he wanted to, so he said nothing.

"Son, please make sure she doesn't show up to the groundbreaking."

"Sure, Pastor."

Antoine was pissed. He couldn't believe Roger had that much influence over his father-in-law. Now, the man was controlling his personal life. He wanted to tell Jennifer but was afraid it would get back to his father-in-law, and he couldn't risk that happening. Instead, he sent her calls to voicemail.

Monica started coming around again, and they kept it a secret. The last thing he wanted was for his father-in-law to find out that he and his former mistress were seeing each other again.

This time their relationship was different. Although he believed Monica had become more thoughtful and someone he could talk to about his problems, he knew she could never replace Michelle. He made it clear to Monica that he was not ready for a committed relationship. Most nights, he wouldn't call her until very late after the kids were fast asleep, and she was never allowed to spend the night. So far, she was fine with the arrangements.

***

This was not a good time for Rachel to request a few hours off, especially with the groundbreaking only a few days away. She was excited to receive a call for a job interview, and she wasn't going to turn down this great opportunity. Rachel tossed and turned all night, thinking of what to say to impress the panel. As she drove to the interview, Richard called to offer words of encouragement.

"Good luck, sweetie."

Rachel's excitement wore off as she sat for about an hour in the lobby, waiting for someone to escort her upstairs to the executive offices. A short blonde woman, who introduced herself as Christine, apologized and directed her to a panel of four people in a small conference room.

"Please have a seat. We are running behind schedule," said one panelist.

Each member drilled Rachel with questions about her educational background and experience. While she thought she answered their questions well, it felt as though they had someone in mind already for the position. One could never tell, but Rachel sensed by the expression of one of the interviewers that he was not impressed. He yawned ten times, she counted, throughout her interview.

"Do you have any questions for us?" Christine asked.

"When will the panel make their decision?" Rachel asked.

"We'll have a decision by the end of this week."

Rachel left the interview feeling somewhat optimistic. She wanted this position so badly. When she returned to the office, she immediately removed her suit jacket in the elevator and placed it in her bag. She didn't want anyone to know that she, too, was looking for a job.

Rachel settled into her office and began answering calls from reporters, who wanted to know last-minute details of the groundbreaking.

Since Mr. Williams had been acquitted, reporters showed more interest in their events. It was as if they were waiting for something else bad to happen.

Claire called and said Mr. Williams wanted to see Rachel. As she walked toward his office, her stomach began cramping. Once again, Mr. Williams wanted to discuss the guest list.

As she eliminated more people from the list, he said, "Starting a new job during this time is probably not such a good idea."

She was so shocked he knew she went on an interview that she nearly fell out of the chair. Surprisingly, she managed to maintain her composure and didn't respond.

"Mr. Williams, is there anything else?" she asked.

His office phone began ringing, and Rachel took that as my signal to leave. She grabbed her notepad and left.

Later, Rachel shared the incident with Richard.

"Honey, I'm not sure what that was about," he said with a peculiar look on his face, "but don't let it discourage you." He kissed her on the lips and spent the rest of the evening distracting her.

She wanted to let it go as easily but knew differently. Somehow Williams found out that she was interviewing, and Rachel knew that meant she had no chance of getting the job. Her suspicion proved right a week later. She received an email thanking her for applying for the job, but she was not selected to participate in the second phase of the interview process. She called Richard and told him the terrible news, but she was up to her neck with work, and she had very little time to dwell on this missed opportunity.

***

Antoine sat watching Williams parade around as if he was the president of the free world. He ignored Antoine throughout the ceremony and had staff escort him to the back of the audience because the seats in front were reserved for dignitaries only.

Williams thanked everyone, including his secretary and Antoine's assistant for their important roles in the project, blatantly excluding Antoine in his speech. Antoine was annoyed that Williams didn't acknowledge his hard work and the hours he spent making sure this project would go on without a hitch, but he wasn't surprised.

During Williams' one-hour speech, Antoine went to the restroom, and while in the stall, he overheard a man talking on his cell phone about how he recently did extensive renovations at Williams' home. Antoine recognized the voice as one of the contractors who had worked on the shelter. He waited to leave the stall until the man left. Antoine wasn't sure what to think of what he heard. The man never stated whether he was paid to do the work, but he found it ironic that Williams mentioned in a meeting that he didn't know the contractors. Yet, it was obvious from their interactions that Williams had a history with the developers.

***

James was released from solitary confinement and came to terms with the deaths of his loved ones. He realized that there was no way he could survive in prison if he continued to dwell on something he had no power over.

He would rather be feared than be fearful, so the first thing he needed to do was regain control. It would take some time, but his enemies would be already after him, so he had to act fast. Some people wanted him out, and he had to make it known that he was still in charge.

Those who had turned against him would be dealt with one by one. Milk, the person he'd thought had his back, had turned on him. His friendship with Milk spanned from childhood and evolved into a brotherhood over the years, so it was painful for James to hear that his brother wanted him dead.

As the men stood around in the recreation yard, a fight ensued with two inmates from opposing gangs. In tangled limbs, the men fell to the ground as others stood by and watched. As the man on the bottom got free, a foot came out of nowhere and kicked him several times in the face. Some inmates threw punches, and others began running toward the melee to help defend their turf. Milk was among the men in the brawl. He fell to the ground with a stab wound to his chest and later died. The correctional officers used pepper spray and called for assistance. By the end of it all, ten of the inmates involved in the fight were either sent to the infirmary or solitary confinement.

***

While there were no leads to pursue a criminal investigation regarding Garcia, Jim continued to search for answers. He visited both places, where Garcia's remains were discovered. The area had no clues that could be traced to Mr. Williams or anyone for that matter. When Jim drove up to the area near the highway, most of it had been constructed. He looked around to see if he could find something. As he left the grounds, Jim ran into Mark, a security guard, who worked the night before the discovery.

"Did you see anything unusual that night?" asked Jim.

Mark puffed on a cigarette, threw the lit butt on the ground and stepped on it. "No, I didn't see anything," said Mark as he blew smoke from his mouth.

"Where were you exactly?"

"I was on the other side of the grounds."

Jim wasn't buying his story. The thirty-five-year-old was acting elusive.

"Look, Mark, for some reason, I don't believe you. If I have to get a subpoena, you'll be forced to tell the truth."

"Look, I didn't want to say anything. I came to work with a hangover, and I parked in the back and went to sleep. I woke up because of a light shining from a car. I saw a man get in a car and drive off. That's all I saw."

"Did you get a good look at the person?"

"No, I was several yards away, and it was raining."

"How about the make of the car?"

"I don't know."

"Was the car a two or four-door?"

"I think it was a four-door, and it was definitely a mid to large size car."

"Are there any cameras on the facility?"

"No cameras," Mark said. Jim didn't have much to go on but was happy there was some movement in the investigation.

***

The construction of the shelter was moving steadily. Roger was excited about its progress and the positive publicity surrounding its development. He believed the project would help change his career for the better.

He didn't feel comfortable having Antoine involved, but he knew how much it meant to Pastor Covington to have him a part of the project. Still, when he saw Jennifer at the yard sale, he knew there was no way he could trust Antoine going forward. Pastor Covington promised Roger that he would have a talk with Antoine and would make certain Jennifer didn't come around, but that didn't mean Antoine wouldn't still have contact with her on his own time. The last thing Roger needed was Jennifer and Antoine teaming up against him, and he wasn't going to allow that to happen.

***

Night had fallen when Roger left the office. The few cars parked in the garage belonged to the cleaning staff. With his briefcase in tow, he walked across the parking lot, reading a text from his wife at the same time.

He quickly returned the text to tell her he was on his way, and at that exact moment, a car parked at the back of the garage turned on its high beams and came at him at full speed.

Roger barely had time to get out of the way. His briefcase went up in the air and landed with papers splattered across the ground, and his cell phone fell under a car parked two spaces away. He wasn't able to get a good look at the vehicle but was relieved he didn't get hurt. The car tires screeched as they exited the garage. Roger retrieved his cell phone and papers and left the garage as fast as he could.

CHAPTER TWENTY-FIVE

-------FACING HIS WRONGS------

"No!" Roger screamed.

Next to him, Sloan jolted awake. "Honey, what's wrong."

Roger sat up in bed, drenched with sweat and panting for air. He looked around to see if he recognized his surroundings. Sloan took hold of his hand.

"You had a nightmare," she said.

"Baby, get me some water, please." Sloan hurried to the kitchen. When she handed Roger the water, he quickly guzzled it down.

"Is everything okay at work? You've had a nightmare every day this week."

"Yes, everything is fine."

"Well, you screamed out Michelle's name."

"Honey, please just hold me," he said. Roger pressed his head into his wife's chest and held her tightly. He was not prepared to tell Sloan that someone wanted him dead.

Since that incident, when he came in the house each night, he peeped through the blinds to see if the car that followed him home was still lurking around and checked the doors multiple times throughout the evening.

Roger yelled from the bathroom, "Sloan, did you lock the front door?"

"Roger, you checked the door before you went into the shower."

Roger came out of the bathroom with a towel wrapped around him and beads of water covering his bare chest.

"Is someone after you?" Sloan asked.

"I told you everything is okay."

"So why are you so paranoid?"

"There are some people who are upset that I was acquitted. I just want to make sure our family is safe."

"Is this why you're having these nightmares?"

"Yes."

"Well, I think you should talk to someone about it."

"Honey, you're right, and I'll look into it," said Mr. Williams.

Sloan knew something was not right with him, but she went along with everything, including agreeing to Mr. Williams stowing his gun in the nightstand, something he had never done before. She wanted so badly to restore their marriage and didn't want to do anything to disrupt their progress. Instead, she spoke with Pastor Covington about her fears.

"Thanks for meeting with me, Pastor," said Sloane.

"What's wrong?" he asked.

Sloan began to cry. "I don't know where to start."

Pastor Covington handed her a tissue. "Take your time."

"Well, after the trial, the kids and I moved back in our home. And for a while, we were happy, but lately, things have gone astray."

"He's constantly looking out the window. He doesn't want the children to play outside. He's waking up in the middle of the night screaming. Maybe I should not say this, but I'm afraid he is using drugs again, or someone is after him. Shortly before we were married, Roger did a stint in rehab for alcohol and cocaine abuse. It was a really tough time for us. I used most of my savings to pay off his debt with drug dealers. I don't know what to do, Pastor," said Sloan.

"I don't believe you have anything to worry about. I know Roger has been busy working on the transitional shelter project. The contractors are a bit behind schedule, and this has stressed Roger some. Look, why don't you and Roger come over for dinner on Sunday? My wife and I would love to have you guys over."

"I'll see if Roger is available,"

"Is this Michelle and your grandson?" asked Sloan, referring to a photograph on his desk.

"Yes."

"Your daughter and grandson were beautiful."

Pastor Covington picked up a photo of Michelle holding an infant James Junior. "I miss them so much," he said as he stared off in deep thought.

Sloan felt bad about baring her marital problems to Pastor Covington. It was obvious he was still mourning the loss of his loved ones. He spent nearly an hour sharing stories from each of the photos in his office. This had become a normal routine for the pastor since Michelle and James Junior died. Sloan was relieved that she had spoken with the pastor and optimistic that whatever was bothering her husband would eventually go away.

***

Roger stood as his secretary escorted the police detective into his office. He reached out, and the two men shook hands.

"Detective McKeon. To what do I owe the honor of your visit?

"There's still an active investigation with regard to the murder of Juan Garcia."

"So what do you need from me? I already spoke to you guys this past summer about what I know."

"Let's get straight to it. We have a credible witness who saw a vehicle very similar to the make and model of your car leaving the construction site the night before Garcia's remains were discovered. "Where were you on this night?"

"I was with my kids that night. Look, Detective McKeon, I have to prepare for a meeting." Roger looked down at his watch, stood, and walked toward his office door, gesturing for Jim to leave.

The detective rose, and with a smirk, he said, "I'll be back."

Roger slammed his door, wishing that he could close the door to all of his problems, but he knew closing the door was not going to stop the police, who appeared to be determined to pin the murder on him.

Knowing he had to do something quickly, Roger gathered his things and headed out the door.

"Claire, make dinner reservations for 7:00 pm for Sloan and me at that new bistro restaurant downtown and cancel my appointments for the rest of the day," he said as he left the office.

"Baby, how do you like your dinner?" Roger asked that evening.

"The food is great." She sighed. "Did something change since this morning?"

"Actually, I'd like to apologize for my behavior lately. I've been under a lot of stress at work, and I don't mean to take my frustrations out on you and the kids. Besides, I want things to work between us."

Roger handed Sloan a gift bag with pink tissue flowing out of it.

"What's this?" she asked, smiling.

"Just a little token of my appreciation."

Inside the box was a charm bracelet with diamonds. Gushing with excitement, Sloan said, "It's beautiful. Thank you."

"I love you, baby," He leaned over and kissed her.

"I love you too."

The night ended with Roger and Sloan returning home, where their bodies intertwined and formed a human pretzel. He pulled Sloan's body closer to him as he passionately kissed her. She wrapped her legs around his body as he gently sucked on her breast while thrusting inside her. She cried out his name as her body quivered in excitement.

Their night of lovemaking did not free Roger from worrying about his future. It was only a matter of time, he thought, before Detective McKeon would start asking his wife questions about his whereabouts on the night Garcia was supposedly killed.

Roger didn't believe McKeon would buy his story if he told him the truth, which meant he had to do something to stop him.

***

Carol was out of rehab and appeared older and robust in stature. Her thinning blonde tresses were doused with charcoal gray. The pale pink lipstick she once wore proudly, now seemed much too young for her age. Carol was anxious to see her son and was unsure how he would react to seeing her after months of being away. She wondered how she was going to convince James that she was ready to stop using drugs. When James walked into the room, Carol's sullen blue eyes lit up. James was equally excited to see her. He realized how much he needed his mom. He knew connecting with his mom gave her the validation that she had never experienced before, not even with her own parents. It was important for Carol's well-being that he showered her with the love she needed to ward off her desire for drugs.

"How you feeling, Mom?" asked James.

He could sense his mom felt uncomfortable about wearing dentures by the way she smiled with her mouth closed.

"Son, I'm feeling much better. I found a new place in senior housing, and I'm one of the youngest in the building," she said boastfully. In mid-sentence, Carol said, "I have something to tell you." She began tearing up.

"What's wrong," he asked with a look of concern.

"James, I know I disappointed you by getting back on drugs."

"Mom, please."

"No, let me finish. I have a lot to get off my chest. When you're father died, I didn't want to live anymore. Even though he was not good for me or our children, I still loved him; I miss him. In rehab, I learned that by not confronting my problems, I would never get past my demons. For the first time in my life, I feel that I can put the past behind me and move forward. I'm your mom, and I want to be here for you. I'm sorry, and I promise I will do my best this time to stay off of drugs."

"Mom, you can do it. I know you can."

James was stunned by his mom's candidness about her drug abuse. In the past, she avoided any discussions about her addiction. Carol's words of atonement helped soothe the wounds of his childhood, and he no longer held any hostility toward her.

They grew closer over time. Every week he looked forward to her visits. She always came bearing funny stories about her occasional run-ins with her neighbors on social nights. Carol even met a man ten years her senior at bingo named David, a retired postman from Virginia with grandchildren. She definitely wore the pants in the relationship. Her boyfriend was nurturing and much more reserved than his dad. In the beginning, James didn't like the idea of his mom dating again, but he grew to like and respect David and how well he took care of his mom.

***

Jennifer was shocked to receive a call from Antoine wanting to meet with her about Mr. Williams. He said he had something urgent to tell her. When Antoine walked into the restaurant, he appeared overwhelmed and anxious to get something off his chest.

"Jennifer, I'm sorry I didn't return your calls right away."

"It's okay. I know you've been busy."

"Yes, I have been. Well, a lot has happened since we last spoke."

"What's going on?"

"I know this is strange, but I believe Williams illegally handed a no-bid, single-source contract to his friend."

"You mean the contract to build the transitional shelter?"

"Yes."

"How do you know?"

"The same contractor did some work at Williams' house. I overheard the contractor talking about it in the restroom the day of the groundbreaking. One of our clients from the work-release program is working on the construction site. The foreman was overheard telling a worker how the contract for the transitional shelter was a gift from Williams for the work he had done in his home. But Williams specifically told Pastor Covington and me that he didn't know the contractor."

"Antoine, the agency's contracting system threshold for bidding is very high. Mr. Williams can abuse his power and hand out contracts to his cronies and get away with it."

"What do you mean he can get away with it?" he asked, raising his voice.

"The contracting system for the agency is very lax, and there's no oversight."

"We have to do something. He can't keep getting away with this stuff."

"I agree. But it would be very difficult to prove that there's an elaborate kickback scheme."

"This contractor is slated to do other projects. I don't know how I'm going to tell Pastor Covington, but he needs to know what's going on. Until we can figure something out, let's keep our meeting between us. Williams has expressed that he doesn't want you around."

"No, problem. Call me and let me know what I can do."

As they walked toward their cars, Jennifer turned to him. "Antoine, please be careful. Mr. Williams is a dangerous man."

"I will, thanks.

CHAPTER TWENTY-SIX
-------BURDEN OF PROOF------

Rachel drove into work with an enormous headache. Richard felt strongly that she stay home, but she knew better. She didn't want to feel the wrath of Mr. Williams. The closer she got to the building, the more she wanted to run back to her car and drive home.

She walked into the lobby, feeling as though she had been run over by a Mack truck. The smell of caffeine lured her into the break room, where she poured a large cup. She knew there was no way she was getting through this day without it. She stayed mainly in her office. Rachel hoped she would not be called to a dreadful meeting. Mr. Williams' emotional tirades were becoming as common as her nagging migraines.

The day slowly slipped away, and no calls from Mr. Williams. Rachel was thrilled when the clock hit 5:00 pm. She and Richard had dinner plans; he wanted to check out a new Argentinean steakhouse in South Beach. Rachel quickly gathered her belongings and practically ran toward the elevator, only to be intercepted by Mr. Williams. He beckoned her to his office while a group of her co-workers walked by with their heads down toward the elevator. Rachel texted Richard to tell him that she was canceling their dinner plans.

This was the fifth time in two weeks that she had to cancel plans with him. Richard had an early flight to catch in the morning, and she had wanted to spend time with him before he left. Rachel followed behind Mr. Williams into his office, where he drilled her for three hours about not following up with him about a reporter's request. She couldn't believe that she forgot to notify him. Mr. Williams mentioned how the reporter was so upset that he threatened to expose how they ignored his public information requests.

Journalists hated reporting anything the agency was involved in because of Mr. Williams' lack of transparency and refusal to provide any pertinent documents. It usually took about two weeks for him to provide a simple spreadsheet on anything relating to funding matters. However, this time he was not the blame. Rachel was.

She knew she would not hear the end of it. The constant ridiculing was enough to drive anyone insane. It was clear Rachel was on a fast track to losing her mind.

Rachel's eyes had welled up with tears and what was left of her mascara made a streaming path on her face. She could hardly see to drive home; she was mentally exhausted, and now she was making costly mistakes at work.

Richard was extremely patient. He was also busy with work at the foundation and running multiple businesses. He was constantly flying to and from Little Rock and other parts of the country for meetings. When she reached home, Rachel called Richard, and he was preparing for his trip in the morning. They decided they would catch up with each other on his return from Little Rock. These days they spent very little time together and mostly connected through Facetime in between flights.

Rachel was so happy to hear from Alice, who was in town for a day. She was on her way to Antigua to speak at a leadership conference. They spent most of the day sipping on mojitos and hanging out at the pool at her hotel, where she was staying.

"How are things at work?"

Before Rachel could even begin talking, Alice added, "Don't tell me. Roger is at it again."

From the expression on her face, she could tell Rachel was under an enormous amount of stress. She filled her in about the trial and Mr. Williams' return to the office.

"Why don't you quit?" she begged. "And please don't tell me about bills. You're dating a retired NFL football player who happens to be one of the most successful businessmen in the south. Not to mention, he's madly in love with you."

Rachel didn't know how to respond to her statement. She couldn't understand it either. Why was she still working for the agency?

"I'm not a quitter," she said out loud.

"Rachel, you have nothing to prove, and you do exceptional work."

Rachel was on her fifth mojito, and the effect of the alcohol was boldly apparent. She couldn't frame her thoughts well and began to cry uncontrollably. Alice set her drink down to console Rachel.

"How much bullshit are you willing to take from Williams? It's not worth it."

Rachel confided in her that she thought her relationship with Richard was falling apart. Alice looked at Rachel with a stunned look on her face.

"What happened?" she asked.

"We rarely see each other."

"Rachel, this man left his home state to be with you. Promise me you will not allow this job to destroy your relationship."

"I won't."

"I'm serious. You may want to consider looking elsewhere."

"I have been looking."

Just then, an older man with sun-kissed skin and a rotund belly that protruded over his speedos walked toward them.

"Would you ladies like a drink?" he asked, his speech slurred.

Alice and Rachel looked at each other then burst out in laughter. "No, thank you," they said in unison.

"Let's get out of here," Rachel whispered.

The next morning, Rachel drove Alice to the airport. She was sad to see her leave, but she knew they would see her at Anita's wedding next month. They were both bridesmaids.

She was right about everything and not allowing the job to get in between her relationship. Rachel had to also focus on looking for another job. In the meantime, she was going to make an effort to spend more quality time with the love of her life. Rachel was anxious for Richard to get home.

***

Jim watched Sloan as she walked the kids into school. Appearing much younger in age, she wore a fitted gray jogging suit with her hair pulled back in a sleek ponytail. Jim waited in his car for Sloan to leave the school building. As she approached her car, he walked over to her and pulled out his badge.

"Sloan Williams. I'm Detective Jim McKeon.

Sloan was shaken by his abrupt approach.

"I'm sorry if I frightened you."

"No, no, it's okay. How can I help you?"

"Do you have a few minutes to spare? I have just a few questions."

"Yes, but not very long. I have an appointment."

215

"I won't take much of your time. Let's take a walk." Sloan nodded, and they strolled along the boundary of the empty playground adjacent to the school.

"Do you know a man named Juan Garcia?"

"No, I don't know anyone by that name."

Sloan's mind began to race, wondering where this conversation was leading. Sloan immediately began thinking about her husband and wondered if this Garcia was the reason for her husband's sleepless nights.

Sloan looked at the photo. "I've never seen him before in my life."

"Your husband met with this man a few times shortly before he was murdered."

Sloan was in shock.

"Was Roger with you on the night of _____?"

"Yes, he came by to visit our children."

"Are you guys no longer married?"

"We're still married, but we were separated briefly last year."

"What time did he leave?"

"I'm not sure, exactly, but I would guess it must have been shortly before the children went to bed."

"What time would that have been?"

"Around 8:00 pm, I'd said. Wait a minute. Is my husband a suspect in this murder?"

"No, we're just asking questions."

"Look, Detective, my husband would never kill anyone. He's not that type of man."

He nodded and handed Sloan a business card. "Thank you for your cooperation, Mrs. Williams. You have a wonderful day."

Astounded, Sloan stood frozen as she watched the detective get in his car and drive away. She couldn't believe this was happening. She hit the unlock button on her key chain and entered her

Mercedes station wagon. As she drove home, tears streamed down her face. When a call came in from her husband, she sent it straight to voicemail.

As Sloan prepared dinner later that evening, the distant chatter between Roger and the children grew closer. Roger opened the front door, and the kids rushed into the kitchen with their book bags in tow.

"Mommy, I got a smiley face today from school," their older son shouted.

"Wonderful. Give mommy a kiss. I'm so proud of my baby boy."

Roger stood by smiling, and the children turned to run upstairs to their bedrooms.

"Guys, don't forget to bathe. Dinner will be ready shortly!" Sloan called after them.

Roger walked over and hugged her from behind, then began kissing her passionately on her neck while she stood over the stove, stirring. She pulled away and went to pull butter from the refrigerator for their bread.

"What are you cooking?"

"Spaghetti," she said.

Roger must have sensed something was wrong because he asked, "Baby, is everything okay?"

"Sure," she said and smiled.

Sloan said very little to her husband during dinner, although he made every attempt to engage her in conversation.

As the two laid next to each other in bed, Roger rolled toward her and once again asked, "Sloan, talk to me. What's wrong?"

She reached over and turned on the light on her nightstand. "Who is Juan Garcia?"

Roger's eyes narrowed. "I take it the detective spoke to you today?"

"Yes, he met me outside of our children's school this morning."

"Allow me to explain. Juan Garcia is some derelict I met a few times at a bar. He was trying to get his life back in order, and I offered to help him find housing. Apparently, he was murdered."

"Do you know who could have killed him?"

"Of course not."

"Why are the police questioning you?"

"I'm not sure, baby."

"Why are you still waking up in the middle of the night?"

"I told you I'm under a lot of stress at work, but I'll be fine. Please, stop worrying about me." He gently kissed her on the forehead.

Roger assured her that everything would be fine, but Sloan wasn't convinced and feared that her husband was in serious trouble.

***

Roger was growing impatient with Monica. Her nonchalant attitude was infuriating.

"Has Antoine told you anything about the construction project?"

Monica looked around the restaurant before answering. "No. The only thing he said was that he was under a lot of stress and that you were making his life impossible."

A waiter came by their table and interrupted their conversation. "Would you like coffee or dessert."

"No. Just the check, please," Roger replied. He took out his wallet and pulled out his American Express card. The moment the waiter left them, he turned his attention back to Monica. "I need more information. I'm not paying you for nothing. Are we clear?"

"Look, I've given you more than enough. I searched his home and gave you Michelle's diary. What else do you what from me?"

Roger slammed his hand on the table. "I need more."

"I want out of this situation." Monica rose to leave, but Roger grabbed hold of her arm and yanked her back into her seat.

"Look, bitch. We have a deal. So, you better work harder to get me what I want."

"Or else?"

"You don't even want to know," he replied with a smirk on his face.

Monica left the restaurant feeling beleaguered. Her heart began to beat fast. She never intended to hurt Antoine and wanted out of this arrangement. Mr. Williams hired her to seduce Antoine and to dig up any dirt she could find on Michelle. He even had her place a tracking device on Michelle's car. It never sat well with her that Michelle and James Junior died in a freak accident. Monica knew Mr. Williams wanted Michelle dead and considered going to the authorities to tell them what she knew, but she was afraid of him. Mr. Williams threatened to kill her if she told anyone about their deal.

CHAPTER TWENTY-SEVEN
--------DEATH KNOCKING AT THE DOOR------

Roger quietly rose from his bed as Sloan lay fast asleep, draped in bed covers. She wore a headscarf that had shifted downward, slightly concealing most of her eyes, and strands of her hair around the outer surface of her rollers were exposed. With one pillow planted between her legs and the other behind her head, nothing could disturb her sleep, not even the sound of her husband preparing to leave for a joyride.

He slipped into his jogging pants, placed his University of Florida gator hat on his head, and gathered his car keys. He disabled the house alarm and quickly made his way to his car in the garage. Most nights, no one noticed him slipping out except for the family dog, but a few treats kept him distracted.

Taking a late-night drive or an early morning run had become customary since he could no longer sleep more than three hours at a stretch. He would smoke a few joints and sip on scotch while his family was in deep slumber.

A few times, he visited Cindy on the street corner, where she strolled the strip. He would gesture her to meet him in the alleyway. Once in the car, he placed her on the back seat of his car, where he pulled his jogging pants down to his ankles, and she lay on her stomach with her butt positioned upward. He grabbed her hips toward him and began thrusting inside her as hard as he could. He grunted at how she felt inside while she let out a passionate sigh. Her long black curls had fallen forward, covering most of her face.

A visit with Cindy always did the job. He could be pleased sexually without having to answer any questions. He would then rush back home and fall right to sleep until it was time to get the kids up for school and himself to work.

This morning it was a balmy night. Roger drove through the city streets, where lights stretched for miles, making sure he didn't go over the speed limit. He didn't want to draw any unwanted attention.

He parked his car and began walking with his hoodie draped over his head through a neighborhood nestled just south of Downtown. The row of graffiti-laden buildings, dilapidated shotgun houses, and abandoned lots were loaded with junk strewn everywhere. Stray cats and dogs rummaged through piles of garbage in search of their next meal.

With his gun in its hoister and no sense of fear, Roger quickly walked by a corner liquor store, where young men with menacing looks on their faces and dressed in sagging pants with their underwear exposed as a badge of honor, boasted about their last sexual conquest as they waited to serve their next customer.

He approached an apartment building, where the door was left ajar. Once inside, he glanced toward the two security cameras on each corner with wires hanging from them, evidencing the cameras had been tampered with. He avoided taking the elevator and instead took the stairwell. As he climbed the stairs, he saw a gray and white kitten curled in a corner. He lifted the kitten into his arms and continued up the five flights. Once he entered the dimly lit hallway, the smell of cigarettes and urine hit him like a ton of bricks.

The apartment he wanted stood at the end of the hallway, adjacent to the stairwell. Roger tried opening the door several times then began tapping on it lightly. When the sounds of footsteps inside grew closer, he scooted to the side of the wall next to the stairwell to avoid being seen through the peephole. The kitten jumped out of his arms.

Dressed in a night rob, Monica nervously peeped out her door and looked at both ends of the hallway to see if she saw anyone who may have been trying to enter her apartment. A few times during the week, she thought she heard someone at her door, but each time those claims were refuted. It was a neighbor entering their apartment, or at best, her nerves got the best of her. This time was no different. When she realized there was no one at her door, she started to close it, then midway she heard a cat purring.

Monica let out a sigh of relief and picked up the kitten. She assumed it was the sound of the kitten that awakened her from her sleep.

"Come here, cutie pie. Were you trying to get my attention?"

The moment Monica picked up the kitten, Roger barged through her apartment door with his .45 caliber pistol in his hand. He pushed her inside, and the kitten fell to the ground.

"If you say one word, I'm going to put a bullet in your head."

"Please don't kill me," she pleaded.

"Shut up!" He shoved her into the bedroom with the gun now pointed to her head.

"Please don't kill me."

"Did you talk to Antoine?"

"No. I mean, yes," she stuttered. "He said he was busy and he would call me later. Look, I need some more time."

"That's not good enough. Your time is up." He looked around the room, trying to decide a course of action. Then, as an adjacent door stood open, he noticed her walk-in closet with a high ceiling. He ordered her to remove her clothes and tossed her shoes to the side. He yanked the top sheet from her bed and handed it to her.

"What's this for?" she asked between sobs.

"Hold onto that end," he instructed, ignoring her question. Then he tied that end of the sheet around her neck and the other to a brass rod perched several feet above her head. He placed a chair inside the closet and forced her to stand on it.

Sweat and tears flowed from Monica's eyes as she pleaded for her life. When she began to fight back, he grabbed her by the neck and squeezed, not releasing her until she was visibly struggling for air.

Then without hesitation, he swiftly removed the chair and stood back.

Roger watched as Monica stared, her eyes wide and her body flinching until finally, she took her last breath. On his way out the door, he snatched her cell phone from the nightstand and once again lifted the kitten into his arms. He stepped into the hallway, looking around to see if he saw anyone, then quickly ran down the stairs. When he reached his car, he discarded Monica's cell phone behind a bush and removed his gloves and hoodie, leaving him dressed only in a t-shirt and jeans and placed the discarded clothing in his trunk.

On his way home, he stopped by the drive-thru of a McDonald's and purchased breakfast for his family. When he arrived home, his wife was in the shower. He prepared himself for the drilling but knew to remain calm. He took the breakfast sandwiches from the bag just as Sloan entered the kitchen, still in her bathrobe.

"Where have you been?"

He leaned over and kissed her. "Where do you think?"

Sloan glanced down to where he'd placed the breakfast items on the table.

"Oh, you got us breakfast!" She smiled. "Thanks, baby. Guys, hurry up," she called to the children who came wandering in, still rubbing their eyes. "Dad bought breakfast."

Dressed in their school uniforms, the kids sat down and began eating.

"I have a surprise," Roger announced, then placed the kitten in his oldest son's arms. His children could barely compose themselves with excitement over the kitten.

"It's so tiny," said his exclaimed.

"You guys are going to be late," Sloan said.

Roger placed the kitten on the floor, where it began sniffing around to become familiar with its new surroundings. After finishing their breakfast, the kids grabbed their backpacks and hurried toward the garage, with Roger following.

***

Jim believed he was close to having enough evidence to make an arrest but wanted more time. His lieutenant rejected his proposal and demanded he close the case and focus on a suspected serial rapist who sexually assaulted several women throughout the downtown area. Jim sat at his desk reviewing messages from the day before. He stumbled across a message that a woman named Monica Atkins had been by to see him. He called the number and left a message. Jim walked over to the officer's desk whose name appeared on the message.

"You took this message," Jim asked.

"Yes, she came by Thursday, and she wanted to talk to you," said a fellow detective.

"Did she say what for?"

"She said she wanted to talk to someone about Michelle and James Porter's car accident.

"If she comes by again, give her my cell number." Jim decided to give Jennifer a call to see if she knew Monica.

"Hello, Jen?"

"Hi, so happy to hear from you."

"Do you know a woman by the name of Monica Atkins?"

"That name doesn't ring a bell."

"Well, she stopped by the station wanting to speak to someone about Michelle's car accident?" Jim entered the court building as he spoke. "Listen, I'm at my location. We'll talk soon," he said.

***

Pastor Covington met with Antoine to go over plans for the Triumph Community Awards Ceremony.

"Don't forget to include Roger on the list of awardees," Pastor Covington instructed. Antoine snorted at the mention of his wife's former boss.

Pastor Covington removed his eyeglasses. "Antoine, tell me what's on your mind."

"Pastor, I don't know how to tell you this, but Roger Williams is not a good man. I have reason to believe he knows the contractors we're using for the shelter very well. They did free work at his home in exchange for the contract."

"Son, do you have proof of this?"

"Yes, I do." The pastor didn't seem concerned at all, which didn't surprise Antoine. Still, he wondered what it would take for this man to be convinced that Roger Williams was an asshole. It was obvious his father-in-law had been seduced by Williams' access to money and gained respect for the man simply because of his power.

"Antoine, I know this project has been very stressful for you. Allow me some time to think about how we should move forward."

Pastor Covington stood and paced to the window. "You've been working late most nights. Why don't you go home early and get some rest? We'll talk in the morning."

"____," Antoine replied before heading for the door.

"By the way," the pastor said, stopping him, "have you seen Monica lately?"

"No, I haven't. Why do you ask?"

"She hasn't been to work in a few days, and no one has heard from her. Could you have Jan stop by her home tomorrow to check on her?"

"Will do."

His father-in-law's immediate dismissal of his concerns annoyed Antoine. Thinking back on the expression on the pastor's face, Antoine was beginning to believe his father-in-law somehow already knew about Williams' personal association with the contractors.

As he drove home, Antoine tried calling Monica, but the recording said her voicemail was full, and he couldn't leave a message.

It wasn't like her not to show up to work. It was more typical that he could never get her to leave to go home. She loved coming to work every day.

Antoine thought about their last time together. Monica had seemed upset and said she had a lot on her mind. He had asked her a few times what was wrong, but she refused to tell him. One thing she did say was that she loved him, but he didn't know how to tell her that he wasn't in love with her, so he'd said nothing. The expression on his face seemed to say it all, though, and she had left his home in tears. He'd tried calling her a few times to see if she was okay since then but didn't hear back from her.

The next morning Antoine received a frantic call from Jan.

"Jan, stop screaming. What's wrong?"

"Monica. She's dead."

"What? Are you sure?"

"An ambulance is on their way," she cried.

Everyone came rushing out of their offices and huddled around Antoine's desk to hear what was happening. "Monica is dead," he cried.

Overwhelmed with anguish, Antoine handed the phone to the nearest person, grabbed his car keys, and ran out.

Malik, the youth pastor, ran after him. "I'm coming with you!"

By the time they arrived, the police had the entire section of Monica's apartment building cordoned off with yellow tape. Antoine approached an officer.

"I work with Monica," he said. "Can you tell me—"

"We're not allowing anyone inside right now," the officer replied, cutting him off.

Antoine and Malik stood by as sometime later paramedics carried out her dead body covered in a white sheet on a gurney. Overcome with emotion, Antoine nearly dropped to the ground, but Malik held on to him.

Antoine couldn't believe what was happening. Every moment he'd spent with her and every conversation they'd shared raced through his mind.

***

Pastor Covington walked up to the scene in disbelief.

Jim was called to the scene and began answering questions from Pastor Covington.

"It appears that it may have been a suicide."

"Suicide," said Pastor Covington with a stunned look on his face.

"Yes, the body is being transported to the coroner's office for further examination.

"This is not in her character," said Antoine.

"Pastor, did Monica know your daughter and grandson?"

"Yes, of course. We all knew her very well. In fact, she has been employed at my church for several years now, I think. Antoine, how long did Monica work for the church?" he asked.

"Hi, I'm Antoine, and I was married to Michelle. Monica worked for us for ten years," he said.

Jim exchanged business cards with Pastor Covington and Antoine.

"I would like to keep in touch," said Jim.

Antoine was stunned to hear that Monica committed suicide. He felt terrible that he may have been the reason she ended her life. Their last conversations replayed in his head like a broken record. The pain of losing Michelle and James Junior was just beginning to subside, and life without them was finally starting to feel normal. And now this, he thought.

He wondered if rumors would begin circulating about the two of them. He believed some staff members suspected that they were having an affair, even though he made sure no one ever saw them out together.

Antoine couldn't believe he allowed himself to become involved with her again, knowing he would never love her. He couldn't allow himself to open up to her that way.

Antoine felt the brunt of her death and would carry the guilt for the rest of his life.

CHAPTER TWENTY-EIGHT
--------PROVOCATION------

An hour passed, and still, Mr. Williams had not arrived at the emergency meeting he requested the entire staff to attend. Everyone sat glued to their cell phones, not talking to each other as they anxiously awaited his arrival. No one seemed to know what the meeting was about, and everyone began speculating that they had done something wrong. The tension in the room was so thick, it could be cut with a knife.

Rachel sat silently, mentally preparing for a scolding. She also feared the emergency meeting could be Mr. Williams' way of springing a last-minute assignment that had to be done before they all left for the weekend. This boot camp style management had become emotionally draining, and she wasn't sure how much longer she could take it.

When Mr. Williams finally walked into the room minutes later, the misery displayed on everyone's faces quickly morphed into forced smiles as he made his way to the head of the conference table. His pheromone-infused scent permeated the already congested room. For several hours, he spoke about how it was important that they performed better than their statewide peers.

"We have a responsibility to our constituents," he said, and the entire staff nodded in agreement. Sadly, Rachel no longer cared about saving the world; she was too consumed with trying to rescue herself from this madness, desperately trying to dig herself of this mess.

The meeting seemed like it would never end. Rachel started daydreaming about lunch. Mexican and Subway were her top choices. The colleague sitting next to her began nodding off, her mouth slightly open. She was seconds away from falling out of the chair. Rachel gently nudged her with a knee to wake her when she saw Mr. Williams shoot the woman a warning glare.

She immediately woke up and began jotting down notes, pretending as though she had not missed a thing. The meeting was finally wrapping up when a man dressed in all black appeared out of nowhere. He had on a mask and called out Mr. Williams' name.

The staff looked frightful of the burly man. He began tossing chairs as he stalked toward Mr. Williams, and everyone ran for cover when he pulled out a gun.

He threatened that he would shoot anyone that got in his way, and pandemonium ensued. People ran screaming at the top of their lungs.

Rachel feared she wouldn't make it out alive, even though it was clear the lone gunman only wanted Mr. Williams.

She ran as fast as she could toward the elevator and looked around to see if the coast was clear. She started for the stairwell then remembered that Mr. Williams had the doors leading out of the building locked. So she stood in front of the elevator for what felt like a full minute, pressing the button several times before noticing it was stuck on the third floor.

Hurrying in the opposite direction of the conference room, she found refuge in a storage closet, where she sat praying for someone to rescue her. She couldn't call for help because her purse had been left behind in the conference room, and it was too risky to go back to get it.

Frantic, Mr. Williams managed to get out of the conference room, although the man trailed behind him with gunshots ringing out. One hit Mr. Williams in the leg. With his hand on his wound, he struggled to find a way out.

With no clear exit in sight, he turned to face the gunman. "What do you want from me?" Mr. Williams yelled.

"I want you dead."

"Look, I'll write you a check. Just tell me the amount."

"I don't want your fucking money."

In excruciating pain, Mr. Williams fled into a stairwell leading toward the outside of the building. Once inside, he was relieved and believed he could escape from this man. It wasn't until he reached the bottom of the stairwell that he remembered the door was locked. He screamed and cried for help.

"Get me out of here!"

The man was right behind Mr. Williams as he pointed his gun and shot him at close range, leaving behind a trail of blood.

"Please don't kill me!" Rachel screamed.

"Wake up, wake up!" Richard urged in a soothing voice.

Rachel woke up startled.

"Are you okay?" he asked.

I had an awful nightmare." Richard wiped away her tears as she recanted her story. She stopped occasionally and began crying uncontrollably.

"What else happened?"

"One minute, I'm driving toward the building listening and singing to Anita Baker's 'You're My Everything.' Then I see paramedics, news station satellite vans, and police officers telling everyone to keep moving. I see my colleagues who appear to be inconsolable and being ordered out of the building with their hands on their heads. I'm panicking and trying to reach someone to find out what happened. Next, I'm sitting in a meeting with my colleagues and Mr. Williams, daydreaming about lunch and hoping the meeting would end."

"Baby, that's terrible."

"I'm done. I don't want to work there anymore," Rachel cried. "I'm leaving. I'm quitting today."

"Are you sure this is what you want to do?"

"Yes, I'm sure. I believe the nightmare was a message to get out of there now. I don't feel safe there. And I have some money saved up," she added.

"Well, you don't have to worry about money with me. You know I'll support us both."

"Thank you, baby." She laid her head on top of Richard's chest and thought about her next move.

She felt weird being in the office after experiencing such a horrific nightmare. She was nervous about handing in her resignation letter. While she didn't know what the future held for her, Rachel was eager to get started with her new life. Throughout the day, she kept busy making sure she completed all of her assigned work. She didn't want anyone to notice that she was also clearing off her desk, and by lunch, most of her personal belongings were stored in her car.

Mr. Williams was out most of the day, and the atmosphere in the office was less tense. Rachel was hoping she didn't have to run into him and that she could leave the letter with Claire, but at five minutes before five. Mr. Williams requested that she stop by his office. Before he could begin talking, Rachel quickly stretched her hand across his desk and handed him her letter of resignation.

"What's this, Rachel?" he asked.

"It's my resignation letter."

"Did you get a new job offer?"

"No."

"Interesting. You know, I never thought you would last a week here," he said and bellowed in laughter.

"Your fucking pathetic," Rachel said angrily.

Mr. Williams leaned back in his chair, appearing shocked by her searing words.

Rachel hurried toward the office door and slammed it behind her. She was greeted by Claire, who winked at her and whispered, "Good luck."

When she walked out of the building, she felt like a load had been lifted.

One by one, text messages from Courtney, Alice, and Anita began flowing in.

"Did you finally submit your resignation?"

"Yes!" she replied with multiple emoticons high fiving.

Before she could complete her text, Richard called.

"I am so proud of you, baby."

"Thank you, sweetie. I'll see you soon," she said and practically ran to her car.

***

Monica's death was ruled a homicide, and rumors spread like wildfire. Details of Antoine's extra-marital affair had been leaked to the press. An officer, who spoke under anonymity, mentioned how Monica's death could be connected to the deaths of Michelle and James Junior, which he alluded was not accidental.

This made matters worse as everyone began to speculate that Antoine was responsible for their deaths. While Pastor Covington had publicly expressed that he did not believe Antoine was capable of hurting anyone, privately, it was a different story. He slowly began stripping Antoine of his duties at church. His friends, who he believed supported him, suddenly were not returning his calls.

The one person he never wanted to hurt was his mother-in-law, who everyone affectionately called Mama Covington. She said she was so ashamed and upset that she could no longer look him in the face.

Antoine felt he was on life support that had been unplugged, and he was now struggling to breathe on his own. After several weeks of intense questioning, he was relieved to hear that he was no longer a person of interest in Monica's death.

Ready for a new start in life, Antoine considered relocating to Detroit to help his cousin run his business there. The transitional housing project had evolved into a rat race, and the wedge Roger Williams had strategically formed between Antoine and Pastor Covington had grown deeper than he had ever imagined. They rarely spoke, and when they did, it was only about the status of the project or the children.

One day after a meeting, Roger Williams cornered Antoine and offered his unsolicited advice dealing with the news of Monica's death. "I know how you're feeling, man. It's no fun having your name dragged in the mud."

Antoine was disgusted and didn't believe a word he said. "Thank you," he replied and quickly walked away. Antoine knew Williams marveled in knowing he'd destroyed the relationship between Antoine and his former father-in-law. He could no longer stomach being around Williams and simply couldn't trust him.

Jennifer and her husband invited Antoine over for dinner. She had become like a big sister and a true confidant to Antoine. When she shared with him how she believed Williams was responsible for killing his wife and stepson, Antoine was speechless. He was so angry that tears streamed down his face.

"I don't mean to upset you. I wanted to tell you but just never felt it was the right time."

"How and why would he want to kill Michelle? As far as I knew, they were very close."

"I believe Michelle and Mr. Williams's relationship had changed, and they were no longer on good terms. Of course, one reason could be that Michelle was expected to be a star witness for the prosecution. She may have been preparing to disclose everything she knew about the misappropriation that was happening in the office, and he had her killed to stop her from testifying. I think Michelle's last call to me was to warn me about him."

"How do you think he caused the accident?"

"By hiring the man who changed her tire and loosened the lug nuts on her vehicle. And that same man was later found dead."

Antoine placed his head on the table and began sobbing.

"Roger Williams is a monster," Jennifer said, trying to console Antoine.

After regaining his composure, he said, "Wait a minute. So, why aren't the police doing anything about it? He needs to be locked up."

Jennifer stood and began collecting the plates from dinner. "Unfortunately, this is all circumstantial."

"I need some time to digest all of this information. I need to get home to put the kids to bed." He gave her a hug.

Jennifer and Seth walked Antoine out to his car. "Are you going to be okay to drive home?" Jennifer asked.

"Yes, I'll be fine. I'll talk to you soon."

Antoine was furious. The thought of knowing Williams could be responsible for killing his wife and son made him sick to his stomach. Antoine didn't know whether to kill him or let the law handle it. But after getting his head together, he realized he had too much to lose. His kids had already lost their mother, and he didn't want to do anything to jeopardize his freedom and his kids' lives.

Of course, that didn't stop him from doing all he could to help put Williams away for good.

The next day Antoine called in sick from work, something he rarely did. He dropped the kids off at school and went directly to the police station, where he met with Jim McKeon and gave him all the information he knew about Monica and the transitional project.

"We'll look into the project," the detective told him. "But I have to tell you, there's not much here to go on."

Pastor Covington rarely shared any information with Antoine, and since Monica died, Antoine had been kept completely out of the loop for most of the project.

"I want to know if Roger Williams had anything to do with my wife's accident?" Antoine asked.

"We have no evidence to suggest that he did. Although, we believe the man last seen helping your wife with her tire change was hired by Williams. He met with Williams shortly before Michelle's accident, and the man was later murdered. But again, we have nothing concrete."

Antoine was frustrated and demanded more answers.

"Why haven't you arrested Roger?"

"Look, Antoine, we can't make an arrest without any evidence. Until then, there really isn't anything we can do."

"Man, I am telling you, Roger can't get away with this."

"Did Monica ever mention she had any enemies?"

"No, I don't believe so. She was friendly to everyone."

"Maybe an ex-boyfriend or someone from her past."

"Well, Monica was a recovering addict, but she had been clean for over a decade. She has an older sister in Ohio that she occasionally visited, and her parents were deceased. But you probably already knew that."

"What was the relationship between Monica and Roger Williams?"

Antoine rubbed his forehead in disbelief. "As far as I know, she didn't even know him. She never mentioned his name. Although, I did complain to her about him all the time. Why do you ask?"

"We found some calls to him on her cell phone records dating back for a period of two years. In the last couple of months, those calls were more frequent, including the days leading to her death."

Antoine wondered what type of relationship Monica had with Roger Williams. Especially one she wouldn't have told him about.

"Could it have been a romantic relationship?" the detective asked.

The thought of being in a romantic triangle with Roger Williams and Monica made him nauseous. "I have no idea. Do you believe Roger killed Monica?"

"We don't know, but we're trying to seek some answers here."

At the end of the interview, Antoine tried to convince himself that he wasn't leaving with nothing as he'd actually learned a lot.

"Thanks for coming by," the detective told him as he walked Antoine to the door of his office. "Let us know if you find any information that could help with the case."

"I'll be back," Antoine promised.

***

It was a bittersweet moment for James. He received a letter from the Pardon and Parole Board stating he was up for parole. He never imagined this day would come. He tried to gauge the likelihood of being released from prison, but he knew his chances were low. He believed the victim's family members would be there to stop it from happening. Still, Pastor Covington and several of his parishioners wrote letters to the Parole Board corroborating that James had accepted full responsibility for his actions and was prepared to become a productive citizen, so he held onto some hope.

James could not imagine being free and not having Michelle and his son to come home to. Either way, he was prepared to give it a try. In the months leading to his hearing, he stayed mostly to himself and away from trouble. His crew from the outside was eager to put an end to Williams' life, but James said no. While deep down, he wanted the man dead, James didn't want any unforeseen mishaps to jeopardize his chances of getting out on parole. He would get Williams back in due time.

Most of his days since Michelle and his son's deaths were spent reading books and writing letters to his mom and Tabatha, a woman he had dated briefly when he was a teenager. Everything about Tabatha was different from Michelle. She was an introvert and had beautiful cocoa brown skin and shoulder-length hair. When they were teenagers, she was curvier than most girls her age, and every boy in his crew wanted to have sex with her. The closest he got to making a move on her was squeezing her butt in the janitor's closet. After giving birth to a daughter by her ex-husband, Tabitha could never get back her pre-pregnancy body weight. In his eyes, she was still fine as hell.

But James loved everything about her and affectionately called her his brown sugar. He could sense her weight made her feel uncomfortable, and he always made a point to tell her how beautiful she was to him. In the beginning, it took him a while to open up to her, but she had been patient. These days, Tabatha was a schoolteacher and loved working with kids. They wrote letters to each other, and she offered to support him in any way she could. They talked about starting a family together.

James didn't want to hurt her. He felt no woman should be tied to a man in prison; it just wasn't fair. Besides, it was easier for him to know there was no commitment between them just in case she ever decided that being involved with a man in prison was too much to handle. That way, the break-up would not be tough to overcome.

James looked forward to her visits, though. She had a smile that could light up a room.

"Hey, baby," he said as he gave her a warm embrace.

"I've been getting my house ready for you."

He held her hands. "Baby, I don't want us to get our hopes up."

"We have to remain positive, James. I spoke to Pastor Covington, and he's made some phone calls. He also has a job lined up for you, counseling youth."

James was nervous and didn't want to disappoint Tabatha and his mom. If he had a second chance in life, he was going to make the most of it, he would later explain to members of the Parole Board. James was committed to becoming a better man.

***

Several weeks later, James received the news he'd been waiting to hear. He was being released from prison and into a halfway house, where he would have to serve a year before he could re-enter society. It was the best news he could have asked for.

When his mom came to visit him, he shared with her the good news, but he couldn't help noticing how frail she looked. Throughout her visit, she kept coughing uncontrollably.

"Mom, is everything okay with you?"

"Yes, sweetie. Don't you worry about me."

James was concerned about his mother. She looked sick. He received a letter from his step-dad telling him that his mom had stage-four lung cancer and was not expected to live much longer. He didn't want him to worry about her, but he felt James needed to know about his mom's failing condition. Her health continued to go on a downward path. Then the night before he was released from prison, James suffered a major blow, learning his mom had died. He was devastated by the news. He realized he had no one now, but Tabatha assured him she would never leave his side. A year later, James was released from a halfway house and would later form an advocacy group with Tabatha, championing the case for prison reform.

CHAPTER TWENTY-NINE
- WHO YOU ARE AND WHO YOU WANT TO BE-

Jim was thrilled to have an arrest warrant for Mr. Williams in his hands. There was no way he was getting out of this one. Monica's sister handed the authorities a safe deposit box that Monica had left for her to open in case anything were to happen to her. A letter detailing how she met Mr. Williams and a recording she secretly made of him threatening to kill her and admitting to setting up the murder of Michelle became evidence. She also wrote a letter to Antoine apologizing for hurting him. Jim had more than enough to obtain an arrest warrant, including a surveillance video seized from a corner store showing Mr. Williams walking toward Monica's building the night she was murdered. Jim notified Pastor Covington and Antoine with the news about the arrest. Pastor Covington was floored and couldn't believe the man he trusted and considered a son was responsible for killing his daughter and grandson. He cooperated with the authorities in making sure Mr. Williams would never see freedom again.

***

When Jim and his fellow officers arrived at the agency, Claire came out to greet them. "Gentlemen, Mr. Williams is in a meeting. Is there anything that I can help you with?"

"Roger Williams, you're under arrest for the murders of Michelle Porter, James Duperville Junior, and Monica Atkins."

"You're mistaken!" Roger bellowed. "I'll get to the bottom of this, and when I'm done, it will be over for you. Claire, call my wife and my attorney."

One of the officers placed handcuffs on Roger as Detective McKeon read his Miranda Rights.

Staff came running out of their offices and stood by gawking as Roger was hauled out of the building.

Roger Williams was denied bail and stayed in County Jail until he was sentenced. The judge announced during sentencing that Roger Williams would remain incarcerated for "a term of your natural life without the possibility of parole." He was transferred to a high-tech, maximum-security prison.

***

Dressed in an orange jumper and shackles on his feet and hands, Roger made his way into the waiting room to meet with Sloan. He had grown a beard and had deep dark circles beneath his eyes.

"I'm so happy to see you. How are the boys?" he asked.

"They're hanging in there."

"My attorneys have filed an appeal. They believe I have a strong chance of beating this." When Sloan didn't comment, Roger asked, "What's wrong?"

"Roger, I only came today to let you know in person that I'm filing for a divorce."

"Look, I know this has all been tough for you and the kids, but you have to trust me. I will get out of this mess. I was thinking that you and I can start all over and maybe move to Georgia to be closer to your folks like you always wanted."

She tossed him an envelope.

"What's this?"

"Photos. You were cheating on me with a whore!"

"Let me explain."

"I don't want to hear anything you have to say. I stood by you like a damn fool, and this is what I deserve. I've been buying into your dumb shit since before we were married. I loved and adored you. You could do no wrong in my eyes. Well, Roger, I can't do this anymore."

Roger leaned forward and spat on her. "You fucking bitch! I hate you. I hate you!" he screamed as he was forcefully taken out of the room by guards.

Sloan was not prepared for his reaction. She divorced him and never saw him again. She moved with her kids to Georgia to practice law and to be with family. Sloan later remarried, and her children remained in contact with their father through letters and occasional visits.

Pastor Covington and Antoine made amends in their relationship. Antoine decided against moving to Detroit, and he continued his ministry work with Pastor Covington.

Jennifer and Seth were ecstatic that Mr. Williams was finally in prison where he belonged. She continued her consulting and launched an organization for the arts with her husband, Seth.

While it took some convincing from Pastor Covington for Antoine and James to trust one another, in time, they grew close and forged a strong brotherhood.

Life got better for Rachel after she left the agency. She became a stay-at-home mom of two young children with her husband, Richard.

Roger Williams fought hard to have his conviction overturned, but his appeals were denied. In the end, he proved that he was the ultimate thug and made his life adaptable to prison life. He shared a six-by-eight cell with a fellow inmate convicted of bludgeoning his elderly parents to death. He spent days on end lifting weights outdoors, boasting to inmates who cared to listen, tales of how he ran Miami's seedy government. His attempt to build a network in prison that could earn him respect and admiration backfired. Instead, he agonized over the fear for his life.

Epilogue

"Keep your face to the sun,
and you will never see the shadows."

- Helen Keller -

The sounds of fireworks from across the river reverberated throughout the concrete walls of the prison. The celebration of July 4, 1776, could bear no significance to the mostly black and brown inmates, especially Roger Williams. For him, it was just a nagging reminder of his life before prison.

It had been nearly five years since he'd been put in this hell hole, and it hadn't been easy. He had a few run-ins with a couple of knuckleheads. Some beefs were squashed, and with others, he still had to look over his shoulder. He'd had a few bunk mates come and go but stayed mainly on himself. He didn't trust anyone. What he did know is that he was happiest when he could see his boys. When he saw them, he saw the best in himself.

Although his relationship with his sons was strained, they were the most important people in his life. They saw him only during school vacations. The little time that he got to spend with them meant a lot to Roger.

He blamed Sloan and her new husband for feeding them negative stuff about him as well as what his sons could unearth on the internet.

His sons did most of the letter-writing as there wasn't much to share on his end. He didn't want to bore them with details of how his was told when to eat and that he shared a communal shower with other men, and that he laid his head next to where my bunkmate took a shit.

His sons were coming today, and he was eager to see the prison barber. There was only one person ahead of him, so he didn't have to wait long. The barber shaped Roger up and tamed his beard that was now practically all gray. He want to look good for his sons as best as he could. When he received the call that he had visitors, he couldn't get out of his bunk fast enough.

A much leaner and toned Roger Williams shuffled into the waiting room, escorted by two husky-looking guards. Constrained by shackles on his ankles, he slowly made his way over to the visiting area, where families sat engrossed in conversation with their loved ones. When he laid eyes on his sons, he beamed with pride. It had been a year since he last saw them, and his sons were young men now. They stood nearly to his shoulders. Rog and Kev's visit was a reminder of his life before imprisonment.

"Dad," they said in unison.

"I'm so happy to see you. You want something to eat from the machine?" Roger asked, eager to make their visit comfortable.

They both regarded the old machine covered with mounds of dust and shook their heads. "No, thank you," they both said at the same time.

"You sure, sons? They have Ding Dongs. Rog, you know you love Ding Dongs."

"Dad, we ate before we got here."

"Okay. You sure now?"

"Yes, Dad."

Roger sat down at the table and gazed at his sons. "When is prom time?"

"Dad, prom isn't until next year, in May."

"You know who you're taking?"

"Not sure. It's too soon. I have options, though."

"That's my boy." Roger laughed. "How about you, Kev?"

"I have two more years before I have a prom."

"Is everything okay, Son?" He knew it was difficult for his younger son to see him practically in bondage, one of the reasons Sloan refused to bring them when they were younger.

Kevin gestured to Rog to answer him. "Well, Dad, we do have something to show you," Rog said before handing him a piece of paper.

Roger assumed it was about their grades. "Let me put on my glasses. They're not Gucci," he said, joking, "but they'll do for now." He laughed and placed his glasses on his nose. As he began to read the letter, he became enraged, then tossed it on the floor and sprung to his feet, knocking his chair over.

"You want to do what?" he shouted. "Take that nigga's last name? I'm your motherfuckin' father, and no matter if I'm in prison or dead, you're my sons."

"We just think it's best that we change our names. He's like our dad, and he loves us just like you do," Rog argued.

"I bet this was Sloan's brilliant idea."

"No, it wasn't, Dad. We both believe it would be good for us to all have the same last name." Rog hung his head.

Kevin asked, "When was the last time you've been to one of my baseball games or Rog's Debate team matches?"

"So, I'm not good enough to be your father anymore?" Roger asked, his voice cracking. He gritted his teeth and looked directly at their faces. "Well, you want him to be your daddy? Go right ahead and do it. But don't ever come back to see me again."

Rog started crying. "We love you, Dad, and we don't mean to hurt you."

"Mom said you would do this," Kevin muttered under his breath.

"Guards! Take me back," Roger shouted. Even knowing it was the last time he would see his kids, he didn't look back.

When he returned to his cell, he yanked his mattress off his bed and began tossing everything to the floor in a fit of rage. He ripped and removed every trace of his sons' photos, report cards, and letters from his wall and tossed them all in the garbage. A few inmates walked by to see what the commotion was, but none interfered.

Later, Roger left his cell to eat, and when he returned, he slept most of the evening.

"Dad, wake up. Breakfast is ready." A younger Roger and Kevin stood over their dad, laughing and nudging him to wake up, while he tossed in his sleep.

Roger woke abruptly to dirty, stained walls around him and the stench of a feces and urine-stained toilet that stood inches away from him. A reminder that he was in prison and not at home with his children. Those dreams never escaped him. Instead, they played over and over in his head like a broken record.

***

"Rog and Kev take out the garbage!" Roger yelled out in the prison yard.

"Can we play one more set?"

"No, take out the garbage."

"Come on, Dad. Please, just one more? I'm close to winning."

"Rog and Kev get in here and take out the garbage. Your mom is on her way home from the grocery store."

Two inmates walked by and laughed at Roger as he acted out every scene in his head.

Those moments were happening more often, and Roger's attorney was concerned for his client's mental health. He demanded that a medical doctor see his client. There were no traces of drugs found in his system, but the prison psychiatrist diagnosed him with bipolar disorder. A diagnosis he was made aware of in his early twenties. Throughout the years, at the urging of Sloan, he routinely took his medicine, but he had never been this long without it. He refused to take his medication after he told his sons not to return to the prison, and his mental condition quickly deteriorated. Roger would talk to himself and easily become agitated at the drop of a hat. Most of the inmates knew to stay away from him.

Like most days at lunch, Roger picked over his food while he spent most of his time talking to himself.

"Rog, good job. Now place your foot on the bike pedal," Roger mumbled over his tray of food. "Keep riding your bike, and now turn around, Son. Babe, I got him. No, he doesn't need your help. Sloan, stay back. Come on, Son, you're almost there. Keep peddling. Keep peddling. Oh no. Don't cry, Son. I am here for you. Rog, come to Daddy. Let me look at your leg. It's just a little bruise. Don't cry, Son," Roger wailed, rubbing his arm as if he was holding his child in his arms.

He became inconsolable, and the guards forcefully removed him from the chow hall and sent him to the infirmary for observation. Later, he was sent to solitary confinement.

"Go, Kev. Run to third base!" he cheered. "You're almost home. That's my boy!" Roger stood and cheered for his son.

"You win this game, and I'm going to take you and your brother out to get your favorite ice cream. *Strike 1.* You got this, Kev. *Strike 2.* Come on, Son. Bring it home. Oh, my God. Keep running, Son. Yes. Yes. Run, Kev. That's my boy. Mr. MVP!" He applauded loudly.

The sound from the corrections officer delivering the food tray through the slot in the door disrupted Roger's imagination. Roger stopped abruptly, pulled the tray inside, and placed it on the floor.

"Daddy is so proud of you. Let's go get your favorite ice cream."

After ninety days in solitary confinement, Roger was released back to the main population. He sat quietly, mumbling to himself in the rec area as inmates were scattered around the room. Some played cards, and others waited to use the payphone. A fight ensued over a card game. One inmate accused another of cheating. The argument intensified, and the two began fighting viciously while other prisoners cheered them on. An inmate from a rival gang jumped into the fight, and a melee erupted. Inmates came from everywhere in the pod to join in the scuffle. The two corrections officers on the grounds could not contain the brawl.

"We need backup right away!" one of the officers shouted into his radio. "This is an emergency! We need backup, copy?"

Dazed and confused, Roger ran toward the crowd, where he wrestled one man to the ground. He punched another man several times before grabbing another inmate and throwing him off a young man in his early twenties who laid bloodied in a fetal position. Roger reached his hand out to the young man.

"Come, Son."

The young man lifted his swollen and badly beaten face.

"Rog, let's go. It's not safe for us here," Roger demanded. As the young man grabbed Roger's hand, another inmate ran toward Roger and stabbed him repeatedly with a sharp, hand-made object to his chest and side.

Roger's eyes widened as he looked down at his bloodied body and fell to the ground. The corrections officers ordered everyone to their cells. As they made their way through the area to render aid, Roger's wounded body laid still in the middle of the recreation room. His orange jumper was soaked with blood.

Tears rolled down his face. "I'm okay," he said, his voice so soft it was barely audible. "Don't you worry, Son. Daddy will be just fine. You'll see."

His breath came in ragged, shallow gasps, and seconds later, his eyes closed.

When the medical staff arrived, they pronounced him dead.

OLIVIA ALMAGRO

Alternate Ending
Unfinished Business

The fall breeze caressed the old oak trees along the narrow, stretched road. Though the leaves were sparse and mostly bereft of their autumnal glory, the few that remained were covered with hues of brown and green.

Roger intently studied the view outside the window, determined to capture the scene in his memory. The rolling hills of trees his family drove past for years reminded him of a canvas that had been painted by Monet himself. Every detail, from the tallest branches to the smallest blade of grass, had to be remembered.

He was filled with despair, realizing freedom had been taken from him. His wife and supporters remained quiet as the judge's words at sentencing reverberated in their thoughts. Life in prison was his future, and it seemed distant and unattainable, like a dream fading in the darkness. The emptiness in his mind embodied the loss of something so sweet and precious as freedom.

The deputy transporting him and two other inmates were more verbose than most of his colleagues. Deputy Willy Jones was a tall, slim, and prideful man with a shiny, smooth, ebony complexion and a headful of wavy silver hair, which he attributed to his grandmother, a full-blooded Seminole, so he said.

Willy had been working for the State of Florida Department of Corrections for thirty years. He proudly shared these intricate details of his life with the men chained to their seats heading to prison with lengthy sentences. "My wife and I have ten children, fourteen grandchildren, and five great-grands," he said. All of whom were college grads, Willy Jones boasted.

Willy was readying for retirement; he didn't move as quickly as before, and as a standard routine, another CO accompanied him to and from the courthouse. Today's route was no different; Willy and Deputy James escorted three prisoners.

Every time he spoke about his loved ones, his gold crowns that were a gap filler for his two front teeth shined luminously. He, too, had a sketchy past more suited to and as intense as a rap lyric, but the path to redemption for him had been surmountable.

Though his mini-size Bible stayed faithfully in his left pocket on his brown uniform shirt, for Willy Jones, it was like a badge of honor. A symbol of protection. He spent most of his lunch break reading scripture out loud, hoping to gain more insight into God's revelation of himself.

Roger had no choice but to listen to Deputy Jones sing along with the praise and worship coming from the tiny radio with a long antenna. He hadn't been expecting any sort of entertainment during his ride, but there Deputy Jones was, clapping and crooning along with the chorus. It was becoming hard for Roger to hide his frustration.

Roger grew even more anxious when a stalled utility vehicle caught Willy's attention from several yards away.

"Hey, Willie, what's happening?" Deputy James asked.

"I reckon the tire blew or something. Let me go ahead and pull on over." He turned down his music and drove the transport bus onto the side of the road, then radioed in. "There's a work truck blocking my way."

"Let us know if we need to send someone out to move it," the female dispatcher replied.

"Copy."

The man from the utility truck wiped his brow in the searing heat as he tapped the door of the transport bus. Deputy Jones unfastened his seatbelt and stood as the door swung outward from the hull of the bus.

The man stepped forward and opened fire with a Glock 45 handgun with an extended forty-round magazine. He shot Deputy Jones twice in the head, and his body thrust upward—hitting the bus floor with a thud. His eyes were opened, and blood flowed from his mouth and forehead.

A shoot-out exchange between the assailant and Deputy James transpired. The inmates ducked and made themselves as small as they could as bullets flew above their heads. Deputy James was hit twice. A roar of jubilation filled the air as Deputy James fell to the ground, slain. However, the enthusiasm quickly morphed into fear and trepidation as the shooter trained his sights on the other inmates, and one by one - they were struck with fatal bullets.

Roger Williams was peeled over in his seat.

"Nigga, what took you so damn long?" Roger spat.

"Man, traffic was horrible," Steve replied. "We have to get out of here." He reached over and dislodged the camera.

Steve was Roger's first cousin on his maternal side of the family. As kids, Roger and Steve were inseparable, but as they grew older, life began to unravel for Steve. He enlisted in the Army and rose to command sergeant major but struggled with a drug addiction that caused him to lose everything, including his family. He received a dishonorable discharge for abandoning his post in Afghanistan.

"These buses have trackers," Steve told Roger.

"Hurry up and take these chains off of me. You got my bag?"

After Steve cut the chains, he handed the bag over to Roger, who rummaged through the leather tote bag filled with money, a passport, a gun, and a change of clothes. "Where did you park your car?"

"Not that far."

"Hand me the lighter fluid, and let's set this shit ablaze.

"Wait, man. Let me see if they got some cash on them." Steve desperately scoured Deputy Jones' pockets as if they may hold the key to survival.

Steve's face grew increasingly desperate as his eyes became etched with worry and anxiety. Roger fidgeted, frantically looking to see if anyone was coming to stop his escape. The minutes were rapidly counting down, leading to a precarious situation. Steve carelessly pulled Willy's wedding band and watch into his pocket, as well as snatching a twenty-dollar bill from his wallet before chucking the Bible across the bloody carnage. As Steve began to move closer to Deputy James, Roger bellowed out a shot, directly hitting Steve in his shoulder.

Steve turned with his mouth hanging open and a look of shock in his frail eyes. "Why the fuck did you shoot me? We like brothers, man. I love you, bro. Please, Rog, man, my kids need me. Don't do it, I beg you.

With tears streaming down his face, Steve was overcome with a feeling of desperation, as if he correctly anticipated the horrific consequences of Roger's actions. Roger motioned to him without mercy, making it clear that Steve had no chance of surviving this.

"Naw, I can't take you with me." Roger coldly uttered as he pulled the trigger.

The bullets tore through Steve's flesh as he fell to the ground.

Roger swiftly removed his prison-worn tangerine-colored jumper and changed into ordinary clothing.

Ignoring the tragedy before him, Roger proceeded to pour a flammable liquid around the bus. He struck a match, and a giant fireball erupted in front of him, engulfing the scene. Roger sprinted toward his getaway car, leaving Steve and the others to an unceremonious demise and thick plumes billowing into the orange-gray sky.

*****

Tonight was a huge night for the Who's Who of Miami. Pastor Covington's Stand Tall Foundation was hosting The Black Excellence Awards Gala, and Richard, Jennifer, Antoine and a few others were among the honorees.

Nerves hit Rachel as they pulled up at the valet. Jennifer and Seth were already inside with other attendees, and this was Rachel's first time back in public since giving birth to their twins. She was excited her husband was being recognized for his charitable work, but the limelight still felt imposing.

Rachel wore a mid-length royal blue sequined gown that accentuated her curves. "Babe, you look stunning," Richard told her. He knew of her insecurities, and no doubt wanted to assure her that she looked beautiful. She smiled, grateful for his support.

Rachel and Richard, along with throngs of guests, made their way into the elegant ballroom while the DJ welcomed them and asked if everyone could have their seats. Waitstaff dressed in black and white hauled huge trays, sometimes on their shoulders, meandering through the ballroom, replenishing water and passing out dinner plates.

Pastor Covington and the First Lady beamed, their faces illuminated with joy. Yet, age seemed to encase the pastor's stature, leaving his eyes sunken and his hair a stark shade of white—caused by the emotional blow of losing a daughter and grandchild so tragically.

The tables held beautiful tall centerpieces filled with white and pink hydrangeas. A female soloist with long rope-looking locks that nearly swept the floor, accompanied by a jazz band, performed. Scented candles with a honey-vanilla scent permeated the ballroom, ideal for weddings, and gold details that referenced the ambiance. Jennifer and Seth were seated with detective Jim McKeon and his wife and another couple associated with the foundation's board.

Rachel and her husband sat across from them at a table with two other couples. Rachel and Jennifer locked eyes and smiled and mouthed compliments to each other.

"Let's chat later," Jennifer said.

"Okay," Rachel replied. Richard looked over his shoulder to see who had Rachel's attention and waved at both Seth and Jennifer.

Pastor Covington stood proudly at the podium, gazing into the sea of people. "Before we get started," he said joyfully, "let's bless the food. Lord, bless this amazing food and the hands that prepared it. In Jesus' name, let everyone say Amen." The guests replied with excitement in their voices. "Amen!"

With a nod, the pastor continued. "Welcome to our twenty-fifth anniversary. The money raised tonight will go toward promising young men and women heading off to college. The Bible says, 'When we serve others, we are serving God.' Philippians 2:4. Amen. Now, the band is going to perform a few songs as we enjoy our dinner, and the awards ceremony will begin shortly afterward. Enjoy, everyone," he added before returning to his seat.

"The stuffed shrimp is delicious," Jim announced.

"I love the baked chicken," Jennifer said.

"You sure?" Seth asked with sarcasm in his tone.

Jennifer sprinkled a ton of pepper and salt on her food. In all honesty, the food tasted bland to my palette. "Do you have any hot sauce?" she asked a passing waiter.

"Let me see if there's any in the back."

"Thank you so much."

"No worries," the young waiter replied before hurrying off.

Seth looked over at Jim with a note of embarrassment in his eyes. Jennifer grinned. "Honey, I'm a bonafide Haitian who likes her food well-seasoned."

"That I know," Seth admitted, breaking the tension at the table, and everyone laughed.

"Speaking of baked," Jim chimed in, "no pun intended, your guy Roger and a few inmates heading to the correctional facility were killed in a fire today."

Jennifer nearly choked, and Seth leaned over to put a hand on her arm. "Babe, are you okay?"

"Yes," she squeaked out as she guzzled down her wine. "What caused the fire?"

Jim dabbed his mouth with a cloth napkin. "It's still under investigation. All of the remains were taken to the medical examiner for further review. Corrections took a hit and are mourning the loss of two of their prized deputies. One of them, Deputy Jones, had recently put in for retirement."

"Excuse me, miss. Here's the hot sauce you requested."

Jennifer's thoughts escaped her. She blinked in confusion.

"Babe, the hot sauce," Seth reminded her.

"Oh, thank you," Jennifer said to the waiter. Clearing her throat, she scooted her chair back and addressed everyone at the table. "Please excuse me. I'm going to the ladies' room."

Seth touched her arm again. "Are you okay?"

"Yes. Just a bit jittery about my speech tonight."

"You'll do fine."

She nodded, retrieved her designer purse, and headed toward the ladies' room. As she entered, Rachel stood in front of a large round mirror, putting on lipstick.

When Rachel saw Jennifer, she stopped what she was doing and immediately hugged her friend. "You look beautiful."

"So do you." Jennifer showed off her elegant off-the-shoulder coco brown chiffon dress with gold embroidery. "How are the twins?"

"They're keeping me busy," Rachel said as she sighed and shook her head with a huge smile on her face.

Jennifer looked around to see if they were alone in the restroom. "Have you heard the latest?"

Rachel had a puzzled look on her face. "No. What happened??"

"Roger Williams, along with three other inmates and two correctional officers, were killed in a fire as they were heading to prison."

Rachel gasped. "What caused the fire?"

"I don't know. It's still under investigation."

Rachel pulled out her cell phone and immediately began searching for information, with Jennifer looking over her shoulder. It didn't take long to find a news article verifying that it was indeed a fire.

Rachel looked up at Jennifer. "Good riddance."

Jennifer nodded in agreement. "I hope he goes to hell." She stared off in deep thought, and a taut silence ensued.

"What's wrong, Jennifer?"

"Oh, nothing. Just thinking."

"Girl, Roger is dead, and we should be celebrating."

Jennifer didn't want to voice her suspicions, but until that man was confirmed officially dead, she wanted to play it safe.

Rachel's phone pinged, and she looked down at the screen. "Richard is texting me that the ceremony is starting. We should get back."

As Jennifer returned to her seat, the waitstaff placed dessert in front of everyone at the table. The plate with her baked chicken was left behind by the waiter.

"Your food is cold," Seth whispered.

"I'm not really hungry anymore."

"Are you going to eat your dessert?"

"Yes, babe." But Jennifer struggled to eat the banana flambé. She couldn't stop thinking about the suspicious cause of Roger's death.

****

Roger was anxious, and being on the run was exhausting. He pulled into a gas station in a secluded spot, where the security cameras were probably broken or non-existent. He grabbed a bag of chips, a packet of Twizzlers, a six-pack of Heineken, a sandwich, and a Pepsi. To disguise his identity, he put on a hoodie and sunglasses, and the baggy jeans slung low on his hips revealed his checkered boxers. This was not the usual well-cut suit look he was known for. Together with his freshly shaven head, the wardrobe took ten years off of him.

The cashier was an elderly man whose dentures lay loose in his mouth and who had a Bluetooth device in one ear while simultaneously watching a baseball game on his cell.

Too laser-focused and engaged in the game to care, the man handed Roger his change and a receipt without bothering to look up. Roger snatched up the bag filled with his purchases and took off toward his cousin's car.

He knew it was just a matter of time before the medical examiner realized that his body was not among the dead.

He pulled up to the single-family home he once shared with his ex-wife and kids. A *For Sale* sign sat on the well-manicured lawn with tall palm trees hovering over the Spanish-Mediterranean-style home.

He sat in his parked car stoic and staring through a big picture window where he could see Sloane and their kids enjoying dinner with some mystery man. Everyone appeared to be engrossed in conversation, and the kids looked happy. The mystery man couldn't keep his hands off Sloane, even with the boys present.

Roger felt betrayed by his family and was instantly fuming mad. "I see this bitch moved on quickly without me. She's got this nigga in my house. The house I paid for, and with my kids."

His palms were slick with perspiration as he gripped the steering wheel. He pulled his hoodie over his entire bald head, slipped on a pair of black leather gloves, and inserted the cartridge in the gun. As he opened the car door, a noise from the neighbor's house startled him. He looked back over his shoulder to see his neighbor rolling his recycle bin to the curb.

"Oh shit."

Seeing the time wasn't right, Roger drove off in a rage and decided coming back wasn't worth the risk of getting caught. Especially not before taking care of some other unfinished business.

****

He entered the hotel from the garage and walked in from the side door to a busy kitchen, where cooks and servers screamed orders. Trays of dirty plates lay mounted in the midst of mayhem. Roger managed to slip through the kitchen into an empty corridor leading to the ballroom. When he heard a familiar male voice talking on his cell, Roger quickly darted into a nearby custodial closet where he could stay hidden and not be detected.

The music and the chatter in the ballroom made it difficult to hear the conversation. The voice he heard was Antoine's. From what Roger could hear, he guessed that Antoine was speaking with his kids on FaceTime.

"Daddy will be home shortly. I want you guys to behave and not give your babysitter a hard time. It's almost time for bed," Antoine said as he entered the men's room.

Roger slipped in behind him, and distracted by the phone call, Antoine held the door for him.

"Goodnight. I'll be home soon," Antoine said and ended the call.

As Antoine stepped into the stall, Roger pointed the gun at his back.

Antoine turned, saw him and took a startled step backward, then raised his hands. "Dammit, look, my wallet is in my left pocket."

"Shut up."

"Please. I need to get back to my family."

"Fuck you. I needed to get back to mine, too."

"Who—who are you? Antoine stuttered.

Antoine looked into Roger's face. When he realized who it was, his expression couldn't have been more terrified. "Yes, it's me, Casper, the motherfucking ghost. You thought you were going to stop me from getting to you, didn't you?" Roger cackled and gripped Antoine, preventing any motion. Antoine fought for a breath, but the chokehold was too tight. Tears streamed from his eyes, and it wasn't long before his body became lifeless.

Roger left him in a locked stall and quickly walked out of the men's room. He glanced toward both ends of the hallway, and with his head down, he walked through the kitchen and out toward the garage.

A security guard standing post in the rear of the garage stopped Roger. "Hey, you have a cigarette?"

"Naw."

The guard nodded. "Thanks anyway, my man."

Roger walked swiftly across the street to where he'd left his vehicle.

****

"Our last honoree of the evening," Pastor Covington announced, "is a man I've known since he was a scrawny fifteen-year-old. My wife and I couldn't keep him away from our daughter Michelle. Over the years, I've come to love and admire him as a son, father to our grandchild, and now community activist. The work he's done since leaving prison has been nothing short of amazing. We see a huge difference in the young men and women in our program, and it's all because of him. Without further ado, James Senior, man, come up here and get your award." James Senior and Pastor Covington embraced. He whispered, "I am so proud of you, Son."

"I remember that knucklehead fifteen-year-old," James Senior began as everyone applauded him. "Had you told me back then that I would be accepting an award for doing positive work in the community, I would not have believed you. I thank God I was given a second chance. Trust me when I tell you I don't take this opportunity for granted.

James had put on a few happy pounds. His face was fuller with a dash of salt and pepper chin-strap beard and a freshly low fade haircut. Most of his tattoos were hidden under his tuxedo. He looked a lot like his father in his heyday. Tabitha was seated at the table, glowing in her third trimester, wearing a beautiful black sleeveless gown. Her hair fell to her shoulders. She couldn't stop smiling. Life with James was everything she had imagined. He was loving and treated her daughter like his own. They both were excited and praying for a healthy baby boy.

Everyone at the table looked on except for the absent Antoine, whose car keys and award sat on an empty chair, having been left behind. Evidently, he was missing from the gathering.

James fought back tears as he talked about turning his life around, and had it not been for Antoine and Pastor Covington guiding him, he could've easily fallen prey to the streets again. "I want to thank my beautiful wife, my rock Tabitha, for her love and support. "I couldn't have done this without you. I love you, babe. To my angels, Michelle and James Junior, I know you're watching over me. To the young men and women in my program, I see myself in all of you. Know that there's a bright future ahead of you." James looked down at the award and lifted it as a thank you gesture to God.

Pastor Covington returned to the podium and hugged James again. "Thank you to our honorees, and thank you to everyone for attending tonight's award ceremony. Until next year, be blessed, everyone."

A group of people stood around Pastor Covington, taking pictures, while Richard and Rachel took photos with some of the honorees and the pastor. Jennifer and Seth were out front waiting for the valet to pull up with their car.

"Did I do okay?" James Senior asked Tabitha as he returned to the table.

"Baby, you did an awesome job."

"I was so nervous." James reached over and kissed her on the lips. "Where's Antoine?"

"Not sure. He said he wanted to check in with the kids and hasn't returned."

"I'll go look for him."

James walked around the ballroom, where there were pockets of guests still hanging around as waitstaff hauled off plates and table arrangements. "Excuse me, have you seen Antoine?" he asked one of the waitstaff and described his missing friend.

"No, not since earlier this evening."

James called Antoine's phone twice, but it went straight to voicemail. Next, he tried the home phone. "Hi, this is James. May I speak with Antoine?"

"He's not home," the babysitter replied."

"When did you hear from him last?"

"He called about two hours ago to check in with the kids."

"Okay, thanks."

Concerned, James did another walk around the premises but couldn't find Antoine. He went into the bathroom and noticed one stall was locked, and there appeared to be someone in the stall. He called out to the person but got no response. "Antoine? Antoine?" he yelled.

He stood back and kicked in the stall door. He saw Antoine's lifeless body slumped over with his face down. Antoine's lips were blue. James started screaming for help.

Waitstaff and the few remaining guests in the hallway ran into the men's room. James immediately called Pastor Covington to tell him the news that Antoine was dead. The paramedics rushed in to remove his body, and the marks around his neck were pointed out to the officer who arrived at the same time. Antoine was pronounced dead at the hospital.

Pastor Covington was distraught and couldn't understand who could do this to Antoine. James held Tabitha tightly as she cried on his shoulder. Nothing could have prepared him for Antoine's death. Antoine had become his confidant and best friend since his release from prison. Michelle and Antoine's kids called James "Unc."

For the first time, James considered returning to the streets. He wanted the person who did this to Antoine to die, but he didn't want to disappoint Tabitha, who was only weeks away from giving birth to their son. Most of all, he didn't want to disappoint Pastor Covington, who minutes before had been taken to the hospital for observation.

****

Jennifer and Seth had already arrived at their home when they heard the news about Antoine. Jennifer was inconsolable. "Roger is not dead," she screamed.

"Honey, please allow the authorities to do their investigation."

"Seth, I am not going to wait until someone else gets killed. I am not going to take any more chances. God, when will this nightmare end," she cried.

Seth and Jennifer sat practically in silence for several minutes while Jennifer calmed down. The mere thought of Roger being alive and on the loose feared them the most. Jennifer's mind was all over the place as she sipped the last of her chamomile tea.

Seth stood and leaned over to kiss her brow. "Babe, I'm heading to bed. Let's talk in the morning. Good night, babe."

His steps could be heard from a distance, and then she heard the bedroom door close. Still, in deep thought, Jennifer quickly washed both cups, dried them and placed them in the cupboard. The red kettle with hot water remained on the stove.

Roger came from behind Jennifer and whispered, "You're a dead bitch."

Jennifer nearly jumped in fear.

"I've got you just where I want you. You better not say a word, or this bullet is going straight through you."

Jennifer bowed her head while her face became wet with a combination of both sweat and tears.

"Remember how I used to bend your ass over across my desk in my office." Huh? You forget about that, bitch?

Jennifer could feel his erection, and her entire body began to shake. She knew she had to act quickly.

She slowly moved her hand toward the kettle. "Roger..." she began, but her voice cracked, and she had to swallow the bile that rose in her throat.

"Shut up, bitch!"

"I came to collect my money. You thought I was going to take the fall alone? You were going to just walk away scot-free?" He laughed. "You took most of the money and begged me to kill Michelle, but I'm no fool. I knew both of you bitches couldn't be trusted."

"Stop it, Roger! Killing Michelle was never in the plan," she whispered. "You are so fucking delusional."

"Hey babe, I can't find the remote anywhere. Seth stood frozen in disbelief. He couldn't believe Roger was alive and standing in front of him.

"What the fuck are you doing here? Get out of my house, or I'll call the police now," Seth said.

Roger pointed his gun at Seth. "Go ahead and call. Let them know to make room for your wife."

"Honey, what is he talking about?"

"I came to collect my money. Tell him how you wanted Michelle dead so you could have all the money to yourself."

"He's lying. I never wanted Michelle dead."

Jennifer grabbed the metal tea kettle and swung it, pouring boiling water over him.

"I'm going to kill you," he ground out.

Jennifer ran toward Seth.

Roger grabbed Jennifer by the hair. She screamed again and fought back by kicking him.

Roger managed to free himself from Seth's powerful grip, seizing the gun and firing a bullet into Seth's body. Frantic, Jennifer charged after Roger as he slipped through the sliding door to the back patio.

"You sick bastard," Jennifer yelled after him.

She ran back to Seth and wept as she cradled him in her arms.

"Seth, baby, please open your eyes."

"I'm okay. Call the police," he murmured.

Jennifer called 911. "Roger Williams is an escapee, and he's alive. He broke into our home and tried to kill my husband and me. He shot my husband and just left. Please send an ambulance right away. We live at Eight Hibiscus Island. Please come right away," she cried.

****

Roger plowed through the security gates with a vengeance and drove as fast as he could along the stretch road, abutting a body of water that led toward the MacArthur Causeway.

"Damn it, I should've killed that bitch when I had a chance," Roger screamed, slamming his hand on the steering wheel.

When he reached midway, a slew of police cars blocked the entrance to the Causeway while a helicopter hovered above, with strobe lights scanning the area. TV news stations were reporting on the scene and had their cameras rolling.

Roger slowed, put the car in reverse, then stopped when he noticed a security vehicle blocked the entrance to Hibiscus Island as well, and he couldn't go anywhere.

He sat in the car with the engine running, guzzled down a few Heinekens, took a few bites of his sandwich, and smoked half a joint found in the ashtray while he plotted his next move.

Police surrounded his vehicle with their guns drawn.

"I'm not going out like no fucking punk," he said to himself.

The police demanded, "Roger Williams, it's time to surrender."

With an emotional scream of, "Oh hell naw," he jumped out of the vehicle and began shooting at the police officers, who returned fire. As Roger attempted to clutch the car door, he suddenly crumpled to the ground, his body riddled with bullet wounds.

****

As Jennifer stared transfixed at the television screen, the soft snoring of Seth's breath acted as a reminder of her reality. Suddenly, she felt a surge of emotion when Roger was on the TV headline news and sprang to her feet. Attempting to not wake Seth, she raised the volume to a low buzz. "It's Roger," she said quietly as tears began running down her cheeks. She watched solemnly as the medics placed Roger's dead body on a gurney. "It's over. It's finally over," she said with a sigh.

Jennifer was relieved that her dealings with Roger had finally come to an end. She no longer had to look over her shoulder or worry that anyone would discover the mischief she and Roger had been engaged in. She was now free to go on with her life.

From Seth's room, Jennifer witnessed Detective Jim McKeon standing at the nurse's station, enquiring about Jennifer's whereabouts. Seeing this, she became worried.

His expression was grim, and her stomach sank as she noticed other police officers nearby. When he called her outside of Seth's hospital room, a chill ran through her body. Jim spoke relentlessly and charged her with co-conspiring to embezzlement and handcuffed her. Everyone stared at Jennifer, and embarrassment coursed through her veins. Tears that she could no longer hold back spilled down her face.

Jennifer mentioned bravely as she passed reporters amid the teeming crowd, "Roger is making every effort from hell to ruin me, but I have faith in my lawyer to help me escape this ordeal unscathed." Countless gazes followed her while she was escorted away.

-The End-

Made in the USA
Columbia, SC
22 July 2024